Sin & Bone

SIN & BONE

Other novels by Bette Golden Lamb & J. J. Lamb:

Bone Dry
Bone Pit
Bone of Contention
Bone Dust
Bone Crack
Bone Slice
Heir Today...
Sisters in Silence
The Killing Vote

By Bette Golden Lamb
The Organ Harvesters
The Organ Harvesters-Book II

By J. J. Lamb:
A Nickel Jackpot
The Chinese Straight
Losers Take All
No Pat Hands

SIN & BONE

by

Bette Golden Lamb
&
J. J. Lamb

TWO BLACK SHEEP PRODUCTIONS
NOVATO, CALIFORNIA

Bette Golden Lamb & J. J. Lamb

Sin & Bone

Copyright ©2012 by Bette Golden Lamb & James J. Lamb

www.twoblacksheep.us

Published March 2012

Cover Designer: Rita Wood www.ritawoodcreative.com

Dedication

For Rita and Mike Wood, once good friends,
who were always there for us through the
good, the bad, and the ugly.

Acknowledgement

If we did not acknowledge the members of
our Critique Group for their comments,
input, and motivation, we would risk
very bad Karma. So, here's to
Margaret Lucke, Pat Morin, Shelley
Singer, Nicola Trwst, and Judith Yamamoto.
Thank you.

Bette Golden Lamb & J. J. Lamb

₪ CHAPTER 1

Gina Mazzio glared at the call-waiting board high above her desk. The flashing red lights signaled every active phone line into the Ob/Gyn Advice Center; the display made her sick. It was a relentless reminder of all the people waiting to speak to a nurse. Speak to *her*.

The Eye of God.

That's what the clinic nurses called it – among other things.

She pushed back into the chair, stretched her neck, and ran fingers through her short, black hair; her eyes fixated on the sea of pulsating dots.

Three desks were crammed into the tiny office, and normally two other nurses would have been wedged into seats on either side of her. But a sick call and a family emergency had pared the Ob/Gyn advice staff down to one – her. Even without her co-workers, the claustrophobic room had about the same appeal as cramming her five-ten bod into a linen closet.

The Eye continued to flash, all her desk lines rang and blinked. She wanted to fling the phone against the wall and run. Instead, she answered the next-in-line call.

"She's all cut up."

"Sir, this is Ob/Gyn. I think you want the ER."

"No!" the caller said. "Listen to me! She's all cut up."

"I'm sorry, sir, I don't understand. Who's all cut up?"

Silence.

"Sir, what's the problem? Is it your wife?"

"No!"

"You're going to have to explain so I can help you."

"She's all cut up."

"I don't understand. I'm going to transfer you to the ER now."

"No—"

The red light blinked out.

She felt uneasy as she glanced at the finger-smudged plaque in front of her that told where *Gina Mazzio, RN,* sat, then glanced again at the two empty desk chairs. A sharp pang of resentment stabbed through her. Alone, she'd handled more than 100 patient calls during her eight-hour shift, with no break or time out for lunch. She was beat. So whoever was at the other end of those flashing call lights would have to wait until she got caught up with her paperwork.

She jerked the cord out of its jack, yanked off her headpiece, and let it dangle around her neck like a funky necklace.

I need to finish these nurses notes:

11/02/09 4:45pm

Margee Donlevy, 32-year-old primigravida, 34 weeks pregnant, complaining of more than 5 contractions/hr. Good fetal movement,

(-) bleeding, (+) hydration. Working two jobs – on her feet all day.

To L&D for monitoring.

As she tapped the info into the computer, the ringing phone lines scrambled her thoughts.

"*Mama mia!* That's enough."

For her sanity, she needed to take the damn calls, get it over with. But exhaustion and pure stubbornness kept her from hooking back into the network. She checked her watch, then ran a finger across a framed photo of her fiancé, Harry. She smiled.

"Four-fifty, baby! Only ten more minutes!"

This was the weekend they were *finally* getting married. Her heart skipped a beat, but the joy morphed into fear and lodged itself at the base of her neck.

Scared? No, she was terrified and willing to admit that to anyone, other than everyone who knew her already knew. She'd re-set the date three times for three different flimsy excuses and it had reached the critical point where Harry had had it with her. He'd told her last night that he doubted they'd ever tie the knot.

Maybe he was right. Maybe she couldn't do it.

But Regina and Bill had gone overboard to make all the arrangements, and she did love the guy, so she *was* doing it. Everything was set—set for them to run away to the Mendocino Coast to become Mr. & Mrs. Lucke, RNs.

Gina continued to study Harry's picture and wondered why he couldn't be happy for them to just go on living together. He'd been a bachelor all these years, and as a traveling nurse, his out-of-town assignments kept him up to his ass in alligators most of the time.

What was the hurry to get married?

She finished her notes, plugged back into the network, and hoped it wasn't the "she's-all-cut-up" thing again. What was that all about, anyway?

"Ob/Gyn. This is Gina. May I put you on hold?"

"Fi-nal-ly. Don't you people ever answer the phone?"

"May I put you on hold?" Gina repeated in a pleasant voice.

"Don't let me wait too long."

The woman's voice bounced with impatience, but Gina could tell she would wait without further complaint. A pang of guilt cut through her.

Give her a break, Mazzio. She's only trying to get some help. Isn't that what I'm here for?

At least at 5:00 pm the 24-hour Call Center would start picking up the incoming calls. Anything in process before that would have to be completed by her, no matter how long it took. And she'd definitely have to take care of the "on-hold" call. But before she could act, three more calls piled up and it still wasn't quite five o'clock. As she pressed the button, she yelled at the empty office, "*Basta! Basta!*"

3

She dispatched the "on-hold" call with a few simple instructions for self-treating a vaginal infection. The second caller was hoping to still get in for an appointment, but was just now leaving San Francisco's financial district.

What is it about clinic hours you don't get, lady?

Gina popped her-complaining-into a Monday slot and took the next caller.

"Nurse, nurse, help me! I can't breathe...feels like someone's sitting on my chest."

"You need to call 9-1-1. Now!"

"No, no! Can't you help me?"

Gina could hear her shortness of breath. "Ma'am, please call 9-1-1."

The caller's voice was faint, shaky. "Can't you call them for me?"

"No! They need a direct line so they can monitor you."

"I can't handle that...those screaming sirens...it's so embarrassing." The woman began to sob.

"Are you alone?"

"Yes. There's nobody here. I'm scared."

"Listen to me: Please call 9-1-1. You'll get help right away."

Silence.

"*Please* call them."

"Okay."

"I'll check on you in a few minutes to see if you're all right, to make sure that the EMTs are helping you."

The line went dead.

Gina would definitely make sure the woman was in the emergency system before she left for the day. Otherwise she'd continue to worry about her the whole weekend.

"Ob/Gyn. This is Gina."

Silence.

"Hello?"

"What did you say your name was?"

Damn! Him again.

4

"Gina. My name is Gina. Did you call the ER?"

"Gina what?"

A creepy tingling crawled up her spine; she shifted in her swivel chair.

"Gina's good enough. I'm the only Gina here."

A long silence was punctuated with labored breathing that made her think of someone running hard down a basketball court.

"Sliced her into pieces."

Gina's mouth turned to cotton. "Has there been an accident?"

More heavy breathing.

"Sir, I don't think I can help you. This is Ob/Gyn."

"Dammit! I don't care. I need to talk to someone. If not you, someone else … someone who'll listen."

Gina stared hard at *The Eye of God*. Why couldn't that thing give her all the information she could use – like Caller ID.

"I'll help you if I can, but—"

"Don't you get it? She's all cut up."

Sweat blossomed on Gina's forehead. "I heard you. But I don't know what that means exactly. Please—"

"It's too late."

Like the night Gina was cut up. It had almost been too late for her, too.

"If this is supposed to be some kind of joke, it's not funny," Gina said, putting steel into her voice.

Loud sobs morphed into chilling, high-pitched laughter. Then came a wheezing so intense Gina felt her own chest constrict with each gasping breath.

"Sir?"

No response.

"Sir?"

"I'm scaring you, aren't I?" he said in a raspy voice.

Yes, she was scared, but she gave it her best Bronx effort: "Listen to me, whoever you are, there's nothing about you that scares me."

Yet the pit of her stomach was on fire; she was more than scared, she was angry. Angry with her vicious ex; angry with street bullies and anyone else who'd ever tried to beat her up, beat her down.

"What do you want? Do you have a medical problem, or are you one of those people who enjoy terrifying women?" She pretended to laugh. "If you are, you sure messed up this time."

She should have been on her way home, but here was this ghoul, wheezing in her ear, holding her hostage. And she still had to check on the 9-1-1 patient.

Whatever was going on in this guy's head was none of her business. Probably gets off creeping out people. Still, something warned her that he might be the real thing.

"Listen Mr. … what did you say your name was?"

"Who're you kidding? You know I'm not going to give you my name."

"If someone's dead or dying, you need help."

Hit the disconnect! Get the hell out of here!

But she knew she wouldn't. Instead, she pushed her chair back and leaned out into the hallway. It was a quarter past five, on a Friday evening—fat chance of finding anyone around the place to help her. The clinic was as silent as a tomb.

She gave it another shot: "Why *are* you calling?"

The wheezing had lost its crowing pitch, the breathing had slowed.

"He says women are all alike. We love them and they fuck us over." A tortured moan raised goose bumps on her arms. "Cut out our hearts and toss them to the dogs."

"Who said that?"

"For God's sake! Knock off the bullshit! Someone has to stop the cutting, the killing."

"What-"

The line went dead.

₪ CHAPTER 2

The caller hung up, distraught, certain the nurse hadn't believed him.

Could he ever make it stop?

He grabbed his inhaler, puffed until his lungs opened and he was able to fully breathe again. His cell phone stared at him, squat, menacing, like a black widow spider waiting to strike.

When will he call?

The hairs on his neck stiffened. His thoughts curled around him like a shroud.

"No-o-o." A familiar, paralyzing vision filled his head:

Flexed muscles, beefy fists, beady lancing eyes, sadistic snorts of laughter, cauterized hatred. Flashes of slashing, boning, chopping; gristle, fat, and raw, red butchered meat from giant carcasses. And always the metallic smell of blood.

The grotesque panorama made him scream; he swatted at the air to rid his mind of the butcher shop, where slaughtered animals enwrapped his memories like a rancid blanket.

He winced as his feet slammed onto the bare floor. A half-hour of rapid walking around the spacious apartment usually lessened the despair. Acrid sweat dripped from his body, splatters dappled the blond bamboo floor. After the final lap, he collapsed on the sofa, wheezing again, barely able to breathe again. When he calmed down, he reached out and placed a tentative finger on the cell phone. He tapped the hard case nervously, a rhythm as fast and as deliberate as a metronome.

How soon?

His reflection stared back from the expanse of the penthouse window that framed a view of The City, from the Golden Gate to the Bay Bridge—he pulled at his red, spiky, hair.

When will he call?

He looked beyond his reflection, studied the native plants he'd bought for the penthouse patio – they loved the rain, heavy limbs thriving, reaching up to the sky.

Restless, he started on another circuit of the living room, still concentrating on the patio plants. The trees attracted the birds – they would stop and rest in the branches, fluffing their gray, orange, white, and black feathers, then dart down to bathe in the large, variegated stone birdbath. Even in the rain they would chatter, peep at each other, then move on to Golden Gate Park.

At least that's where he would go if he were a bird.

He envied them, envied their freedom.

Freedom.

* * *

He tugged nervously at his hair as he waited in his Jaguar sedan across the street from the main entrance to Ridgewood General Hospital.

He finally caught a glimpse of the nurse, the one he'd seen while passing through the ER last week—red hair, petite. Another one who matched his memories of Mother.

"Bring the package," Father had said when he called an hour ago.

And he would have to do it.

He closed his eyes, remembered Mother. She used to protect him, absorb the fists meant for him. They would turn her soft, white skin purple

Shifting in his seat, his heart thrummed. He continued to stare at the nurse.

He told himself he had to do this. Told himself the same thing every single time. If he didn't please Father, he would never find Mother. Father knew where she was hiding, but would *never* tell him if he didn't help with the packages.

The washed-out blue scrubs draped the softness of the nurse's small frame. Even before he'd seen her face in the ER, he'd stored the image of her body—young, pretty, red hair.

8

Mother's red hair. He concentrated on her chest, where large breasts were now smothered by the London Fog raincoat she'd wrapped tightly around her.

He sniffed the air, as though some aromatic secret was waiting to be deciphered, some special scent that would riffle the cells, bring back another vision of Mother. Instead, his brain conjured up one of the bad memories: *A girl in the butcher shop. Naked. Gray tape smothering her mouth. Hands tied behind her back. Father yelling. Calling her Mother's name –Lola.*

He sucked in more air, deeper, deeper. Tried to switch the vision back to Mother. But all he sensed was heavy moisture laced with the nauseating smell of billowing bus fumes.

He concentrated on the red-haired ER nurse's face; it was animated, yet kind. She stood out among the three or four other nurses around her.

Wide-eyed, vulnerable.

One by one the others departed as their rides appeared, or they rushed to the nearby bus stop, or simply walked away.

She pulled a cell phone from her purse, held it to her ear. When she folded it, her shoulders drooped in apparent dejection. She ran toward an arriving bus and got on board.

He made a U-turn and followed the bus as it moved slowly along the busy street; watched her get off in the Diamond Heights district and start walking uphill.

He drove past her, pulled into a space guarded by a yellow fire hydrant, and surveyed the neighborhood. Even though it was still early, all he saw were wet deserted streets and sidewalks. He got out quickly, smiled without humor, and waited as she walked toward him.

The sky opened up and rain crashed down on his head, leaving him drenched and cold. Just before she was even with him, he raised one arm and held it straight out to block her progress.

She looked at the obstructing arm and gave him a startled, then angry glare. Her eyes widened in recognition.

"You!"

He smashed her in the face.

He expected her to cry out, scream, fight back. But she dropped in her tracks, out cold; blood streamed from her flattened nose.

His breath caught in his throat. He turned away and vomited in the gutter. After wiping his mouth with a handkerchief, he bent down and scooped her up in his arms. He hauled her back to the Jaguar, grunting all the way, then held her upright against the back of the sedan. He opened the trunk and lowered her inside.

Sitting in the soft leather driver's seat, hands clenched around the wheel, he tried to stifle the tremors that rippled from head to toe. His breath caught, he choked; two quick puffs from his inhaler and he was able to breathe again.

"Calm down," he whispered. He forced himself to slowly inhale and exhale until he was in control. On the move again, he obeyed every stop sign, every red light, the posted speed limits.

If only he could turn around, go back to where he'd grabbed her and dump her there.

It was too late for that—she'd recognized him.

₪ CHAPTER 3

Gina's hand shook as she unlocked the door of her ancient red Fiat Spider. Sitting behind the steering wheel, she was numb, her fingers tingling with fear. The caller's words repeated and repeated in her head-*cutting, killing*.

Get going, Mazzio. Harry's waiting for you.

But she sat frozen in the seat of the Fiat, staring at the dashboard.

Most days she was tough enough to stand up to any challenge that fell into her court by the mere act of forcing her body into motion. Movement could catapult her through most problems. But she knew the toughness was just a veneer, created long ago to camouflage her insecurities. At the core lived a little girl, no different today than when she was a scared kid growing up in the Bronx—run from danger, keep your fists up high, fight as dirty as it takes to escape. Inertia was the enemy.

So why was she just sitting here?

Because a few menacing words had stripped away her armor, stripped away the cover-up that said she was strong, that fooled her into believing she was safe.

It took only one disturbing telephone call to reveal that she was made of hot air. There was no getting around who she really was—a terrified woman on the run from a dark memory.

That alone had been a good enough reason to move to the West Coast. But the geographic escape had also given her hope, provided an opportunity to define herself and find some kind of peace.

At least that had been the plan.

Her stomach cramped as the black memory blossomed. She tried to shove it back into the past where it belonged, to squash it,

1

to snuff it out. She breathed deeply, squeezed her sweaty hands together, and hurriedly looked around at the deserted streets where predators could be hiding in any alley, behind any wall. It had been the same kind of night then, a night like this—damp, forbidding. Only worse because it was a Bronx winter night with piles of dirty snow on the ground.

* * *

Gina and another nurse always shared a ride to Jacoby Hospital. But the Bronx facility was short-handed that night; she was fast-talked into an extra four hours, and lost her ride home. The threat of another snowstorm was in the air but she'd decided to walk back to her apartment anyway. It was only a couple of short miles and she needed time alone to come down from all the tensions of the day.

She was in a particularly good mood, had the next two days off, and much to her relief, Dominick was going to hang out with a bunch of his drinking buddies, go down to Atlantic City to gamble. She planned to meet a friend and go to the Metropolitan Museum, maybe even take in the Museum of Modern Art, where a traveling exhibit of Toulouse-Lautrec's work was getting smashing reviews—mostly his popular bigger-than-life posters of brash women. She'd always felt more of a connection to Lautrec's prostitutes than with the delicate female portrayals created by most artists of that era.

When she arrived at their apartment building, exhaustion hit her hard as she climbed the four flights of stairs. Dominick was standing in the doorway, holding a beer bottle by the neck, slapping it repeatedly into his palm.

"Where the hell you been?"

Alcohol fumes polluted her space; she wanted to turn tail and run. He quickly yanked her through the doorway and flung her into the living room. Off balance, she stumbled, smashed her head against the coffee table, and crashed to the floor. An explosion of light assaulted her, everything became blurry.

Her husband's voice was low, tense with anger. "Tell me why I shouldn't bash in your fucking head?" He threw the beer bottle across the room; it shattered against the wall, splashing beer everywhere.

She started to scream, but he backhanded her into silence. She tried to see his face, to plead with him, but everything became lost in a haze. Sound diminished until all she could hear was his incoherent shouting and her hammering heart. She squirmed on the icy-cold floor, trying to get away. Dominick ripped off her panties, fell on top of her and rammed himself deep inside.

"That's the last decent fuck you're ever going to get," he said as he rolled away.

She heard a crash, then pain ripped through her. Red, orange electric flashes of searing fire burned from deep within.

She screamed and screamed until everything shut down.

A buzz of frantic voices broke through: "Stop the goddam blood! Get me more packing! Dammit, she's gonna bleed out!"

"Help me," Gina whispered.

"She's awake!"

Someone took her hand. "We've got you, Gina."

"Who?" She tried to open her eyes, started drifting away. Words were running together, fading.

"Asshole … broken beer bottle … she's not gonna make it. get her to the OR … now!"

* * *

Neighbors had heard her screams and called 9-1-1. Otherwise she would have bled out on the apartment floor.

It had taken two days, six units of blood, and two surgeries for the medical staff to put her back together. They even saved her uterus, though being able to have children was still an unresolved issue. But she knew it was not likely.

Her breath caught between uncontrollable sobs. Could she ever rid herself of the terror that Dominick would find her now that he was out of prison? Could she ever rid herself of the fear of

3

being totally helpless again? Could being with Harry finally make her feel safe?

She wiped her tears on a sleeve. A spike of anger stiffened her spine. She pulled a business card from her purse, bit down hard on her lower lip, and punched the phone number into her cell.

"San Francisco Police Department."

"Detective Mulzini, please," she said, looking at his card. He was the only cop she knew by name.

"Sorry, ma'am, he's off duty for the next few days."

Gina paused, unsure how to proceed. "I need to speak to someone about a telephone incident."

"Obscenities?"

"No, no! Worse than that. Weird, scary stuff. Someone might even be dead."

"A possible homicide?"

"Yes."

"Then you want Detective Yee. Hold on a sec."

Gina tapped a finger on the steering wheel, thinking about the wheezing voice. It made her jumpy. She listened again for any signs of life near her car. It was quiet around the hospital. By now the day staff was either in a favorite hangout, getting a head start on the weekend, or curled up with a good book and sipping on a glass of wine.

"Detective Yee here," said a female voice.

"Yes, hi! My name's Gina Mazzio. I work…I'm an advice nurse at Ridgewood Hospital."

"Would you spell that, please?"

"What, Ridgewood?"

"No, *your* name."

"Mazzio. M-a-z-z-i-o."

"And what can I do for you?'

"About an hour ago I had this call on the advice line that was really disturbing."

"And you say you're a nurse?"

4

"That's right."

"What about this call?"

Gina could tell she didn't have the detective's full attention. She pictured the cop sitting with a take-out dinner, just waiting to get her off the line.

"The man who called said a woman had been … sliced."

"I see."

Right then, Gina knew Yee *didn't* see, didn't believe, didn't care.

"When will Detective Mulzini be back in the office?"

"He's not going to be much help to you. He and his wife are off to Hawaii for the next week." She gave a self-conscious laugh. "'Fraid you're stuck with me."

"Is there anything you can do?"

"Well, tell me, did you get a name or call-back number? Anything that could help us identify the caller?"

"No. He hung up on me."

"And you expect me to do what?"

"I was hoping there might be *something*."

"Without more information, Ms. Mazzio, there's nothing we can do. I'd say you were a victim of some loser starting out his weekend with a crank call." She paused. "There're plenty of those around."

"I thought that, too, at first. But, if you'd heard him—"

"I'm sure it was scary. But you haven't given me anything to work with."

"I see."

"Listen, if he calls again, give me a call. How long you gonna be there?"

"I'm already off work, calling from my car."

"Wish I could be of more help, but this kind of thing's pretty hard to track down." She paused. "Let me mull it over. Call me if it happens again. Okay?"

"I suppose that's what it'll have to be."

Gina started the Fiat and drove off into the darkness, her mind racing far ahead of every intersection. The detective hadn't believed a word she'd said.

If she and Harry weren't getting married tomorrow, and out of town until Wednesday, she would have talked to her manager first thing Monday morning, or even now. But Lexie Alexandros was also going away for the weekend, might have left town already.

She glanced at her watch. Late. She wondered if Harry was back from his travel assignment in Denver. If so, he was probably pacing the living room, wondering where she was. She sped up and gave a sigh of relief as she turned onto her street, and miracle of miracles, a car pulled away from the curb in front of the apartment building. She nosed into the empty space, avoiding having to do the dreadful parallel parking thing.

When she entered the lobby, Harry was standing by the elevator, suitcases on the floor. "Great timing," he said, giving her a huge grin.

She ran toward him and launched all 5'10" of her into his arms.

Harry squeezed her, nuzzled her neck. "Hey, beautiful, I wasn't gone all that long. Just another out-of-towner." He leaned back and looked straight into her eyes. "I sure did miss you, though."

"And I was afraid you'd be upstairs wondering what the heck happened to me." She buried her fingers in his black hair and tousled his curls.

He looked at her with dreamy blue eyes. "If you don't stand on your own two feet soon, we're both going down for the count."

She loosened her hold and allowed her feet to slide to the ground. He tightened his grip on her waist.

"I'm so glad you're back," Gina said. Tears rolled down her cheeks; she pulled a tissue from her pocket.

6

"Hey," he said, pulling her into the elevator, "what's going on?"

She tapped the button for their floor. "I'll tell you upstairs."

* * *

"So, how was Denver?" Gina asked. They sat at the dinner table, bathed in the glow of candlelight. From the time they'd sat down, she'd merely picked at her food.

"Another fiasco, but then what else is new?" He reached across and took her hand. "That's not really important. Tell me what's got you so upset."

"Later." She still couldn't talk about it. "I want to hear about your two-week stint in the Mile-High city."

He rolled his eyes to the ceiling, let out a deep groan, and put down his fork.

"As usual, I couldn't keep my big mouth shut – dared to question the ICU manager about her out-dated protocols for sepsis," he said. "She all but told me to shove it and shove off. 'What does a traveling nurse know anyway?'" He gave Gina a brilliant smile. "But the mountains were spectacular, covered with fresh, glistening snow. It was so pristine. I kept wishing you were there with me."

When she didn't respond, he looked at her plate of pasta, which she'd still barely touched. "Hey, you usually like my Italian. Now I know there's something seriously wrong."

Gina quickly stuffed a forkful of spaghetti into her mouth, chewed, then smacked her lips. "You're the best Italian cook in the world. Next to me, of course."

She dipped her garlic bread into the sauce and took a big bite. She knew the concoction had its origins with an off-the-shelf brand that had been tastefully enhanced by Harry's own combination of herbs and spices. It was pretty good *ersatz* Italian.

"You've become even more adept at changing the subject than I am," he said. "If you don't want to talk about whatever it is, just say so."

7

Gina shrugged, took another bite of spaghetti, and started collecting their plates.

"So, that was it with the ICU manager?" she asked as they rinsed off the dishes, put them in the dishwasher.

"Unfortunately, no," he said. "Actually, I sort of pulled a Gina."

"And what does that mean?"

He ran soapy water into the pasta pot and swirled it around with a brush. "I did what I thought needed to be done."

"Oh-oh!"

Harry kissed her cheek. "Anyway, instead of a reprimand, I got bamboozled into going before the hospital's Future Health Care Committee. Jumped right in and told them how inadequate their provisions were for the community's underprivileged. And I suggested that maybe the docs should step up to the plate and become more vocal if they wanted to see any real change."

"Are we the only ones who actually think a change in health care for the poor is going to happen?"

"I hope not."

"Don't know why you go to meetings like that. It's always talk, talk, talk. Nothing ever seems to get done."

"Yeah, but just think about it: Out on the road, *I* get a nice variety of bureaucratic bullshit, while at Ridgewood, you get the same old crap over and over. How boring is that?"

Gina stretched and headed for the living room. "Let's have some music to soothe the savage breast." She set the player on random after selecting a number of their favorite CDs.

"You got Santana on there?" he asked.

"That and some Gato Barbieri."

Harry leered at her. "Ah, wild romance to a Latin beat."

Gina smiled, but avoided saying anything about their plans for the next day.

"I've seen that look before, Mazzio. You aren't going to do it again, are you?"

"Do what?"

"C'mon! Regina and Bill have gone to a lot of trouble to make things happen." He straightened the scatter of magazines on the coffee table, a little more forcefully than necessary.

"I know," she said. The Latin beat floated through the small apartment.

Grabbing her hand, he pulled her down onto the purple sofa they'd recently found at a garage sale. He tossed the yellow throw pillows on the floor and nodded at the print of Chagall's *Lovers in the Night* that hung over the sofa.

"I still think that's a portrait of us," he whispered.

They kissed until Harry pulled away. "I missed you, beautiful, and I really want to talk about our wedding, but before we do anything, you have to tell me what has you so down."

It took a moment for her to get the words out. "Something happened; it triggered some old memories. That's all."

"The woman I ate dinner with tonight is not the woman I'm planning to marry tomorrow. *My* fiancée would have given me a half-hour discourse, with flying hands, for God's sake, in a lousy Bronx-Italian accent about my hybrid spaghetti sauce."

He tilted her chin; they gazed into each other's eyes. "Now tell me what's going on. Please!"

She struggled up from the sofa and walked to the window. Rain was coming down hard again, cascading from the eaves and rushing furiously into the street. The streetlights made it look as if someone was pouring water from a huge bottomless bucket.

"I spoke to a crazy man today."

"A man? I thought most of the nutcases you spoke to in Ob/Gyn were women."

"Ha, ha! Aren't you the cute one?"

Harry held up his hands in mock surrender. "Just trying to be my usual humorous self."

"This guy wasn't funny. He said a woman had been cut into pieces."

Harry rescued a pillow from the floor and tossed it back onto the sofa. "Come on, Gina. He's not the first nitwit who's tried to get his jollies by shaking you up on the phone."

"True. And it takes a lot to get to me, *really* get to me. But this was different."

He moved next to her at the window, slipped a hand into hers. They both watched the rain and wind tear at an umbrella a woman was struggling to close before dashing into an apartment building across the way.

"You should have heard his voice, Harry. He was having so much trouble breathing it intensified everything he said. Made it even creepier."

"Why would he call a female advice line?"

"Wish I knew."

Harry wrapped his arms around her, crushed her to him. "I haven't seen you so wrought up, so troubled since the last union negotiations."

"I wanted to let Lexie Alexandros know about it, but she was gone at five … on the dot. I tried the hospital's Security Hot Line. And guess what? It was busy. I even tried Administration, if you can believe it."

Gina said in a falsetto voice, *"Ridgewood General's administrative offices are closed for the weekend. Please call back during regular business hours."*

"I felt like I was the only one left, not only in the clinic, but the entire hospital."

"What about the police?" Harry said.

"All I had was a wild story to tell, with no facts to back it up. Besides, I'd had it. I needed to get out of there. I called the cops on my cell in the Fiat and the detective I talked to treated me as though I was mentally challenged. She basically blew me off."

"There's nothing you can do now. Tell your manager about it when you get back to work on Wednesday. You know, after everyone has finally started calling you Mrs. Lucke."

"I can't let go of it, Harry. What if there *is* some sicko out there."

"And what if it's just some Neanderthal playing a rotten prank?"

Gina kept hearing the caller's words as a replay, over and over and over: *Someone has to stop the cutting, the killing.*

"But suppose he's murdered a woman?" Gina returned to the sofa and plopped down. If Harry didn't believe her, who would?

"Okay. So on Wednesday, tell Alexandros—"

"And she'll tell the administrator, and neither of them will believe me. This time I'll probably get tossed out into the street. Good ole troublemaker Mazzio."

Bette Golden Lamb & J. J. Lamb

₪ CHAPTER 4

Three times the caller circled the block, slowing down as the *St. George Specialty Meats* sign came into view. Instead of turning into the parking lot, he floored the accelerator, taking another spin around the block. He wracked his mind, went thought of every possible scenario to keep from doing what had to be done. It was too late. The ER nurse had recognized him, could tell the world what a monster he really was.

Maybe that would be better. Just get it over with.

But he finally drove through the opening in the chain link fence, parked the Jaguar in the shadows at the rear of the building, and walked to the back of the car. When he lifted the trunk lid, the woman unfolded like a striking viper – teeth bared, fingernails extended. She lunged for his eyes.

He flinched, held her off with one arm, and punched her hard on the side of the head. She whimpered like a small puppy and collapsed back into the trunk. He stood transfixed, looking at her closed eyes, her limp body. The back door to the shop swung open, slammed into the outer wall with a bang.

"It's about time," a gruff voice shouted. "I've been waiting more than an hour."

Eddie St. George yanked the woman from the trunk, carried her inside, and dropped her onto a large, scarred cutting table.

"Can't even get here on time. Jeez, you're useless as tits on a boar."

Eddie ignored the tirade, used a boning knife to cut away the raincoat and scrubs. When she was naked, he duct-taped her ankles together, hoisted her on his shoulder, and hung her upside down between two sides of beef.

"Get out of my way!"

Eddie stepped back, dropped onto a stainless steel stool.

"Look at her! What have you done to her face?"

"I had to—"

"How many times have I told you to stay away from their faces?"

"I thought—"

"You thought?" Jacob sneered at him, flicked the back of his hand at Eddie.

"Maybe we should let this one go, Father." Eddie clutched hard at the sides of the stool.

Jacob laughed, fingered the woman's arms, then squeezed her thighs. "No, she's ours now."

Eddie fed a spark of rebellion. "You promised you'd tell me. Where is she?"

Jacob leveled a burning gaze at him. "I'll tell you where your mother is when I'm good and ready. Stop asking me every damn time we do this."

"You've been promising that for ten years."

"So?" Jacob swung the naked nurse into one of the beef carcasses, waited for her to bounce back before pushing her again. "And during those ten years you've been up to your ass in this whole shtick." Jacob pointed a finger at him. "Right?"

Eddie closed his eyes, nodded his head.

"I still remember that first little tasty piece you brought me." He started swinging the woman again, back and forth, back and forth. "Little Eddie will do exactly what I tell him to do. Now get off your ass and get things ready. Milty Hiller will be here any minute. He'll expect the packages to be sealed and ready for pick up."

The woman's eyes fluttered, opened wide. "What?" She stared at them from her upside down position.

"This is how you treat them. Watch!" Jacob spun the woman around and kicked her in the back of the head.

"Please," she pleaded, the word barely understandable. "Let me down. Please!"

14

Sin & Bone

Another harsh bark of laughter cut through the room.

The woman continued to spin. "Stop! Stop!" she screamed. "Please stop! I'll do anything you want."

"You're not fucking your way out of this, Ms. Nightingale."

High-pitched shrieks lanced Eddie St. Georges' brain.

₪ CHAPTER 5

Gina had backed out of their wedding again.

Harry walked out on her Friday night after a horrendous fight, convinced she was never going to marry him. She'd never seen him so angry

She spent the weekend hiding out in the movies. All she wanted was to forget her own problems, get lost in someone else's story. But each time she left the theater's cocoon and headed home, the reality that Harry might be gone forever hit her hard – her head ached, her stomach roiled, and her legs trembled.

Monday morning, dressed and ready for work, she called her manager at the stroke of 8:00.

"Lexie? Gina! I'm going to make you an offer you can't refuse."

"Really? I hope this doesn't have anything to do with your derriere not being where it's supposed to be on Wednesday morning."

"Sort of."

"Not one extra day off. That's final!"

"Not what I had in mind," Gina said. "I'm home and available to work today, if you need me. But we have to talk later."

"Home?"

"Like I said, we can talk later. Do you want me or don't you?"

"Gina, you know damn well the answer to that. It's Monday!"

* * *

When Gina entered the Advice Center, her two co-workers were stunned into a rare silence. She said nothing as she slipped into her chair and began taking calls.

"This is Gina. Yes, I do remember. We talked last week. You still have that infection? Even after you tried what I suggested? Guess we better bring you in and have a look. How about tomorrow at ten?"

While she waited for the patient to check her schedule, she started entering notes in the computer.

"Okay. Sorry things haven't cleared up," she said. She clicked off, and said aloud, "I swear, if I have to talk to one more female about a yeast infection, I'm going to go bonkers."

"Yeah, you're already bonkers," Shelly said. "Besides, you're supposed to be on your honeymoon, not here taking yeast infection calls."

"Cut to the chase, Mazzio," Tina said. "What happened? Why no big, rosy I-got-fucked expression?"

Tina and Shelly cocked their heads, waited for her to explain.

"We didn't get married. That's it! What else do you need to know?"

"So the Bronx bombshell really bombed, huh?"

"Just like you to blame it on me, Tina. How do you know it wasn't Harry's fault?"

"Give me a break," Shelly said. "That guy would do anything for you."

"Admit it," Tina said, "you don't want to get hitched, no matter what kind of bullshit story you make up."

"You have such a professional way of expressing yourself."

"If you don't grab that guy while the grabbin's good, someone else is going to come along and steal him right out from under you ... so to speak."

"Man, he can park his naked buns between my sheets any time," Shelly said, shaking her shoulders to jiggle her ample breasts.

"Don't you guys ever listen to me? I'm seriously gun-shy about getting married again."

"Oh-oh!" Tina said. "I think we're back in the middle of that boring, never-ending 'Will Mazzio Ever Get Married Again' soap opera. I can hear the violins now as you chatter on about the abusive ex-husband."

"You don't know the whole story."

"So you've been messed with, been through the wars," Tina said. "It's time to move on, baby."

"The milk of human kindness just gushes through those skinny veins of yours," Gina snapped.

Shelly pointed at Tina. "Hey, she's got a point there, girl."

"So, maybe you're both right." The room turned silent except for Gina blowing her nose into a tissue.

"It's not that we don't empathize with your past," Shelly said, "it's just that you keep living in it."

"I wish it were different, but when it comes to marriage, something always makes me turn and run."

"To hell with that," Tina said. "Marry them and worry about it later."

"Stop, already."

"*Madre de Dios.*" Tina pretended to pull her hair out. "Why do you always have to be such a drama queen?"

"Look, something creepy happened here Friday. It scared the bejesus out of me. And Harry was anything but supportive."

Gina swiveled back and forth, her chair squeaking, echoing in the room. After a couple of minutes, she got up. "I'm going to take the early break."

"Oh, no, you're not," Shelly said. "You're not going anywhere until you finish telling us what happened."

She hesitated, reluctant to relive the moment. Both the women sat on the edge of their seats, staring intently at her.

"Look, it was like a graveyard around here when I took my last call. This guy came on the line—"

"Guy? Wouldn't mind talking to a few more of those," Tina interrupted. "At least the ones who aren't calling for the little woman because he thinks the poor thing can't handle herself."

19

"Let her tell the damn story," Shelly said.

"Believe me, I wish it'd been you here instead of me. This was one scary dude. He started right off talking about a woman being all cut up."

"All cut up?" Tina said.

"That's what the man said. Kept wanting to know my full name."

"God, you didn't tell him, did you?"

"I know you both think I'm nuts, but I'm not *that* nuts."

"Why didn't you call for help?"

"Like who? Lexie left on the stroke of five, and you know how this place is on a Friday evening—like a tomb. You two were out, I was here by myself. I don't think there was a living soul in the whole clinic except me."

"Not even Security?"

"Couldn't get through."

"What about those over-paid pencil-pushers in Administration?" Tina asked.

"Hah! Their weekend starts at 4:55. Besides, I didn't want to risk having to talk to Vasquez."

"Rumor has it the two of you don't exactly get along," Shelly said.

"Damn straight. Our dear administrator would love to find a reason to fire me, won't even look at me when we pass in the hallway."

"When all else fails," Tina said, "There's always *la policia.*"

"Been there, done that. I spoke to a Detective Yee, but she didn't seem terribly interested, brushed it off as a crank call."

"You should have pushed her harder," Shelly said. "Cops are usually pretty helpful to nurses."

"It was late and I was in a rush to get home to Harry. I got rattled."

"Probably just some idiot jerking off," Tina said.

"Well, I told Harry about it. He thought it was a prank, too. Didn't think it was worth worrying about."

"So that's the reason you didn't get married?" Shelly said.

"Isn't that reason enough?" Gina couldn't look at either of them. Instead, she glanced at the call-waiting board. It was a sea of blinking red lights.

Shelly leaned over and whispered, "I'm really fond of you, Gina Mazzio, but I gotta say, you confuse the hell out of me."

"Have you and Harry really broken up?" Tina said. "Like, forever?"

"I don't know."

Gina blew her nose again. She could barely get the words out: "I need him to believe in me. Or I don't need him at all."

* * *

Gina clutched a damp tissue as she caught the elevator to the cafeteria, ripping mad that Tina and Shelly had treated her like an emotional lightweight. The fact that they found her mostly amusing was not amusing at all. It was damn insulting.

And as for Tina? Gina wanted to treat her to a Bronx blue plate special – a whopping knuckle sandwich, with a dropkick on the side. Maybe that kind of indigestion might dull her appetite for flippant remarks.

And what about Harry? Accusing her of making up an excuse, any excuse, just so they couldn't get married? What was that all about?

Asshole!

She kicked hard at the wall of the empty elevator.

Asshole!

This wasn't the first time Harry hadn't seen eye-to-eye with her. He hadn't exactly believed her when she thought her patient's bone marrow was being held for ransom. And it still stung that he hadn't backed her innovative ideas as the lead contract negotiator for the nurses' union. He'd claimed she was being too aggressive, was making Vasquez and the hospital negotiators turn a deaf ear to the union's requests. He suggested more than once that she should back off. Instead, she'd pushed even harder for the things the nurses wanted, particularly a comprehensive pre-school childcare package. And she'd won.

Did she have to prove herself with every breath?

Well, screw you, Harry Lucke.

In the cafeteria, she grabbed a cup of coffee and whizzed through the line looking for a place to settle in.

"Hey, over here, Gina. Grab a seat." It was Arina Diaz.

Gina wanted to be alone, to think about a life without Harry, to think about the nutcase who called Friday. But she smiled at Arina, who waved her to the table.

Gina set her cup down and slipped into the chair opposite the Labor/Delivery Room nurse. It didn't take long to realize Arina was also upset or why she wanted company.

"Jorge just takes me for granted, Gina. Can you believe it? I moved away from my parents just so we could spend time alone. Only now I'm the one who's alone."

Gina tried to look sympathetic, but her mind was on her own problems. She couldn't come up with an appropriate response.

"Hey, here I am running on and on about me when the word is that you married Harry Lucke over the weekend."

"It didn't happen, Arina, no matter what you may have heard." Gina's voice caught in her throat.

"You gotta be kidding! I've seen that *hombre* with you. He absolutely worships the ground you walk on. What happened?"

Gina checked her watch, pretending to be on a short break. "Maybe when I have more time we can talk about it."

Arina looked disappointed, but smiled. "Let's get together for lunch sometime. That would be cool."

"Ciao," Gina said, barely making it out of the cafeteria before tears gushed down her cheeks.

₪ CHAPTER 6

CHEMwest's oval conference table spread out before Eddie St. George – a freshly polished, satin surface without a scratch or finger smudge on the solid teak. He jammed his sweaty palms underneath it and took a trio of deep breaths.

The regional sales manager had yet to arrive and, in fact, he wasn't due for another five minutes.

The clock took on a stern face, shouted the current minute: **7:55.**

Robert Merz would cross the threshold and take his place at the head of the table, primed and ready for his ritual Monday morning let's-start-the-week-off-right meeting. The sales staff hated the mandatory get-togethers and the buzz was that most didn't sleep well the night before.

Everyone's eyes watched the doorway as they topped off their coffee cups, stuffed last minute muffins or bagels into their mouths. Anything solid had to be finished before the boss arrived. No spitting mouths or loose food crumbs around *his* conference table.

Eddie followed the second hand's smooth circuit, then watched everyone settle down as they got ready for the hammer of evaluation. Nothing new, just the usual monthly trash-your-performance-to-pieces.

The room was getting hotter, the air foul with crackling fear, excitement, and ugly tentacles of sexual heat that smacked of raw competition. Scrutiny was the name of the game and Eddie hated the sense of doom that permeated the conference room.

Why should I be nervous?

He was one of those unique birds that flew in the upper stratosphere. No one was going to pull the rug from under *him*.

The company's monthly sales graphs, prominently displayed on two large easels, were there for everyone to see; they not only made him king of the mountain, but showed a reign of consistency that defied the competition. Rarely did anyone come close to the revenues he generated. He'd been awarded four free trips to anywhere in the world, and though he'd never taken advantage of these outstanding performance bonuses, he had taken a few free weekends to Vegas, New York, and Los Angeles. But it was no free ride for him—he paid a high price in verbal abuse from Father each time he dared to leave the Bay Area.

Yes, his performance demanded a grudging respect from every sales rep in the room. And while they were all nice enough, he'd made it plain he didn't want or need their friendship—and especially the questions that came with it.

His stomach howled an audible growl; he searched the room to see if anyone heard or cared.

No. Everyone was too caught up in his or her own thing to acknowledge anything that occurred beyond the space they occupied.

St. George took more deep breaths and forced a casual glance at the four men and three women that made up the sales staff of CHEMwest-Northern California Region.

All the reps were going into hyper drive, shifting in their seats, taking notes, repeatedly lining up pens and pencils, tapping fingers on their notepads, and laughing a little too loud, too often.

7:57.

Three more minutes and Regional Sales Manager Robert Merz would appear, take his seat and begin the two-hour session.

St. George tried not to think about it, but his mind drifted to the last woman he'd snatched, taken to the shop. He couldn't get her face out of his head.

She'd looked at him with, what was it?

Betrayal?

Her eyes screamed: I know you. How could you do this?

24

Squirming in his seat, he tried to focus on something else, but he couldn't block the memory of those questioning, accusing eyes. They haunted him:

Why? Why me?

If he could have told her, would she have understood?

She was a nurse, like Mother. Nurses were supposed to understand, Father said. Nurses knew life wasn't a Disney fantasy. And if Eddie could, he would have helped her, would have helped all of them. He closed his eyes, shut down the image, and forced his mind back to the present.

The other CHEMwest NorCal reps had his attention again. He concentrated on each person, spaced around the table, as though set equidistant on a three-dimensional chessboard. St. George could visually define the territorial borders each had mapped out.

The women were clones of each other. Young, seductive, but still business-like in their dark suits and expensive, muted silk blouses. There was little to differentiate one from the other. St. George sometimes wondered if they checked with each other in the morning before going to work. On any day no two ever wore the same color blouse. He studied each in turn, focused on the brunette who sat directly across from him.

You think being a woman gives you a leg up, don't you, Martine Yamada? How many of those docs have made it into your panties? And you're still not top dog, are you?

He wondered if she remembered their one night together. She turned her head just then, almost as if she knew what was on his mind. He nodded and gave her a quick thumbs-up, but she averted her eyes and began rearranging the pencils in front of her.

The men were beardless, with close-cropped hair. All of them dressed in custom tailor-made suits, with rep ties that were expensive, subdued, and conservative. He took satisfaction in the fact that he was the only one with even the slightest offbeat appearance: his red, gelled hair often brought snide remarks, especially from Merz. But he knew that man was never going to mess with success. St. George brought in enough money to leverage some individuality, as long as it didn't get out of hand, and he continued to be a winner.

8:00

Robert Merz burst through the door, quickly covered the length of the room with long strides, and took his seat at the head of the table.

"So, Marti," Merz said without any preliminaries. "I see your stats are still hovering over the toilet. What's the problem?"

Yamada's skin lost all its color. "I'm on it, Bob. You'll see a big turn-around next month."

"What's your criteria for handing out these expensive perks?" Merz said sharply, consulting his notebook computer. "Let's see, two trips to Paris for the good doctors Grandemange and Farkas at Ridgewood, yet, their orders aren't worth mentioning. Looks like you're trying to frost the cake before it's baked."

"I just need a little more time, Bob."

St. George looked at Marti's animated face.

Did he feel sorry for her? He considered that for a moment.

In a fair world, all the reps should have occupied the same playing field, but the fact that Marti was so young and beautiful should have nudged the odds in her favor. Yet here was Merz roasting her over the coals.

"Time?" Merz leveled a finger at St. George. "Does Eddie ask for more time? No! He does his job, stuffs the big bucks not only into CHEMwest's pocket, but into his own." He swung the finger around and leveled it at Yamada. "Get with it, little girl."

Merz moved on without missing a beat. "So, Archie," he said, taking a quick glance at his open laptop.

The moment was filled with tension; everyone held their breath. Archibald Jervis had been low man on the sales stats for three months running. Merz had been increasingly harsh following the posting of each month's results.

"Archie, when are you going to finally show me those big guns you keep bragging about?" Merz said. "Right now you're only shooting blanks."

The sales manager loosened his tie, getting ready for battle, then sat upright in his seat. "Between you and Marti, CHEMwest NorCal is going down the chute faster than a snowboarder."

Jervis did not change expression. The wide smile he'd walked into the room with took up the same spread of space from cheek to cheek.

"Man," Merz said, "don't just sit there with that shit-eating grin. What's going on in that overly-educated head of yours?"

Jervis flushed, then his skin turned pasty, but the smile remained. A sheen of perspiration oozed on his forehead and St. George could smell the fear two seats away.

"You can't know what a nightmare it is out there," Jervis said.

Merz leaned forward in one quick, threatening motion. "Are you kidding me? It's my business to know exactly what's going on out there."

"I didn't quite mean it that way."

"Well, how the hell did you mean it?"

The tone of Merz' voice caused St. George's chest to clamp down.

No. He's not Father. You're safe here.

St. George pulled his inhaler from a jacket pocket, took two solid puffs. For several seconds he tried to quash the wheezing that squeaked out into the room. They all turned their attention from Jervis to stare at him. Their eyes were merciless, did not waver until his chest eased and silence returned to the conference room.

"Well, Archie? I asked you, just what *did* your dire comment about what's happening out there mean?" Merz demanded.

"The fact that we left the negative results from the latest clinical trials off the informational insert is making the docs suspicious of our big money maker, Longinal," Jervis said. "They're not putting in orders like they did in the past."

"I see."

"Those class-action suits against us aren't doing us any good either," Ellen Carrie blurted.

"And it doesn't help being accused of having the FDA in our pocket, either," Monique Larkin said. "We're getting a whole lot of static about corporate policy that tends to make the job twenty times more difficult."

"What a bunch of whiners. Do you stay up nights thinking up this bullshit?" Merz said. "You're all supposed to be professional sales people. Sales mean selling. Sell the goddam products!"

"We're trying," Yamada said.

"Did you hear what I said?" Merz stood, leaned over, rested his palms on the table. "You need to sell more. Do you hear me? More! MORE!"

Goose bumps rose on St. George's arms. He stared hard at the manager. Agitated coughs from other reps rippled throughout the room. Some started to get up, assuming the meeting was over.

"No, no, no!" Merz shouted. "Stay right where you are." He turned his attention directly to St. George.

"I've got a biggie for you that's going to make your month, Eddie, maybe even your whole year. And you've earned it. If you think your cohorts are envious now, they ain't seen nothin' yet."

Merz let his eyes roam from St. George to each of the others in turn. Those who had left their seats quickly sat back down. Everyone's attention was hard on the sales manager.

"As we're all painfully aware," Merz said, "the patent will soon expire on CHEMwest's successful and highly profitable lung cancer inhibitor, Pneucanex."

"Zyloctine, right?" said Terence Hawks.

"Forget the generic. Let's stick with our trade name: Pneucanex," Merz said.

This should be interesting, Eddie thought. Merz, in a rare weak moment, once confided that he was often at loss as to how to deal with Hawks, CHEMwest NorCal's only Afro-American detail man. "Really want to get him out of the middle-of-pack in stats," Merz had said, "but I'm afraid if I push too hard I'll get hit with a discrimination suit or some other anti-black nonsense."

"How long before the altered version of Pneucanex is ready?" Larkin said. "And what's the new name?"

"Hold off! I think I can answer all your questions so you don't waste any more of my time," Merz said.

"Essentially," he continued, "the new polymorphic form of Zyloctine-to give it its full, legal, generic name, for the moment, is ready for field trials."

"Thank God!" said Yamada. "When can I start telling my customers?"

Merz glared.

"Sorry," she said.

"Marketing is in the process of putting together a series of pre-launch events, to be closely followed by a launch program to heighten interest and enthusiasm for the altered product."

Merz nodded at several of the reps. "I know many of you have commented that you would like to see marketing come up with a new name for the Pneucanex replacement, and I don't totally disagree. However, what we have is a recognized, mature brand. While we all might have preferred a brand new drug, with a brand new name to fight lung cancer, we go with what we've got.

"So, as they say, if ain't broke, don't fix it-the new name will be Pneucanex-CW."

He held up a hand to stop the moans. "Live with it!"

"And what does the tacked-on CW represent?" Yamada asked.

"And what's the name of the company you work for, Marti?"

"CHEMwes—Oh! Sorry."

"Now, back to you, Eddie," Merz said. "A week from Wednesday there's going to be a nice little ceremony at Ridgewood Hospital. It will involve the head of their Oncology Department, the president of CHEMwest, and an economically challenged lung cancer patient. Plus, as much of the local and national media as we can turn out."

"And my part in this?" Eddie said.

"You'll be point man responsible for delivering the first batch of Pneucanex-CW to Ridgewood. Marketing is putting together a script for you on how to interact with the patient and all the dignitaries involved. Got that?"

"Yes." Eddie was about to say something else when he felt his cell phone vibrating in its holster.

Father!

"Good," Merz said. "Now not a word of this to anyone outside of this office or you can kiss your ass goodbye."

₪ CHAPTER 7

Harry Lucke's focus on a travel brochure was interrupted when the winter rain came crashing down on the roof of the oceanfront cabin Gina and he had planned to share during their four-day honeymoon.

He stared at the colored pictures of Florence, a city Gina had talked about incessantly for the past couple of years.

Would serve her right if I took off for a riotous couple of weeks in that fabulous city and came back speaking Italian like a native.

He flung the literature out into the middle of the room; it hit a Barcalounger and dropped to the floor.

"Who am I kidding?"

What would he do in Italy without Gina Mazzio by his side except wander the streets and moon the days away?

Can do that right here. Save a few thousand bucks.

He moved to the window and stared out at the panorama of the Pacific Ocean. The water was gray and moody with tumultuous white caps; thunderous waves crashed against the rugged shoreline. The random, natural violence suited his mood.

He grabbed a Gortex hooded shell and went out into the rain; the wind-blown drops pelted his face, trailed down under the collar of his corduroy shirt. His feet sank as he trudged along a narrow strip of sand that wove in and out of strewn boulders. The driven rain stung his face; it was what he needed to clear his head and think about his life with or without Gina. He sat down on a wet rock and watched the clouds merge with the ocean.

This time, he feared, his Bronx bombshell had become too much for him. Maybe he needed time away from her.

Usually he could adjust to her mood swings because the flip side brought him the most loving person he'd ever known. It had been that way since the day they met, almost three years ago when he was working Ridgewood's ICU. She was floated in from Oncology to help cover an overflow of new admissions.

They'd clashed right from the start.

* * *

"We need him hooked up now!" Harry yelled.

Gina was struggling with a gurney that was caught in the elevator door. "I just got him here," she yelled back.

"Move!" Harry insisted. "Can't you see this guy's hypoxic?"

She glared at him. "Just tell me where you want him and I'll perform like the puppet you seem to think I am."

He leaned over and read the identification card clipped to her scrubs. "Pop him into the slot next to the nurse's station for now, and for God's sake hook him up to the O2. Got it?"

Without a word, she spun on her heel.

At the end of the shift, Gina cornered him in the elevator.

"Who the hell did you think you were talking to? Don't ever yell at me like that again! Understood?" she said. "Not if you want to leave this place in one piece."

"If you can't keep up, you don't belong in ICU."

"Look, buster, I don't *belong* in ICU. Got it?"

"Oh, yeah. That much was obvious."

"Like I said, don't ever mouth off at me again. I've probably got as many years in nursing as you have, and I expect some respect, especially from another RN. *Capisce?* "

"Hey, I was hassled. I'm sorry."

"Come over to Oncology tomorrow and let me return the favor."

"I said I'm sorry."

"Damn straight."

They turned their backs on each other as the elevator made its descent. Despite their clash, Harry hadn't been able to keep from sneaking a glance at her now and then. He found her very

32

attractive. And once he thought he'd caught her looking at him, or perhaps it was only wishful thinking on his part. He had to admit that for being out of her element, she'd caught on quickly and appeared to be a damn good nurse.

As the elevator came to a halt and the doors slid open, he allowed her to step out first. She didn't look at him as she moved briskly past him.

"Ms. Mazzio?"

She stopped, turned toward him. "Yeah?"

"In an attempt to make up for my knuckle-dragging earlier today, I would very much appreciate it if you would allow me to take you to dinner."

Her steely glare relaxed, she burst out laughing, and agreed to go out with him.

At dinner, he apologized again. "It's a family thing," he said.

"Apologizing?"

"No, acting boorish." And before he realized it, he was telling her about growing up in San Francisco where the men in his family worked the port docks loading and unloading cargo.

"Part of their Saturday night entertainment was to pick on me for going to nursing school."

"And the women?"

"Cook, clean, patch up the men, and have babies."

She laughed.

"You find that funny?"

"No," she said. "A picture flashed in my mind of you in your scrubs exchanging punches with some bearded guy in filthy jeans."

"You mean, with a background like that, how'd I ever decide to become a nurse?"

"Something like that," she said.

He told her about the football scholarship to the University of New Mexico, how he'd majored in sports training, and how that led to thinking about becoming an MD.

"What changed your mind?"

"The scholarship wasn't hefty enough. It wouldn't cover medical school, so I gave nursing a try. Came back to San Francisco for my first job."

"No girlfriends along the way?"

"A date here and there, nothing serious. Most gals aren't too crazy about a guy who's always too broke to take them anywhere."

"You make pretty good money now," she said.

"Haven't met anyone I want to spend it on."

Before long they were seeing each other exclusively; then they moved in together.

* * *

But there was a well of depression from her disastrous first marriage; memories would sprint to the surface at the drop of a wrong word. She would lash out, leave him feeling helpless. At times she would cry, become fearful, not want to leave the bedroom, much less the apartment. It was hard to be objective, to figure out what was real or imaginary.

He'd gone into their relationship with his eyes wide open, understood from the beginning what he was facing. It would take a long, long time, if ever, before Gina would fully trust him, or any man.

Harry looked up at the sky, let the rain wash away his despair.

He wasn't sure exactly what happened Friday night – they were talking, then all of a sudden they were arguing, and then, bam, he was out the door with a half-packed suitcase.

One thing he knew for certain: the wedding was definitely off.

What was it they'd been talking about? He forced his memory to respond: A telephone call. One that came in just before Gina got off work. Some jerk-off trying to pull her chain. That took him back to other times when he hadn't taken her seriously: The bone marrow incident, her work on the union contract. Both had caused terrible rough spots in their relationship, particularly after Alan Vasquez almost fired her.

Mazzio was a serious woman, didn't want to be considered a light weight. Treating her that way wasn't even like him. It was a stupid mistake!

And now, some creep on the telephone was pushing her buttons, causing her to sense danger.

Real or imagined?

"Cutting up women? I don't think so, Gina," he'd said in their apartment living room.

Wrong move again, Lucke.

Still, she should have just given him hell, allowed him to apologize and gone on with their plans.

Or, if she flat out didn't want to marry him, she should just say so and be done with it.

He walked back to the cabin, picked up the brochure he'd tossed aside, and put it in his suitcase next to his laptop and smart phone.

What was he going to do with the two-week break he'd arranged with the traveling nurse registry? The plan was to either work on their apartment, or look around for a new, larger condo. He certainly wasn't going to call in and make himself available for a new assignment right away, and when he did, he would request someplace far, far away, like Alaska.

But he did need a place to stay. Maybe he could hang out at his brother's place for a while.

Harry looked out at the ocean, watched ten-foot waves crash against an outcrop of offshore rocks, spray high into the air.

On a stormy day like this, the two of them should have been tucked away in the cabin, warmed by a roaring fire, making love.

"Shit!"

Bette Golden Lamb & J. J. Lamb

₪ CHAPTER 8

The Ridgewood nurses loved the Swiss chocolate, personalized notepads, and expensive pens that Eddie St. George dropped off on Mondays. Best of all, Oncology's Mike Cliffords had gone ballistic over the free Warriors tickets – floor level, right behind the home bench. In fact, the doc was in such an up mood, he signed off on one of the largest drug orders ever written for Ridgewood's Oncology Department.

Eddie hadn't lost his touch and couldn't wait to see the transaction posted back at CHEMwest so the others knew it, too. Merz would make some kind of phony congratulatory display, then try to grab some of the fame and glory. Eddie was still pissed at Merz for sandbagging him into doing the ridiculous marketing ploy to introduce the designer alteration of Pneucanex. All it would do is eat up time he could be devoting to sales calls.

He entered the elevator, reached for the "G" button, paused a moment, and punched "C" instead—that would let him off at the overpass to Ridgewood's clinic wing. It wasn't a part of the facility he visited very often, but that was where he might find Gina, the OB/Gyn advice nurse who had taken his call Friday evening.

A wave of weariness swept across his shoulders. The physical and mental stress, plus the accelerated pace of Milty Hiller's demands for more packages was exhausting.

And the dilemma of Father's brain tumor. Was it only four months ago he'd learned about it? The shock had worn off as the guilty relief grew. Soon Father would be dead. Yet despite the tumor, nothing seemed to change. Father was the same physically. In fact, he seemed stronger than ever, and even more vicious.

Eddie couldn't face it anymore; it had to end now, and he needed to find Mother as soon as possible, or he might never find her.

Why did she leave? Was it really as Father said? Does it matter? I need to see her again, to hear her voice.

His briefcase became heavier and heavier with every step even though it was actually some ten pounds lighter than when he'd started that morning.

He tried to distract himself by looking out the windows that lined the bridge to the clinic wing, but the height caused an unexpected sense of vertigo. The dizziness passed as he pushed through the swinging doors.

A tall, long-legged woman walked up to him; her name was stitched across the breast pocket of her white coat: Lexie Alexandros, Manager. She gave him a brief up-and-down evaluation, pausing at his red, gel-spiked hair before carefully reading his visitor's identification tag.

"Are you lost, Mr. St. George? We usually don't see CHEMwest reps in the clinic."

Perspiration trickled down the small of his back. He made a quick evaluation as to whether this woman represented a danger to him.

"I know." He smiled, looking deep into her eyes. "Mike Cliffords has been hounding me for months to check out the clinic wing. Said he would appreciate my input with respect to future renovation plans."

He waited a moment for Alexandros' reaction. When none came, he added, "Guess that's because I walk the halls of just about every medical facility in the Bay Area." He waited again. "Anyway, he thought I might have a fresh idea or two."

Her features relaxed; she flipped a lock of hair out of her eyes. "We're pretty low down on *that* totem pole. No money, no new clinic." She laughed out loud. "But that's Clifford's pet committee. He plagues everyone for ideas." She ambled away.

"Have a look around. It won't take long to see the obvious." She tossed a goodbye wave over her shoulder.

Eddie set his case on the floor, pulled a notebook from his pocket, and scribbled a bunch of nonsense, waiting for the pounding in his head to stop.

He peered down the clinic's two corridors: one with offices that alternated on either side of the hallway, the other with a continuous stream of patient examination rooms.

He put away the pad, picked up his briefcase, and edged past several empty offices. Checking his watch, he realized he might be out of luck. It was still the lunch hour.

Then he heard *her* voice—Gina!

She was in an office, explaining to someone why she didn't get married over the weekend. He could tell from the timbre of her voice that she was close to tears.

"…what do you want me to say?" Gina said. "We didn't get married. That's it."

He looked down the corridor, afraid someone would catch him standing there eavesdropping. But this room was at the far end of the hallway and he'd only passed three other offices directly before this one, all of them empty, at least for the time being.

He pulled out a pad and pen again. If anyone showed up, he would pretend to be thinking, taking notes.

"... something happened here Friday. It scared the bejesus out of me. And Harry was anything but supportive."

She's going to tell them about my phone call. Who else has she told besides her boyfriend?

"…why didn't you call someone? … like who? … don't think there was a living soul … not even Security? … couldn't get through … Administration? … didn't want to risk having to talk to … with our history … I wouldn't even try … there's always *la policia* ... spoke to a Detective Yee ... she didn't seem terribly interested; brushed it off as a crank call."

The jumble of voices convinced him that the other nurses didn't believe her.

"I'm really fond of you, Gina Mazzio, but I gotta say, you confuse the hell out of me. Have you and Harry Lucke really broken up?"

Eddie's hopes fell. No one had believed her. Yet, what had he expected, that some magical savior or non-existent exit would appear with one telephone call? That he could then find Mother and they would disappear together? Escape from Father?

What a fool I am.

Father was right: Eddie would continue to get away with everything. He'd be clever, look innocent, and most people will never see a thing, even if it's right in front of their noses.

He pressed against the wall, moved in closer to hear the rest of the conversation. He lost the thread of what they were saying. Remembered with little boy eyes when he hid in the butcher shop and watched Father:

Peek around the corner, hide among the aprons on fat wooden pegs. They hang nice. The red stuff makes funny pictures on the cloth.

Father left me in the office with my crayons.

He would beat me if he knew I snuck out. Don't matter. Father beats me anyway.

Mommy used to save me.

Mommy's gone.

Miss Mommy.

Want to cry, to scream at Father. But hide so he can't see me.

Promised not to come into the shop. Promised to be good, stay in the office.

Always tell Father I don't want to come here. Brings me anyway. Brings me every day except Sunday. Here, with the bad smells.

See a girl with no clothes on

Sin & Bone

Blink, rub my face. She looks right at me. Tries to tell me something. The smell of the aprons makes me dizzy.

Father walks up to her, calls her "Lola," Mother's name. But she's not Mother.

Her screams are loud, hurt my ears.

"Let me go, you bastard!"

Father laughs. Laughs the same mean way he laughs before he hurts me. Hurts me bad.

The room spins. Don't like Father hitting her.

Squint, make everything turn blue to cover it all up. Blue is nice. A shiny blue like the broken crayon I left in Father's office.

More screams. Cover my ears, cover my face. Peek through my fingers. Have to see.

Fingers spread wider.

Father throws her on the table. Climbs on. Rides her like a cowboy. Want to yell but must be quiet. Father will find me, beat me.

Don't want to look. Throat closing. Can't breathe. Gulping. Choking. Need air.

Try to make it go away.

Make the blue darker.

Darker.

The girl screams louder.

Louder.

Her eyes burn me. Feel my tears dropping, spilling on the aprons.

The cowboy gets up, roars like a lion, carves a dripping red smile on her neck.

Father turns, looks right at me, points.

He's coming for me.

* * *

Gina raced from the office, a bundle of flailing arms as she rammed into Eddie outside the door.

"Sorry!" she tossed over her shoulder as she spun away and hurried off down the corridor.

He could still feel the place where her breasts had crushed against his chest; still sense her female pungency.

He took off after her but the distance widened as she sprinted across the bridge connecting the clinic to the hospital. His heavy leather sample case cut down his speed, banged hard against his leg, making it awkward to close in before she ducked into the elevator.

"Hold it!" he yelled.

When he entered, he was sweaty and breathing hard. She released the hold button and the door clamped shut; she dabbed at her eyes with a soggy tissue, barely looked at him.

"Thanks." Eddie eyed her nametag to make sure it was the right nurse: Gina Mazzio, RN.

Could this really be the same person who took his call on Friday? He'd visualized a short, stocky, blonde nurse with a fat marshmallow face, although he couldn't think of a single reason why he'd thought that. This woman, with her black, cropped hair, was tall and athletic. Her eyes were sad but fiery.

How could his impressions have been so far off?

Father would have been unimpressed with such a question; he would have demanded that Eddie stick to the facts:

– Gina Mazzio's fiancé had walked out on her;

– No one believed her about his "crank" call, thought it was just another crazy person of some kind; and

– Some misstep in the past made her vulnerable to losing her job, made her reluctant to go to the Administrator.

Hairs on the back of his neck prickled.

He wanted to jab a finger into the nurse's chest, tell her what had been drummed into him ever since he could stand: Depend on no one. Not a single soul.

He watched her continue to wipe away the tears running down her cheeks.

The clunk of the elevator brought him back to the moment; thoughts vanished as the door opened at the entryway to

Ridgewood's large cafeteria. They both stood looking for places to sit.

"Kind of crowded," Eddie said. "Would you mind sharing a table?"

The nurse's eyes burned into his; he felt naked, exposed, as if she knew he was the one who had called Advice.

He forced himself to look directly at her without blinking. Her answer was cool, to the point: "No, thank you. I'd rather be alone."

"Problems?"

Tears welled again as she glanced at his visitor's pass: "Mr. St. George," she said, her voice quavering. "You obviously can't take a hint. I don't want to talk to you. Or anyone. If that hurts your feelings, I'm sorry."

Without another word, she stepped away to join the cafeteria line, dismissing him.

* * *

Gina grabbed two servings of raspberry Jell-O and ordered a double shot of espresso before staking out a table that had emptied near the garden window. As she sat, she stared blindly at the view, then back at the red quavering blobs in the dessert dishes.

Why on earth did I take Jell-O?

She pushed the gelatin away, sipped her espresso.

"Hi, Gina!" said a voice from behind her. "Mind if I share the table with you?"

She turned to see who it was Megan Ann Hendricks from Oncology.

Was she up to a conversation with the nurse who had her former job? But there she stood, enviably petite, with gorgeous flaming red hair, waiting politely for Gina to answer.

Gina waved a hand. "Sure! Sure!" She'd wanted to talk to her friend Helen in Oncology, to catch up with all the gossip, but it hadn't happened. Maybe Megan Ann could fill her in; take her mind off her disastrous morning.

"Thanks!" Megan Ann sat down, spread her napkin on her lap, and immediately started in on her tray full of the day's special: tortilla soup and tacos. She seemed preoccupied as her gaze drifted around the cafeteria.

Gina studied the deep lines in Megan Ann's forehead, the smudges of darkness under her eyes, and a mouth that drooped at the corners. She knew a troubled face when she saw one.

The first time Gina met Megan Ann, she'd wondered why her shoulders seem to slide down into a sadness that was open and raw. Not much different than the way Gina felt today.

She followed Megan Ann's gaze and watched her stop to stare at the CHEMwest rep, who was still looking around for a place to sit.

For no apparent reason, St. George made her think of her fiancé, even though this man was tall and extremely handsome. And Harry? Harry was Harry.

"Look at him," Megan Ann said. "Isn't he the most beautiful man you've ever seen?"

Gina pushed her Jell-O farther away and studied the "beautiful" man—expensively dressed, long and lean, with shoulders that went on forever. And there *was* something else. Even with his funky gelled hair, he exuded an innocence, a boyishness that made him look endearing and vulnerable. Against all reason, Gina felt protective toward him; she could see why Megan Ann was attracted.

"He's all right," Gina finally said.

Megan Ann's arm shot up; she waved furiously at St. George. "Eddie! Over here!"

The hunk's eyes lit up in recognition. He smiled at both of them as he strolled over to their table.

Megan Ann seemed to be melting right before Gina's eyes. Against her will, she felt a twinge of sexual heat herself.

"Man, I've never seen it so crowded in here." He set his tray down on the white Formica table and dropped his sample case next to the vacant chair. If he harbored any resentment over

Gina's earlier rejection, he hid it well. With a sigh, he eased his long frame into what became a tiny chair. He immediately used his fork to seriously dig into a large Caesar salad.

All Gina could think about was Harry. Harry, who had disappeared, leaving only a note in their mailbox. She'd read the note over and over. The words still burned in her head:

I can't believe you would make up such a crazy story to get out of marrying me. All you had to do was tell me the truth, whatever it is. Anything is easier than living with this kind of uncertainty, never knowing from one moment to the next when it will be over between us. I need to be alone to think about things. Think about us. If there is an us.

She pinched her arm. Maybe she'd cancelled their wedding one time too many, maybe he would never believe in her again.

Why can't he understand, have enough faith in me to know I love him, would never lie to him about anything?

Gina stood, tears blinding her. She abandoned her tray and ran from the cafeteria.

* * *

"I hope my sitting here didn't upset her," Eddie said.

Megan Ann looked up from her soup, her face a mask of bewilderment. She turned to watch Gina disappear through the exit.

"That's not like her."

"Well, she did seem very unhappy," Eddie said.

"I didn't notice."

"Is she a friend of yours?"

"Not really." Megan Ann picked at the crisp edge of her taco; thin bits of half-melted cheese hung over the sides. "I used to work in the Ob/Gyn Advice Center, where she works. We sort of swapped jobs." She left the spoon in her soup and took a small bite of the taco, chewed slowly. "She seems like a very nice person. I don't think she blames *me* for what happened."

"Blame you? For what?"

"The administrator tossed her out of Oncology. The word is he has a grudge against her, that he forced her out of the department; would love to find a good reason to get rid of her."

"What happened?"

"Don't know. Heard it had something to do with her not being cooperative."

"Hospitals usually try to hang on to their floor nurses."

"No one talks about it much anymore."

Eddie let his thoughts about Gina Mazzio drift away. He gave his full attention to Megan Ann.

₪ CHAPTER 9

Most of the time Megan Ann Hendricks accepted the screams in her head; they were constant and shaped each and every one of her days.

At her best, she could cope with the noise and seductive whispers begging her to forget about staying clean and sober. At her worst, she was overcome by a secret self that binged on alcohol, binged on drugs, binged on sex.

And she never knew what would set her off: too much rain, a patient who looked at her in a desperate way, or memories of her lost husband and child.

One moment she was in control, the next, voices would whisper:

Where were you while your family was burning?

Always the same question, and the answer was simple – she'd been enjoying herself at a movie, sitting with a friend, laughing at funny images on a screen, never knowing she'd lost everything.

At work, she would bolt to her locker and dip into her cache of Valium and vodka. The combination obliterated the panic and the pain, made the rest of the day bearable.

Often, she would call in sick and stay away from work, succumbing to her addictions until the screaming in her head was finally reduced to a murmur.

She'd reluctantly agreed to take a position in the Oncology Unit a year earlier, hesitant to leave the safe haven of the Advice Center. She wasn't sure she could handle bedside nursing again, particularly with cancer patients. But to her relief, she was getting great satisfaction from the personal interaction, receiving far more from them than she gave.

Today, she was proud of herself, almost happy – it was a little more than three months since she'd last called in sick. Her reward was Eddie St. George, the CHEMwest rep.

Earlier, she'd seen him in Oncology, had come up behind him, and playfully poked him in the ribs. He was so startled by the physical contact that he lost his footing, and had to reach out for the wall to keep his balance.

"Hey!" Megan Ann said. "Didn't mean to startle you." She looked into his innocent sea green eyes, eyes that made her long for sensual Hawaiian beaches. "I was wondering if you'd be coming in today."

He smiled widely at her. "Ridgewood Oncology, Monday, rain or shine."

Was she coming on too strong? So? She'd wanted him from first sighting – he was tall and carried himself like her lost husband, and that was reason enough. She hungered for Eddie St. George.

"How was your weekend?" she asked, now sitting across from him in the cafeteria. It had to have been much more exciting then hers—doing chores and shopping for groceries.

His smile faded briefly, only to return as he said, "I spent most of my time with Father."

"That's sweet. What did the two of you do?"

He stabbed a leaf of lettuce and pushed it into his mouth.

She repeated her question.

"Oh!" His attention returned to her. "He, uh, worked around the place; I did a lot of studying. We have a new product coming out soon."

"A new breakthrough?"

"I wish that were true, but it's really just a variation on an old theme. Although I suppose I shouldn't say that." He lifted his glass and took a sip of iced tea. "How was your weekend?"

"Definitely not worth discussing."

Megan Ann glanced at the wall clock, saw that her lunch break was almost over, and chastised herself for wasting it on small talk.

"Hey, I've enjoyed having this time with you," she blurted. "Could we continue this, meet for a drink after work?" Her cheeks burned.

"Uh, sounds like a great idea, but not tonight."

She'd upset him, made him uncomfortable. She wanted to run from the cafeteria. Instead, she stood, picked up her purse, and started for the doorway. She was embarrassed when he got up and walked with her to the elevator.

"How about in a week … next Monday?" Eddie said. "Wish I could do it sooner, but ..."

She looked up to see him smiling. Her heart ran wild. "Yeah, Monday would be good." She wished it were sooner but she did have a firm date with him. She dug into her purse, found a slip of a paper, and quickly wrote down her cell number. "Call me. We'll set up a time."

* * *

And he would call; he'd have to keep his word. If the RNs complained about him, the MDs would soon find some reason to pull back on their orders. Merz called that the Trickle U p Syndrome. Eddie found that funny at first, but his manager was right: If the troops weren't happy, no one was happy.

He walked with Megan Ann to the nurses' station, said goodbye, and continued on.

Most of the nurses he passed in the corridor slowed to look at him, most smiled. He knew exactly what they saw: A good-looking, rich bachelor. Someone they could sink their teeth into.

Women who come on to men are tramps.

Eddie didn't believe that, but he never argued with Father.

He thought again about Megan Ann, and how she met Father's requirements: petite figure, flowing red hair, and penetrating hazel eyes. Then ugly visions of other women he'd taken to Father flashed in his mind: lifeless bodies, unseeing eyes, teeth frozen in a death grimaces.

He blinked away the specter and tried to blank out the graphic vision of dissected body parts spread across the butcher shop cutting block.

His chest became heavy as though some giant force was squeezing him.

Sharp twinges curled painfully through his groin. Despite the gross images that disturbed him, he could still smell Megan Ann's seductive scent, hear her voice floating in the air:

"What did the two of you do?"

He heard her ask the question over and over and over.

And he knew he could never answer it, for her, for anyone.

Those answers existed in an abyss, a black hole in the center of his mind where all his darkest memories lived.

₪ CHAPTER 10

Eddie returned to his Jaguar, slipped into the rear seat, and napped in the underground hospital garage until five o'clock. He then moved the car outside to a side street near an exit used by Ridgewood Hospital personnel. He waited, tapping his fingers continuously on the leather briefcase on the passenger seat, watching every female that left the building.

Gina Mazzio and another woman, a strawberry blonde, walked out together, then parted. Gina yelled out, "See you tomorrow, Shelly. Sure you don't want a ride?"

"I'll take a rain check. And I do mean rain, sleet, earthquake, tornado. That's what it would take to get me into that wreck you call a car."

Gina frowned, gave Shelly a thumb down and climbed into a small, red Fiat. He listened as the roadster made loud chugging noises even after it was warmed up.

"So that's Shelly," Eddie mumbled. He waited until Gina was a block away, then began to track Shelly as she ambled down the street.

She had an umbrella that she alternated between swinging in a carefree manner and using as a serious walking aid. Her hips swayed confidently, but every few steps she would noticeably limp as though her leg had given out.

Eddie looked up at the darkening sky. It held rain-filled clouds that could open up at any moment.

After five minutes of watching Shelly, trailing about a half a block behind her, his mind zoned into a hypnotic cadence. Stop. Go. Stop. Go.

"I need to get out of here," he said aloud, his voice shaky and unrecognizable even to himself.

No. He would have to stay.

Father's message continued to flash on his cell phone screen; each letter branded into his brain:

M-O-R-E.

He clutched the phone. One word.

MORE.

Since that summer evening when he was ten, the very last time he saw Mother, Father's demands had inundated him, controlled him, made him a slave.

Hot and sweaty, Eddie yanked at his collar.

He was again in that time and space long ago when Mother had bent over to kiss him goodnight after tucking him into bed. Her eyes were glassy, as though she didn't really see him. She was looking at something, someone far beyond him, far beyond the room. The next morning she was gone.

"What were you looking at?" he said out loud; repeated it louder. A woman crossing the street gave him a funny stare. He shrugged and smiled at her, saw her visibly relax.

Need to pay closer attention to what's happening now.

Shelly ducked into a doorway. A neon sign overhead blinked: THE HIDEAWAY.

Eddie found a parking space, beat out someone who hadn't moved quickly enough.

"Hey, what's the matter with you?" the man in the other car yelled. "That's my parking place. I was here first."

Eddie got out of the driver's seat, gave the man a wide-eyed look of discovery and said, "Sorry." He shrugged and strolled towards the bar.

Even though it was Monday, the small local lounge was busy, crowded with people who had obviously just come from work. Most of the men and women wore business suits; there were flashes of smart phone screens everywhere. People nodded, smiled, talked.

Probably telling lies, every one of them.

Eddie stood behind Shelly in the crowd, then eased into a vacated stool next to her. He listened to her and a guy standing on the other side of her bounce small talk back and forth, the kind of bull men and women indulge in before getting to the serious business of hooking up.

Shelly was about forty-five, wore her hair in a ponytail that shone even in the diminished light. Under her unbuttoned raincoat, a gray knit shirt and light green scrub pants looked wilted, and there were large areas of stippled ink markings on the thigh area, probably from tapping a pen on her leg. She lifted her arm to the bartender to order a drink and Eddie caught not only a waft of stale perspiration, but also a scent of female sexual excitement.

What was he doing here? He was exhausted. He closed his eyes, saw the message on his cell phone again:

MORE.

For years Father would demand that he bring a woman to the shop every other month or so. But recently he'd become insatiable. Nothing was enough. It was getting harder and harder to find the type of redheads that Father insisted he bring. Even though his sales territory stretched from San Francisco to San Jose, there were only a limited number of large medical facilities to draw from.

He couldn't understand the increased demand: Father was supposed to be very sick, but the shaking hands or troubled speech he'd expected as a result of the tumor had not happened. Had Father lied to him?

A cellular phone rang out a merry-go-round tune and the man Shelly was talking to raised a phone to his ear.

"Yeah?"

"Okay. I'm on my way."

The man leaned over to Shelly and said, "Sorry, honey, I've got a sick kid at home."

Shelly held his arm briefly and Eddie noticed a large diamond engagement ring on her right hand. Like her opalescent fingernail polish, it flashed in the diminished light.

"Do you really have to go?"

He shrugged her arm off and without another word headed for the exit.

Shelly took a couple of large gulps of her Margarita.

"Better off without him," Eddie said to her. "Seemed kind of like a jerk."

"And who the hell asked you?" Shelly said, her hazel eyes glaring like a striking viper. She turned away and tossed down the rest of her drink.

He leaned back and forced a smile, but he could feel his scalp wrinkling with dissatisfaction. "Sorry! Just trying to make small talk."

Shelly turned back to him, studied his face again, didn't recognize him. But she seemed to like what she saw; she caught the bartender's attention: "Another one, please."

When her drink arrived, Eddie said, "Take it out of this." He handed over a twenty. The server moved away from Shelly's stash of money on the counter and swiped away a crisp Andrew Jackson.

Eddie wanted to leave, wanted to rush outside the bar. He didn't want to pick up Shelly, didn't want to bring any more women to Father. But the insistent cell phone was vibrating inside his pocket.

People were packed in tight around him and the noise level was making his ears ring. He shifted in his seat, focused on the discomfort—made it step back, far back. Soon, he was able to raise his glass of Merlot as she lifted her salt-frosted Margarita. They clinked glasses.

* * *

Shelly leaned on Eddie as he walked her to his car. She gave him her address and immediately passed out, sleeping soundly during the ride to the concrete block building. The roofie he'd slipped into her last drink had worked immediately on her.

When he opened the gate and pulled into the back of the shop, a crash of rain battered the windshield. As he stepped out, the deluge on his neck startled him, added to his misery.

He gagged, retching alongside the car. He couldn't stop. He dry heaved again and again.

"I don't want to do this," he muttered, leaning against the car. "I just want to go home."

But his brain echoed with the insistent admonition: **MORE**!

He was afraid, afraid someone might remember him leaving the bar with Shelly. But there would be a more immediate price to pay if he disappointed Father, and he couldn't face paying it.

A sudden violent energy sprang from nowhere, zigzagged through his arms. It gathered a furious momentum and a chaotic buzzing hummed in his head.

Women are all like your mother. Liars, deserters, users.

Only when he reached into the car for Shelly, yanked her out, and tossed her up and over his shoulder did the noises stop.

She grunted as her gut hit hard against him, but her hand swung listlessly, back and forth, back and forth.

All at once, his chest opened up and a rush of air forced its way through his lungs. He screamed with a strange exhilaration. She became light as a feather as he swept through the smelly lockers into the processing room. Sides of beef and cuts of pork still hung on hooks in the chilled cutting room; fresh sawdust was scattered on the floor. He dumped Shelly onto the hardwood cutting table.

An array of containers filled with organ meat was carefully lined up on an aluminum cart. Next to them were scalpels with various size blades mingled with boning and sawing knives. Eddie cringed, knew he would have to assist Father. They would be there past midnight preparing the packages.

Shelly was moaning and starting to wake up.

Father stepped from behind a swinging side of beef, quickly pulled a pair of poultry shears from an overhead rack, and expertly cut away her clothing as if it were a loose coat of fur. She lay naked, her skin forming goose bumps up and down her arms and legs. Pendulous breasts drooped to the sides of her ribcage; her gut bobbled as she coughed and rubbed her neck.

"Red hair! How many times do I have to tell you? Red Hair!"

"She is a redhead," Eddie mumbled.

Jacob pointed to Shelley's mouse-brown pubic hair. "Wrong! Wrong! Wrong! Just can't get it through that muddled head of yours—red hair, small, attractive. God but you're stupid."

Father duct-taped her wrists and legs to the table, pausing once to look at the large diamond ring on her finger. She was now awake, staring at him.

"Where the hell am I?" she said, looking around the room. First she glared at Eddie, then at Jacob.

"Son-of-a-bitch! What the hell do the two of you think you're doing?"

She yanked against the silver-gray tape; her face turned purple with exertion and rage. Every part of her trembled as she tried to pull free. Father leaned over and licked her face; she turned her head sharply away.

"Sit!" Jacob said to Eddie.

Eddie was shaking but he eased down on a high stool.

"Touch her, you wimp. Touch her!"

He ran a hand lightly across her thigh, across the soft flesh of her stomach.

Father was laughing, but the voices in Eddie's head boomed even louder:

Miserable brat. Stop whining. Do it. DO IT R-I-G-H-T!"

"Let me go!" Shelly screamed.

Eddie's head buzzed, buzzed with a never-ending accusation:

Sin & Bone

It's your fault your mother left me. Left me with YOU.

Jacob's voice was nasty and sweet at the same time. "Nurses should understand the values of anatomy and physiology," he said. "Learning with the real thing is always best." Father twisted, then yanked the diamond off Shelly's finger, held it up to the light, then tucked it away in a pocket.

Shelly was silent; her eyes followed Jacob's every move.

"Think of it!" Jacob said. "Your miserable body will teach future nurses everything they need to know about their insides … with your insides."

Shelly's short, stabbing scream filled the room.

Eddie smashed his hands over his ears, released a loud wheeze.

The elder St. George frowned at him, then turned back to Shelly. His hands poised over her like a surgeon ready to operate. He smiled.

₪ CHAPTER 11

Gina slipped into her apartment and quickly shut the door. She clenched her teeth and tightened her muscles to quell her shaking body, then drifted through the vast pool of darkness she called home. If Harry were here, the living room would have held a warm welcoming light and the rich aroma of one of his many spicy concoctions.

She groped for the lamp switch, allowed the light to pierce the blackness. Everything was as she had left it that morning—coffee table filled with magazines that spilled onto the floor, the morning newspaper folded and unread on the sofa, and a throw blanket on the scruffy chair she kept threatening to replace. It all stared at her reproachfully, including a framed photograph of Harry, with his soulful eyes that seemed to follow her every movement.

When she finally removed her raincoat, she realized the apartment was damp and cold; it also smelled sterile, like some important human component had been drained from the place.

Just four walls.

Her gaze jumped to the answering machine, but there was no blinking light. No new calls. There would be no sound of Harry's voice.

Loneliness washed over her as she sprawled across the sofa, the chill of the room raising goose bumps. Limp, wasted, she felt small and vulnerable, like a child who sprinted home after school to be in a safe, warm place and found herself alone. How many times had that happened to her as a child growing up in New York City, with both parents working?

But there were also many good moments being part of a large extended Italian family of parents, siblings, aunts, uncles, and friends. Together, they created a world of trust, creature comforts, and the wondrous abundance and flavors of Italian cooking. It was as if she and those in the neighborhood had been intermingled during some ritual prenatal exchange, then delivered so tightly bonded they even thought alike most of the time.

Now she was on the other side of the continent, away from her roots. She glanced at Harry's picture again and sighed softly. He was gone also.

Harry!

Another vital connection that no words could explain, but whose loss endangered her sense of belonging.

She sat up, pulled his picture to her. He was the only man who made her feel secure, even if she refused to commit her soul to him. It wasn't his fault—Dominick had ruined that kind of surrender.

Sometimes when she was scared and alone, she shook with fear as she thought about her ex-husband. Memories of that final night with him would flash through her head like a looped, slow motion film.

She started to cry, stopped herself, started again. The worst thing was knowing that the man who brutalized her was her husband, someone she had once trusted, had placed her total faith in.

And the betrayal of her mother and father, who acknowledged what had happened to her, but did nothing. Her parents and in-laws were *paesanos* from the same little village in Italy and that seemed more important than her life-threatening situation.

"You can't put your husband in jail. It was just a misunderstanding. These things happen sometimes with newlyweds." She could still see them standing by her bed, watching a unit of blood flow into her arm as she lay in the hospital, torn and bruised. At the same time, her brother patrolled up and down the streets in his Chevy, looking for Dominick. He'd come back alone, unsatisfied and defeated

For the first time in her life, she identified with the ravaged women of Africa and the non-existent or lowly status of women in the Middle East. She/they had no value except for the children they could bear. And for her, that dubious value might never occur.

Later, they learned that Dominick had holed up in a fishing buddy's upstate cabin. After Gina pressed charges, they picked him up and dragged him off to jail.

Then came his threats of what would happen if she testified, followed by the trial, and sentencing – for the minimum term allowable: two to five years.

Maybe her life, like those of other abused women throughout the world, did have less value in the eyes of the courts.

She clutched Harry's photo tighter to her chest and in spite of herself, smiled. Harry didn't have one drop of Italian blood flowing through his veins, yet he happily merged his identity with hers and allowed her background to embrace him.

"You're my rock, my home," she said to the photograph. "Why didn't I grasp that before?"

The telephone rang. Her heart raced as she grabbed the receiver.

"Hello! Harry?"

"It's Regina. What happened to you? We were supposed to have a wedding this past weekend. I mean, *you* were supposed to have a wedding. I've been calling and leaving messages since Saturday. Don't you ever listen to your message machine?"

"I should have returned your calls, I know." Gina could barely speak, had difficulty swallowing the lump that rose and threatened to choke her. "I'm so sorry."

"Don't tell me you got cold feet again. How on earth could you not want to marry that incredibly cool guy?"

"No, no. It's not that, it's something else. It's complicated."

"Gina, I swear, *you* can complicate the simplest of things. You either love the guy or you don't."

She stood, stumbled over her own feet, and reached for the other lamp.

"I know. And you and Bill went to all that trouble to set up the ceremony. I feel just awful."

"So Harry's not there, huh?"

There was a long silence before Gina answered. "No. I guess I've managed to mess up our relationship, along with everything else."

"Everything else?"

Gina swiped at the tears that spilled down her face. "I'll call you tomorrow, Regina. Can't talk about it right now. Please tell Bill I'm sorry. I'll make it up to the two of you."

"You better call."

"I will. I will."

"Promise?"

"I promise."

Gina gently hung up the phone, slumped onto the sofa, and sobbed until there were no more tears.

She dragged herself into the kitchen, opened the refrigerator, and pulled out a container of vanilla soymilk and fixed herself a bowl of cereal. After a couple of spoonfuls, she pushed it aside.

"*Mangia!*" she muttered, remembering her mother, who would circle the kitchen table like a vulture, demanding that she eat. She started shoveling in spoonful after spoonful until the bowl was empty.

Standing in front of the sink, she pushed aside the crisp, white curtains at the kitchen window. She watched the rain pour down on the cars under the street lamp; they were jammed together next to the curb and seemed to bear the brunt of the cascading downpour. Her little Fiat was standing like a brave soldier, but she knew the one small rip in the vinyl top would allow water to slowly puddle on the floorboard.

She smiled when she remembered how Harry would force them out into a storm just like this one, in whatever they were wearing. He said it would make them feel more alive. And he was right. Her skin would tingle as the icy rainwater spilled over her. And how they'd laugh as they raced around the block, then dash inside to take a long, hot shower together.

During those times, she was much more than alive, she was safe. She was with Harry.

* * *

After a soak in the tub, Gina tried to read herself to sleep, but it wasn't until after 1:00 AM that she turned out the bedside light.

The telephone rang.

She grabbed up the receiver. "Harry?"

Silence.

"Harry, is that you? Please talk to me."

"Gina?"

That voice. It was *him*. Her throat tightened. "How did you get my number?"

"Please, I need to talk to you."

"I'm hanging up."

"I know all about you, Gina."

She froze, stared at the receiver. "What do you know?"

"You help people."

"I'm going to call the police."

"They're going to keep dying." His voice was soft, but intense.

"Who?"

"Shelly's gone. You'll never see her again."

"I don't believe you. You're just trying to satisfy your own sick needs by trying to scare me."

"She won't be at work tomorrow. She's all cut, cut into pieces."

"Why are you doing these terrible things; why are you calling *me*?"

There were several beats before he responded. "I do it for Father."

"Father?" Gina clutched her pillow to her. "Like God?"

"Not God. Father. What *he* says must be done."

Gina looked around the room, tried to focus on a single object, something that would allow her mind to stop jumping from one thought to another."

"You're cutting women up because your *father* tells you to?"

"No, he…"

She waited, then said, "He what?"

"He … he promises to tell where Mother is, but he never does. I beg him, but he won't tell me."

She heard the wheeze. Small squeaks grew in timbre until Gina was struggling to stop a sudden tightness in her own chest. She could barely speak.

"What can I do? You haven't even told me your name." Her hand was dripping wet from clutching the receiver tighter and tighter

"Help me make it stop."

The line went dead.

₪ CHAPTER 12

Car keys in one hand, a piece of toast in the other, Gina tried once more to call Pepper Yee before leaving for work.

"I have your other two messages, Ms. Mazzio," the police receptionist said. "I'll give them to Detective Yee as soon as she comes in."

"It's really important. Can't you radio her?"

"She's in the field, ma'am. If this is an emergency, give me the information and we'll have someone else handle it."

Gina needed to leave immediately if she expected to meet with her manager before her shift at Ridgewood began. "Just tell her it's important that I talk to her."

"Like I told you, ma'am, I *have* your messages ... all of them!"

Gina started to respond, then hung up the phone.

* * *

The caller's words continued to echo in Gina's head as she pushed through the doors to the Clinic: *They're going to keep dying.*

Three large mugs of high-test coffee were propping her up—the only thing that kept her going after being awake most of the night. Her eyes were dry and scratchy, felt like they'd been stretched to their limits in all directions.

She tapped lightly on Lexie Alexandros's office door, knowing that her manager habitually came in early. A wavy shadow moving back and forth behind the frosted glass confirmed she'd been right.

"Come in!"

Gina slipped into the office. Alexandros didn't look up from her computer keyboard, pointed to the uncomfortable hospital-issued armchair opposite her desk. Gina sat, waited impatiently for her manager to finish.

Alexandros was a couple of years younger than Gina: about thirty, with long, dark blonde wavy hair, and a trim body. As the manager typed, engrossed in the monitor, she curled and uncurled a flyaway strand with a nail-bitten finger. Finally, she looked up.

"Sorry! Had to finish entering a report while everything was still fresh in my mind, otherwise I'd have to go back to my handwritten notes later and start from scratch. And you know what my handwriting is like."

Gina shifted in the chair as Alexandros' dark eyes appraised her. She knew she'd dressed haphazardly, thrown on clothes with no thought as to her appearance. But once she put on her white staff jacket, no one would even notice, but she hadn't even looked in a mirror, and she knew she probably was a mess. Although she'd done nothing wrong, she felt like a little kid sitting before the principal.

With jittery fingers, Gina tried to arrange her short, curly hair, tried to ease her tension-ridden back.

"So what's happening?" Alexandros' face relaxed, she gave Gina her full attention.

Gina had promised herself that she would be calm, explain the situation without being her usual bombastic self, but the words sprang from her mouth, like water spewing from a broken faucet. "I think Shelly Wilton may be dead. I tried to call her last night. All night. Right up until I left this morning. No one answered. No one."

"Dead?" A frown etched Alexandros' forehead. An expression of concern, then disbelief feathered her face. Gina knew she had to slow the torrent of words. She had to get herself under control.

Alexandros placed both palms on the desk, leaned forward, and stared hard.

"What on earth are you talking about, Gina Mazzio?"

"He called. Again. That same maniac who called on the advice line Friday. Told me Shelly was dead. Cut up into pieces. For God's sake. Cut up!"

"Friday? Why haven't I heard about this before?"

"I tried to report the first call when it happened, but you'd already left for the weekend. Then we couldn't seem to get together Monday, so I left a written report on your desk." She pointed at Alexandros' IN box. "Now it's happened again."

"Oh, shit!" Alexandros riffled through the papers in the box, pulled out a sheet of paper. "You're right. Here it is."

"You haven't read my report?"

Alexandros held up a hand. "Give me a moment. Let me scan this."

When she finished she said, "Sounds like a crank call to me."

"You and everyone else, including the police."

"What *did* the police say?"

"I just told you … they shucked it off as a crank call."

"And last night, it was the same guy?"

"Damn straight!"

"The same kind of bizarre call?"

Gina glared at her manager. "You don't get it, do you? He called my home! He said more people would die."

"Did you slip up and somehow give him your full name Friday evening?"

"I'm not an idiot."

"Sorry. But did you try the police again?"

"Of course. I've left several messages with a Detective Yee. But I haven't heard back."

"Let me know what happens when you do."

"And that's it, that's supposed to make me feel better?"

"I don't see there's much else we can do." Alexandros' eyes continued to appraise her. "You know, you never did tell me why you and Harry didn't get married last weekend."

67

"What the hell does that have to do with the price of onions in Maui? I know you think I'm a numskull when it comes to male-female relationships, but this phone thing has absolutely nothing to do with my love life."

Alexandros started to speak but Gina interrupted, "Why on earth would you even bring up my personal life?"

"I was trying to give you the benefit of the doubt," Alexandros said, leaning back in her chair.

"Do I look like someone who would make up a ridiculous story just to divert attention from the fact that my love life sucks?" She stood and looked down at her manager. "Do I?"

"Sit down, Gina!" After a beat, "Please!"

Gina plopped back into her chair. She knew if the tables were turned, she would want to know what was going on. She would never react this way to such a disturbing story, no matter how far out it sounded.

"Well?" Gina said.

"You're right, I owe you an apology."

Damn straight!

Gina shifted in the rigid chair. She needed to calm herself. As usual, it wasn't working. Her sleep-deprived, caffeine-soaked brain was holding her hostage. She took a couple of deep breaths.

"I probably should get back to the phones."

"Right," Alexandros said, "we'll talk later, after you've heard back from the police."

* * *

Gina stared at Shelly's empty chair, her brain on autopilot as if another entity was taking the advice line calls. Only yesterday Shelly was sitting there, laughing and giving her a lot of lip about not getting married.

Everything was all just as Shelly had left it the night before: papers scattered across the desk, pens and pencils flung here and there. A wilted rose that one of the RNs had given her was hanging limply in a bud vase half filled with cloudy water.

Sin & Bone

Sadness curled around Gina's heart; she couldn't stand to look at the drooping blossom any longer. She reached over, grabbed it, and tossed it into the trash.

"Have you spoken to Shelly this morning?" Gina asked Tina between calls.

"No."

"I just wondered," Gina said. "It's not like her not to call in sick."

"Are we talking about the same nurse?"

"Well, yeah."

Tina gave a wide smile, her green eyes flashing with mischief. "I've known her to hook up and forget to call in at all."

"Hook up?"

"Oh, shoot! The woman is a bar hopper. You never know who that chick might take a shine to ... have a few drinks ... shack up ... and forget all about work."

"I never thought she was that way. We walked out together last night. I offered her a ride home, but she wanted to walk." Gina reached over and put an incoming call on hold. "She said she didn't trust my little Fiat and that's why she wouldn't go with me."

Tina laughed. "Probably hoofed it to *The Hideaway* looking for someone to take her home for the night."

Gina bit down too hard in the middle of her pencil, then picked splintered wood from her mouth. "How come you're so savvy and I'm totally in the dark about what Shelly does or doesn't do?"

"We used to spend a lot of off time together. Besides, most days you're floating around somewhere up there near the ceiling because of Harry. You don't hear or see half of the things going on around you."

"What's that supposed to mean?" Gina snapped.

"It means you'd better pick up that 'Hold' call.

* * *

The Ob/Gyn manager sat across from Alan Vazquez, the Ridgewood Administrator. Lexie Alexandros had thought long and hard about calling him for a meeting. In the end she hadn't; she'd merely arrived unannounced at his office in the administrative wing of the hospital.

Vazquez had a corner suite with a view of Golden Gate Park. It was a beautiful view even though the day was dreary with another winter storm coursing through the city.

Among the array of diplomas on the wall behind him, the one that interested Alexandros the most was the certificate from UC Berkeley. Even if he was a business major, she couldn't place this straight-laced, humorless man on that particular campus.

He must have been a barrel of laughs during his college days.

Just as she was rethinking her visit, he looked up and gave her a serious, if distracted, smile.

"So, Ms. Alexandros, how are things going in your part of the Ridgewood world of medicine."

The administrator's shirt was heavily starched; he wore a traditional rep tie that would never dream of encountering a stray splatter of food.

"Things are going well, the department is within budget." She laughed softly, but realized business humor was not his thing. He stared at her, waiting for the reason for her visit. "There was an incident last Friday that I thought you should know about."

"Last Friday?" He leaned back and steepled his fingers under his chin, and questioned her by raising a single eyebrow.

"It involves one of my RNs. Gina Mazzio."

Vasquez's hands abruptly fell to the desk and he flipped opened a notebook to a fresh page. "And what has our Ms. Mazzio gotten herself into this time?"

Alexandros didn't like his tone; it made her even more uncomfortable. The administrator's obvious distaste for Gina flavored every word he said. She'd come to him for advice but it

70

was apparently the wrong thing to do. She had no choice but to go on.

"Well, it seems that last Friday night a man called on her advice line and intimated he might have killed somebody. Then last night he called her at home and said that one of Gina's co-workers, Shelly Wilton, was murdered."

"Do you believe her story?"

"I have no reason not to. But it does seem a little surreal."

"Well, let me tell you something: That nurse Mazzio is a nutcase. Why do you think we bounced her out of the hospital and into the clinic?" He shoved the notebook to the other end of the desk. "Now it seems she's going to be disruptive no matter where we put her."

"She's under a lot of stress; she was supposed to get married last weekend and it fell through."

"Probably because she wasn't minding her own business." He pulled a tissue out of a box and blew his nose. "Married? To that male nurse who used to work in ICU?"

"Yes. Harry Lucke. I hear only good things about him."

"Well, if he's that close to her, chances are he's going to be a pain in the neck, too." He blinked away what appeared to be a discomfiting thought. "Anyway, forget Lucke – tell me more about Mazzio's latest misadventure."

Alexandros hesitated. The administrator was tense, sarcastic, territorial. "I thought we were lucky to have her in the Advice Center."

"Lucky? Is that what you think?"

"She does good work: patient surveys have her at the top of the list, and her stats for handling calls are the best in the region."

"Regardless, she's nothing but trouble," Vasquez insisted.

"You couldn't prove it by me."

"Trust me, Ms. Alexandros, Gina Mazzio almost brought down this hospital with her costly union negotiations and there are other matters that I don't wish to discuss. How the hell she has the time to cause so much disruption and still do her job as a staff nurse is beyond me."

"What did she do?"

Vasquez turned towards his window, his face a bright red. "I've told you all I intend to, other than to repeat that she's a troublemaker. I would have fired her on the spot if it hadn't been for the union; they stick their noses into every part of our operations. It wasn't worth the hassle at the time. Maybe it is now."

"There's nothing to fire her for. She's worried, that's all."

"Maybe, maybe not. But do let me know the minute you've heard from your *murdered* Nurse Wilton."

Vasquez turned back to the desk and tapped the top of his notebook. When he spoke again, his voice was reasonable, but there was an undercurrent of menace accenting every word:

"I want to hear from you if *anything* ... let there be no mistake ... I said if *anything* more comes up about Ms. Mazzio. Is that clear?"

Lexie stood and headed for the door.

"Perfectly."

₪ CHAPTER 13

Gina tried to remain rational, but a mixed agenda fragmented her thoughts. First, it was Harry, then the grisly telephone calls, then the possibility that Shelly was dead, and now a killer might be stalking her.

"Indifference is the epitome of evil," she mumbled as she walked to her car, her step a little firmer. She tried to live by that quote from Elie Wiesel, and since coming to Ridgewood, she'd definitely pushed Wiesel's credo beyond anything she'd ever dared before. But maybe a little indifference at this point might relieve some of the pressure.

So far she'd landed on her feet, but what would tomorrow bring? The direction of her life had changed again mid stride – she was disconnected, unsure, and way over the edge.

She fired a backward glance, first to see if anyone was following her, then to observe the gloomy, ominous hospital in the fading light.

Ominous?

When had she begun to feel that way?

Being away from the Bronx and her marital memories were only part of the equation. Coming to Ridgewood was supposed to be the answer to everything—a teaching institution, a place she could learn new techniques, meet world-class doctors and researchers, be involved in advanced studies. Most of all, she hoped it would be a place where she would receive the respect a professional deserved. Instead of being enclosed in the hospital's protective circle, she'd been slapped in the face, hard.

A year ago, her union involvement had turned unhappy nurses into proud people, excited to be a part of such a progressive staff. Morale had never been better. But instead of thanks, she'd been tossed out of the hospital, with its intense patient involvement and tight staff relationships, and shunted off to the isolation of Ob/Gyn Advice, a service she never once contemplated.

It wasn't that she didn't like being an advice nurse – it was a challenging job. It simply wasn't what she'd signed on for.

Ridgewood had betrayed her.

She yanked up the collar of her coat against a sudden sharp breeze. It had rained heavily earlier and the beads of moisture covering her car flew into the wind as she opened the door and settled into the damp seat.

She pulled out her cell and punched in Shelly Wilton's home number – one she now knew by heart.

Still no answer.

The key slid into the ignition smoothly and, for a change, the car started without its usual complaints.

"Hah! Take that, Harry Lucke." She loved the recalcitrant Fiat and hated it when Harry kidded her about it being old enough to be classified as an actual antique.

The light moment passed quickly. She'd made up her mind—she was going to contact the police again, and this time she wasn't going to be brushed aside. Pepper Yee would have to listen to her, show some real interest. Either that or she was going to become the biggest pain in the ass Yee had ever encountered. It was past time to really get into the cop's face.

When she arrived at the police station, it was pouring rain again. She looked fruitlessly for her umbrella in the car, then pictured it in the locker room at Ridgewood. She was drenched before she reached the station entrance, and in rotten humor.

She signed in with the desk sergeant, asked to see Yee.

"I'm off soon," said the roly-poly officer, ogling her. "Won't I do?"

"Sergeant, I'm in no mood to have you hitting on me."

"Com'on, beautiful, give a guy a break. I'm just looking for a little conversation and companionship."

Gina read his nametag. "I'm sure you are, Sergeant Ober. I'm not!" She shoved the sign-in clipboard back at him so hard it bounced off his rotund gut. The sheet was now covered with dots of moisture from her dripping hair and arm.

The cop tried to stare her down and gave her a sleazy smile while punching in numbers on the desk telephone. Gina stood her ground, her eyes burning into his as she tapped her finger on the counter.

He spoke, then hung up. "Detective Yee'll be with you in a few minutes."

* * *

Pepper Yee scrawled Gina Mazzio's name on a scratch pad, frowned at it, and punched the *Hold* button to resume her telephone conversation with her lieutenant:

"We got a hot tip about a suspect," Yee said. "Not only that, we nailed a name … a guy we think is a key player. I need to connect the dots."

"A raid?"

"Not necessarily. I'm thinking more like a sting operation … maybe set up a phony buy. But, if I can't bring that off, it'll have to be a raid."

"I hope that nets us something," the lieutenant said. "We need to hook into the source for all these unaccounted cadavers and body parts."

"That's what I'm shooting for." She drew circles around Mazzio's name, put a star at either end of the note. "Give me a few more days to look for a go-between—someone who knows all the players and can be coaxed—"

"—or coerced."

"Right. Someone to play nice with us."

"Make it quick, Yee. Complaints coming in about these bodies have been increasing monthly. We need to act quickly on this."

"Top priority, Lieutenant."

"Good! I'm counting on you, Yee."

"Yes sir!" She was also counting on being at the top of the list when the next First Grade slot opened up.

* * *

The desk sergeant continued to glance at Gina in between dealing with people stopping at his desk and taking phone calls.

About ten minutes had elapsed when a tall, skinny blonde, definitely non-Asian, came through a set of swinging doors.

"Yee," the detective said as she came around the counter and offered a hand.

"Gina Mazzio."

"The advice nurse from Ridgewood Hospital, right?"

"Right."

"Nice to meet you. That doesn't always happen in my line of work."

"Mine either."

"Thought I'd be Chinese, didn't you?"

Gina forced a small smile. "Crossed my mind."

Yee led Gina back through the swinging doors and wove a path through a haphazard placement of desks that nearly filled the large room. She stopped at an untidy cubicle in a far corner of the area.

"Have a seat," Yee said, pointing to a straight back wooden chair. She plopped into a wheeled desk chair with well-worn vinyl upholstery. "Got your messages. Sorry I haven't gotten back to you. It's been a killer couple of days, if you'll pardon the pun." She pushed her hair back and re-clipped it. "What's going on?"

Gina unfastened her raincoat belt, undid the buttons, and sat down. She gave the room a closer look: it was grungy, like no one had really cleaned it in a long time; take-out cartons rested on several desks, and, from the aromas coming from the detective's desk, Gina would have bet Yee's dinner was stashed in one of the metal drawers. She glanced at her watch: About the same time she'd called Friday night. Maybe Yee *was* eating her dinner as Gina had suspected when she called.

76

Same time, same game.

"You know, detective," Gina said, "I'm not a happy camper. You were flippant with me on Friday, and I had to come in here to get you to respond to my phone messages."

Yee gave her a so-who-the-hell-cares kind of look.

"I really wanted to get a hold of Detective Mulzini, who helped me about a year ago, and was very kind."

"You and Mulzini have a thing for each other?"

"Hardly," Gina said.

Yee opened her notebook to a fresh page. "So what was that all about?"

He looked into some death threats that came my way because of a union situation. He also handled an extortion and murder situation involving the hospital's bone marrow cancer treatment patients. It was pretty wild. Anyway, I always felt he had me in his sites. He was great."

Yee's face relaxed. "Yeah, he's one of the good guys, but don't ever quote me. I'd deny it to the end." She tapped a pencil from end to end, briefly studied a picture on her desk that Gina couldn't see. "So what's happening to bring you here tonight? Not the same problem, I hope."

Gina slipped out of her raincoat, mostly to stall while she thought about what she was going to say. She would have to be logical, not run off at the mouth as she had with her manager.

"You remember the call Friday when this … this creep told me a woman had been sliced up?"

Yee nodded.

"Well, late last night, the same weirdo called me at home. Told me another woman had been cut into pieces, a nurse that I work with, Shelly Wilton."

"Called at your apartment, not the hospital?"

Gina nodded. "It was scary … scary to know he could find me so easily, that anyone could find me so easily." Gina bowed her head, covered her eyes to hide the tears that welled up without warning

"It's okay. I understand. Go on."

"I didn't want to believe him, but when I went to work today and Shelly didn't come in, I was frantic. Tina, another coworker, said it wasn't unusual; Shelly is supposedly known for taking time off unexpectedly."

"You work with her and never noticed?"

Gina reached for a tissue from the detective's desk and dabbed at her eyes. "When I thought about it, I realized it was true. But it's not my thing to get into other people's business. As long as we're fully staffed," Gina shrugged, "life goes on."

Yee looked around the squad room. "Sort of the same thing here."

"I tried to call Shelly on and off all night, then again today. No one answers. Something's happened. I just know it."

Yee continued to write as Gina spoke. "First of all, I'm going to have to do a fly-by and see if this Shelly Wilton is there, or if someone knows where she might be. Maybe she *is* sick."

"I'll go with you."

"No, you'll stay away. I'll let you know what's up."

"God, it would be such a relief if she was there," Gina said.

"Is your address in the phone book?"

"No! In fact, not even my telephone number is in the book. It's been that way since I moved to San Francisco."

"Do you live alone?"

"No. My fiancé lives with me, but he's not always in town."

"Name?"

"Lucke. Harry Lucke."

"Occupation?"

"Travel Nurse. Goes all over the country on assignment."

"Where is he now?"

Gina thought for a moment. "He's in town, but we're, uh, taking a time-out … for the time being."

The detective closed her notebook, leaned back in her chair and leveled her gaze at Gina: "Does he know Shelly Wilton?"

"No! And what the hell's that supposed to mean?"

₪ CHAPTER 14

It was almost 4:30 when Tina told Gina there was a personal call waiting for her on Line #3.

Harry!

The thought gave her a momentary high that crashed with the reality of their situation. She wasn't ready to talk to him, and she had the disturbing thought that this time they might not find their way back together. Still, where was he? It wasn't like him to stay out of touch this long.

She became transfixed by the blinking light.

Maybe it was Yee, finally getting back to her. If so, the cop had taken her own sweet time about it. She was antsy to find out what Yee had discovered during her so-called fly-by of Shelly's apartment—if the detective even went there.

Mostly, Gina didn't want it to be *that* voice again. She held her breath and took the call.

"I stopped by Shelly Wilton's apartment about an hour ago," Detective Yee said without preliminaries.

Gina's throat constricted, she squeezed both hands into tight fists until her knuckles turned white. She waited, expecting Yee to lower her voice, then tell her that Shelly was not only dead, but cut up and scattered all around the apartment.

"What did you find?" Gina whispered rapidly. "Is she all right?"

"Everything appeared to be in order. No sign of anything unusual. But no sign of Ms Wilton, either. Or any clue as to where she might be."

"Did you speak to the super?"

"Ms. Mazzio, I did what needed to be done."

"Then what do you think?"

"It's too soon to think anything."

"But we can't just ignore the nut who called me at work, and then at home. And we can't ignore the fact Shelly hasn't come into to work for the past two days."

"We'll let it play out a little longer. She may turn up."

Gina hated the way Yee retreated into a condescending mode. A voice riddled with a there-there-you're-a-nut-case cadence.

"Easy for you to say," Gina snapped. "No one's stalking you ... you with your big gun and badge." Then in almost the same breath, "Why did I ever think you'd do anything helpful or significant?"

She punched the disconnect button. The line lit up almost immediately. She refused to pick it up; she would just have to find out for herself what was going on with Shelly.

Gina turned and stared at Chelsea, who'd been called in to take Shelly's place. But seeing the on-call nurse only accentuated her fears about the missing nurse.

And as for Yee? Screw her!

"Stop looking at me that way," Chelsea said. "I'm only here because Shelly didn't show up for work. Would you rather be understaffed?"

Gina held up a hand. "Sorry, Chels. I'm just worried about Shelly. Believe me, I'm glad you're here."

"Don't pay attention to her," Tina said. "She's a born complainer. Kvetch, kvetch! Never satisfied about anything. Aiyiyi!"

"Bite yourself," Gina blurted.

"There goes the drama queen. Always a sage word for us lesser people."

Gina wanted to punch her out, but instead of taking the Bronx approach to settling things, she headed for the door. "It's five and I'm out of here." Her eyes bored into Tina's. "And I wish you'd stop taking those nasty pills. They're much too efficacious."

As she walked out the door, she heard Chelsea say, "What nasty pills?"

* * *

The Fiat coughed, spat out billowing exhaust smoke and fumes, then shuddered into silence. Gina pounded on the dashboard, tried again.

"What's with you? Why can't you do smooth? Why can't you do easy? Why can't you do what the hell you're supposed to do?"

The starter whirred away, paused as though the car was actually considering her litany of questions, then the ignition caught and fired. The engine roughness smoothed out quicker than usual; the tach needle trembled only slightly, then settled in to indicate a steady rpm.

She let loose a huge sigh. "I knew you could do it, baby."

She entered into the flow of traffic, a vision of spaghetti doing a number in her head. But instead of pulling a hard right to take her home, she headed straight out toward the Sunset district.

Twenty minutes later, after a ferocious search for a parking place, she climbed a long flight of concrete stairs and stood at the doorway to Shelly Wilton's apartment building. The structure dated back a few decades, but it had been recently renovated and the smell of fresh paint permeated in the air. She peered at the metal mailbox and studied the names of the occupants.

She pressed Shelly Wilton's apartment buzzer, tapped her foot as she waited for a response. Giving up, she rang for the super and within a minute a man wearing a grimy, almost threadbare, gray sweatshirt popped his head out the door.

Gina wanted to smile at the work of the amateur embroiderer who had stitched "Maxxy" around the neck of his shirt in ugly shocking pink. Instead she concentrated on how the garish color highlighted his sallow completion.

"We're all outta apartments, honey," he yelled.

Gina stared at the big scruffy man, eyed the stenciled *Shit Happens* on the front of his well-worn sweatshirt, then pointed at his chest:

"Ain't it the truth," she yelled back And then, even louder, "Don't call me honey."

He gave her a blank stare, then started to close his door.

"Wait!"

"Did'nya hear me, lady? Ain't got a single empty pad right now."

She motioned for him to open the outer door. He gave her a perfunctory nod, the door lock buzzed, and she stepped into the foyer.

"Listen, Maxxy," I need you to hear me out, okay?' I'm not looking for a place to bed down. I'm looking for Shelly Wilton in 3C."

"Yeah, you, the police, and my grandmudder. So what?" He held his door half open. "Far as I'm concerned, her rent is cool for another month. She pays the dough, she gets her privacy. If you ain't got a warrant, go 'way!"

Before he could slam the door in her face, Gina blurted, "So where you from Maxxy? You don't sound like you're from around here. Maybe back East?"

"Yeah, so what's it to ya?"

"Nothin,' nothin.' Just that I get lonely for my home turf. Hearing you talk is music to my ears."

He took a closer look at her. "Yeah? So where you from?" The door opened an inch or two more.

"The Bronx ... Grand Concourse."

"Gidouttahere! You, too?"

"Moved here a couple of years ago." Gina smiled. "Beats shoveling snow."

The super opened the door all the way and gave her a you-ain't-shitting-me-sneer while he pulled a ring of keys from the loop on his jeans, motioned for her to follow him. She started up the steps, tried to avoid smelling his trail of stale sweat.

"So what's up with Shelly? Seems like a good kid to me."

"Yeah, I like her, too. But I'm worried. She hasn't shown up for work for two days. I've called her. Not a peep."

"Thinkin' about her myself since the police came by."

Gina ran her hand along the freshly painted banister as they climbed two flights of newly carpeted stairs. The rug was already spotted from foot traffic carrying the dregs of bad weather.

Shelly's name was typed on a card above her bell. He knocked, waited a moment, then turned a key in the lock.

The first thing that hit Gina was the feeling that no one lived here anymore. It felt empty, sterile. She shrugged off a chill of fear that told her Shelly was dead and started looking around the one-bedroom apartment.

The place was surprisingly tidy. Gina always thought of Shelly as a kind of sloppy character, judging from her desk at work. But the person here was more artistic than messy.

Several of the paintings scattered around on the walls were signed by Shelly in bold letters. That was a total surprise. Gina couldn't remember Shelly ever talking about being an artist. They were interesting paintings, mostly nudes. The fleshy subjects had tentative stares that gazed into space. Something had them puzzled.

Probably a statement about life; I'm sure as hell puzzled by it most of the time.

All seemed in order. If Shelly was murdered, it didn't happen here, even a clueless amateur could see that.

Maxxy's restless jingle of keys told her that he'd had enough. Before he could say anything to move her out of the apartment, she hurried into a bright, spacious bedroom.

The first thing she saw was a jumble of paint tubes and a dozen well used brushes in a jar. They were on a color-splattered drafting table next to a wooden easel that held a large, partially completed painting. Again, a nude.

A double bed at the other end of the room was a scramble of burgundy sheets, with an orange comforter half-on, half-off. A small teak dresser held a few novels and one framed picture of Shelly posed between an older couple. Probably her parents. Perched on the end of the dresser was a telephone and message machine. There were no blinking lights.

"Whadaya say, Bronxie? Had enough?"

Gina wanted to stay, wanted to learn more about the woman who had worked with her for the past year, someone she knew so little about.

Are we all destined to be strangers? Walk around smiling, nodding, thinking we know so much about each other when we know nothing about what really goes on in each other's heads or in each other's hearts?

She looked at the super, noticed the gold band around his left ring finger. His eyes held dark circles, the kind of hollowness earned from pacing the floor with a sick child night after night.

"You have children, Maxxy?"

His chest seemed to expand; he laughed. "Oh, yeah! My little six-year-old boy did this." He pointed to his name on the neck of the sweatshirt. "Not too much of a guy yet, but he'll catch up later."

"Sure he will."

"And I have a beauty of a deuce. She's already breakin' hearts."

He shut the door behind them and they went down the two flights. Gina realized there was nothing here to explain Shelly's disappearance. Just as Yee had said. She'd hoped for at least some kind of clue, but there wasn't even a telephone message on her answering machine. All she really knew was that Shelly had disappeared without a clue.

"Thanks for helping me out, Maxxy."

"Anything for a Bronx pal."

At the front door she shook his hand.

"You're a lucky man to have that family."

"Bet your sweet ass, kid."

84

₪ CHAPTER 15

The cafeteria was quiet, about an hour too early for the surge of noon-hour traffic. There were a few clusters of people here and there, but still plenty of empty places to sit. Gina, who'd opted for the early lunch slot, grabbed a bowl of minestrone and an espresso, then claimed a window seat. She stared out at Ridgewood's native California-style garden—usually vibrant, it looked sodden and miserable from the constant dousing of the past few days.

She held up a spoonful of the thick vegetable soup, but couldn't bring herself to eat it. The utensil sank back into the bowl while she filtered events of the past few days.

"Hi, Gina!"

She turned—Eddie St. George.

"You look lonely," he said. "Mind if I join you? I could use some company." He stood next to the table, looking down at her, then quickly glanced around the room before returning his attention to her.

Gina was surprised he wanted to sit with her after she was so rude the other day

She nodded. "Sure. Why not?"

He lowered his tray, which was filled with some kind of Chinese concoction—plenty of crispy noodles spread across over-cooked vegetables. Then he eased his long, lanky body into the molded plastic chair. When he was comfortable, he looked at her with soft green eyes that again made her think of Harry. As he started to eat, she studied him more closely. There was sadness in the droop of his shoulders, and he continually released a barely audible sigh before he took each bite of food.

Troubled man.

The moment forced her to stop thinking about her own problems, made her realize how much she missed direct patient contact, the opportunity for insight into human suffering. The world needed more compassion, not the misdirection of indifference and compulsive anger.

Her thoughts eased the tension of the Gordian knot in her skull. Suddenly she was hungry, the first time in several days. She picked up her spoon and dipped into the minestrone.

She noticed the CHEMwest rep was staring at her, a forkful of food poised in front of his face. Megan Ann was right: he was very attractive.

"What would it take to convince you to have a drink with me after work?" St George said.

Her first thought was: was she or wasn't she still engaged to Harry? Second thought: would going out with him be fair to Megan Ann, who was seriously into this guy? Without really sorting it all out, she decided it might be good to kick back with someone for an hour or so.

"We could do that," she said.

* * *

The rest of the shift was dismal. She and Tina barely spoke to each other. Chelsea, caught in the middle, tried to mediate, but soon gave up and spoke only when spoken to, or when taking a patient call.

Alexandros popped into Advice around **2:00**. Gina took call after call and barely nodded to her. At one point the manager indicated she wanted to speak to her and Gina reluctantly put the next call on hold.

"How are you doing?" the manager asked

Gina forced a smile, one she didn't remotely feel like giving, and in a neutral voice said, "It's a busy day."

Alexandros sat down next to her. "Not what I meant."

"Oh, I know what you mean: Am I still thinking about the big, bad boogie man? Worrying about imaginary scary things that

86

go bump in the night? Or, have I crossed the line and gone totally nuts?"

Alexandros flipped a strand of hair away from her eye, said nothing.

"I'm fine," Gina said, "just doing my job."

"If you need me, I'm in my office." Without another word Alexandros walked out of Advice.

"What was that all about?" Chelsea asked.

"You don't want to know," Tina said.

* * *

Five on the dot, Gina edged out from behind her desk and left the Clinic, another day without settling her disagreement with Tina. As she walked to her car, she made what was now a routine check to see if anyone was following her; everyone seemed to be in after-work mode that didn't include her: Get out and get gone. She slipped into the Fiat and sat behind the wheel, cell phone in hand.

There were no messages from Harry, or from anyone else.

She ran her fingers through her hair several times, grateful it needed so little attention. Then she opened her purse, and without checking in the mirror, put on fresh lipstick. She sat for another few moments, then with determination, pulled away from the curb.

* * *

Eddie St. George sat in his Jaguar and watched Gina enter The Hideaway. He'd deliberately forced himself on her in the cafeteria, curious as to whether she would recognize his voice from the phone calls. He was drawn to her and wanted to put his trust in her, tell her he was the one who had called. But the cafeteria hadn't been the right place. He again noticed how attractive she was; the kind of woman he always thought would be the right fit for him.

No! He could not get involved with this woman, or any other—it only made what he had to do for Father that much more difficult. He would have a drink with her, make up an excuse for having to leave early, and then be on his way.

His cell vibrated in his pocket. He pulled it out. The message screamed:

MORE. TONIGHT.

Leave me alone!

He glanced at his watch. Too late to visit any of the other medical offices and clinics up and down The Peninsula, where he could slip in without being noticed. And he was too tired to troll the streets and bars to find the right woman for Father.

Before he could change his mind, he got out of the car and, with long, determined strides, entered the cocktail lounge.

Right away he spotted Gina. The Advice nurse had settled at one of the small tables in the back; a waitress was taking her order. As he approached, he heard her order a Margarita.

"Make that two," Eddie said.

The waitress wrote up the ticket, flashed a perfunctory smile, and moved toward the bar.

The tables were like oversized dinner plates, jammed together in a crowded dishwasher. Eddie could not only hear the patrons next to them, he could smell the nearest woman's perfume.

Gina eased out of her raincoat and draped it across her shoulders. A Kelly-green polo shirt contrasted with her dark eyes, making them piercing, yet somehow soft.

"I didn't think you'd show," he said.

"Same here." She laughed. "But against my better judgment, here I am."

"I'm glad." He reached for her hand; she pulled it out of reach.

"It's just a drink," she said. "Don't put any more into it than that."

"Sorry. The Ridgewood rumor mill has it that you broke up with your boy friend. I guess not."

"Maybe the rumor mongers will figure it out for me. As it is, *I* sure don't know."

"Well, it's still good to just sit back and relax after an unusually difficult day."

"Something special going on for you?"

"New chemo product. I got tapped to set up a special presentation involving Alan Vasquez, Michael Cliffords, a financially challenged patient, and a couple of our bigwigs. Took hours, but we finally agreed on a time that would fit everyone's schedule."

"Glad it was you and not me," she said. "I used to work for Cliffords; good guy, but busy, very intense."

"I agree. But I couldn't figure out Vasquez. What's he normally like?"

Gina gave a curt laugh. "You're asking the wrong person when it comes to the Ridgewood administrator."

He was going to ask for details, but the waitress arrived with their order and scooped up the twenty-dollar bill he'd placed on the table.

Gina lifted her drink and they touched glasses. "To friends."

"Are we friends?" The cell phone vibrated in his pocket. His chest tightened, he covered his shortness of breath by coughing as though he'd swallowed wrong.

"Do you need a good whack on the back, or would that really make you wonder if we're friends?"

He waved away her offered treatment. "I'm okay, but I'm still wondering why you agreed to have a drink with me?"

She took a long sip of her Margarita, looked at him thoughtfully. "I don't know, guess you looked like a man who needed some company." She glanced away, lowered her head. "Truth is, *I* needed some company. Couldn't stand the thought of going back to an empty apartment."

He felt the cell vibrate again, stopped listening to her. He knew what was on the message screen:

MORE! TONIGHT!

She smiled, stood. "Would you excuse me for a moment?" He managed to nod, watched her zigzag through the tiny tables to the restroom—tall, athletic, dark haired. Not at all what Father would expect.

Colors flashed in his head, blossomed from everywhere in the room. He pulled out his inhaler, rapidly pushed the pump. A few moments passed before he could breathe freely again.

MORE! TONIGHT!

TONIGHT!

He hesitated, then reached into the side pocket of his jacket, trapped a roofie with thumb and forefinger, and then dropped the hypnotic sedative into Gina's Margarita.

When she returned, she slipped back into her seat, folded her hands in front of her on the table, and looked at him with sad, red-rimmed eyes.

It was me. I'm the one who called you.

But he couldn't say it out loud, couldn't trust anyone to know who he was, what he'd done.

Gina lifted the glass to her lips, sighed, then set it down.

"Maybe we'll do this some other time." She stood and walked out.

₪ CHAPTER 16

Gina drove a practiced route around her apartment complex, searching for *the* parking place. Tonight, even sacred hydrant slots were violated by illegal parkers. Then the windshield wipers stalled; she could barely see a thing.

"Damn Italian electronics!"

She toggled the switch several times but the blades refused to move.

"Keep this up and I'll turn you into a pile of scrap metal, you neurotic monster." The wipers immediately went into high speed.

"That's better."

She finally found a spot and shoehorned the Fiat into a space that really needed to be at least a foot longer.

"Idiot!" she chastised herself. "Drinking with some guy you barely know? What's that all about? What a loser you've become."

She tromped through the rain, wiping the water out of her eyes, picturing Eddie St. George. He looked like a regular guy, typical of most of the pharmaceutical reps who paraded up and down the hospital halls drumming up business. He was well mannered, expensively dressed, attractive. And ready to do almost anything to make a good impression.

She hadn't seen many of his kind since leaving Oncology to work in the clinic, but she knew they were still out there, lugging their heavy satchels up and down the long corridors, wearing pasted-on smiles even when their clothes were soaked with perspiration. And she knew what was in those cases — samples of the popular, the newest drugs their companies had to offer so the Docs and NPs could not only satisfy patients that were ever alert to the advertising that saturated the media, but continue to prescribe their company's ongoing line of products. And, of course they carried, all the goodies for the RNs and other staff to insure the reps were always welcome wherever they turned up.

Gina, on more than one occasion, had gone with Cliff Michaels, along with other doctors and nurses, to weekend Giant-Dodgers games after several big CHEMWest drug orders had been placed. Best seats in the stadium, of course, and free.

Several of the Oncology MDs she'd worked with took their vacations in Hawaii, Hong Kong, Tokyo, or Paris, at CHEMwest's expense. Sort of a 'thank you' for having used the drug company's efficacious chemo therapy rather than some other company's efficacious chemo drug.

But it was the sales reps that were at the front. They carried all the bits and pieces that kept a huge inter-dependent machine well lubricated and functioning smoothly. It was business, big business. And the doctors were the targets.

She'd noticed, however, that up close and personal, Eddie St. George wasn't as typical as he tried to make people believe. Sitting at that little table in *The Hideaway,* he was attentive and distracted at the same time. Her problem was that being with him only made her think about Harry.

She'd needed to get out of her own skin for a while and the rep had made himself available. But for reasons she couldn't quite pinpoint, it was as if he was forcing himself to only make casual conversation when there was something more he wanted to say. Or was it that she'd been out of the dating scene too long?

Well, enough of Eddie St. George. She needed to get on with her life.

Go, Megan Ann, go. Good luck with that dude.

The street was empty, dark, and the air heavy with the smell of moss, supersaturated plants, humus, and mold. Just what her allergist ordered.

The thought made her sneeze.

She used her key to enter the lobby, quickly closed the door behind her, and waited for the elevator. Lack of sleep made her legs heavier and heavier, and when she stepped out of the elevator, she almost collapsed and had to grab for the wall to keep from falling. Total exhaustion swept over her; she was lightheaded and weak. Two nights without her standard eight hours of sleep and then a frustrating date, was dragging her down.

She jammed the key into the door, stepped inside, and stopped in her tracks. Harry sat on the sofa staring at her. He dominated the half-lit room.

"Bottom line, I can't live without you, beautiful." His face was all eyes, like a vast ocean, blue-green and watery.

"Is that a fact?" She turned away from him, slipped out of her raincoat, and draped it across the back of a bar stool in the kitchen; it left a puddle of dripping water.

He crossed the room and slipped an arm around her waist. "I shouldn't have walked out."

"Damn straight."

"Try to understand. I was crushed. I've waited a year to marry you, Gina Mazzio. You know how much I love you."

"A helluva way to show it." Relief and anger fought for her attention, but the right words wouldn't come.

"Where have you been, anyway? I've been worried about you."

She planted both fists on her hips. "Did you think I would sit around here and mope, pine over you? Is that what you thought?"

"Of course not. It's just that I was concerned."

She reached into the fridge, pulled out a container of yogurt, flipped it open, and stuffed her mouth with it.

"If you must know, I was out having a drink."

Harry barely nodded.

"One of the drug reps." She licked the spoon before setting it down. "Kind of cute, a little on the young side, but who cares. I'm not going to marry him ... or anyone else."

"That hurts."

"Really? Funny, I thought it was just the opposite: you not believing in me and walking out when I'm trying to deal with some maniac."

"Please, Gina."

"And what's this shit about being worried about me? And did you really say you were concerned?" She raised a hand, cutting off a retort. "You weren't *worried* Friday when I talked to that nutcase." She thunked her head with a palm. "Oh, I forgot. You weren't *concerned* because it was only a crank call."

"Gina, I'm sorry. All I could think about was that we were finally going to get married."

She snatched up the spoon again and pushed another glob of yogurt into her mouth. "Not good enough, Harry Lucke."

"All I can do is apologize."

"You can do more than that. You can leave ... leave me alone."

"Gina."

"I don't want to marry you," she said. "You or anyone. Relationships are too complicated for my simple mind, too messy for my need of orderliness."

He reached out and pulled her to him. "Don't make up your mind right now. Please!"

She held back an angry response, squeezed her eyes shut to stem the tears. "Leave me alone, Harry." She pushed him away.

"Please, Gina."

"Just go."

"I'll call you tomorrow. Maybe we can talk then."

She bit down on her lip to keep from screaming at him.

"Don't count on it."

* * *

Gina had just entered her bedroom when she heard her computer chime the arrival of an e-mail. She hurried to her desk and clicked to see who was sending her a message.

Sin & Bone

It was from her brother, Vinnie, stationed in Afghanistan. She hadn't heard from him for a week and her hands shook as she read his letter:

Hey, Big Sis,

It's me, the big shot (did I misspell that?) from the hellhole.

As you can see, I haven't flamed out yet. Some bitchin' moments, but looks like I'm still gonna kick your butt at handball again.

Been worried about you. Not like you to carry a grudge. Almost two years and you still haven't buried the hatchet with Mom and Dad? I know they should have stood up for you, not try to push you back to Dominick, for any reason. But we both know they're religious, hung up on that old-fashioned, stand-by-your-man crap and we also know that shithead ex- of yours belongs six feet under, but I'm still staying away from telling them about your plans to tie the knot with Harry—I'm not pissing grease on a bonfire.

Crazy part, your ex-father-in-law still thinks you'll make up with Dominick. And get this. So does Dominick! The jerk plugs me with e-mail, begging me for your address, begging me to sway you. Man! Get a life! Does this guy even have a clue about what he did? All that asshole sees is his "possession" walking out the door. Maybe we ought to fit you for a burkha? No, no. Don't hit me! But the fool still refers to you as his pretty wife. I know you're not a dog, but pretty? Ha! From this distance, I can call you anything. I mean ANYTHING.

Kidding aside, I only communicate with him to know what's on his mind. The fact he's out of prison now means I gotta know what he's up to. You're the biggest reason I wish I was back in the good old USA. Wonder if I'd like living in Frisco?

You can't hide from Mom and Dad forever. Gonna have to cut the folks some kind of slack. At least drop a line. It's almost Christmas.

Enough about you. Let's talk about me. Been thinking (just like you asked me to) about what I want to do after I get home. IF I GET HOME. Now don't go all snively on me. Just talkin.'

Guess I'm confused. You'd think having bombs tossed at me, bodies flying all around, something radical like this nightmare would set me on some kind of righteous path. But, you know, sis? I don't seem to give a damn about a future. Only getting back in one piece. That and beating your silly ass at handball.

Don't make me hurt you. Write to Mom and Dad. At least they're now in the 21st century in some things. They're sending e-mails. Can you believe it?

And for chrissakes, don't beat on Harry too much. Give the guy a break.
Love,
Vinnie the terrible.

Gina plucked a tissue from a nearby box and dabbed at the tears spattered on the keyboard.

"Men! Who needs the bums? All they do is mess up your life."

She wandered into the small kitchen and pulled out a can of Chef Boyardee spaghetti and meatballs. She grimly remembered how she'd had Harry over on one of their first dates. She'd prepared homemade pasta but brought out this very can to break the ice.

"You've got to be kidding," Harry had blurted, laughing so hard she thought he'd burst.

"Whaddayamean," she said in her best, straight-faced Bronxese.

"Oh, I'm sorry. I guess the promised home cooked meal made me think real I-T-A-L-I-A-N, not vintage hospital cafeteria. But what do I know?"

They'd both roared when she pulled the hidden plates of food from the oven.

Sin & Bone

Now, Gina opened the can and dumped the contents into a saucepan. When it was barely warm, she picked up a fork and started eating directly from the pan.

She stared at a picture of Harry on the refrigerator door. It was under a magnet, along with a picture of her brother in uniform.

She forced a forkful of the canned pasta mixture into her mouth and chewed slowly.

Bette Golden Lamb & J. J. Lamb

₪ CHAPTER 17

Jacob St. George clawed at his head, yanked out clumps of hair, watched as the strands slipped through his fingers to the wooden floor.

Where the hell is he? Hiller will be here first thing in the morning.

He unlocked the big walk-in cooler, strained hard to pull open the heavy door. His flesh was searing from flashes of white-hot lightning that struck randomly at his neck, eyes, and gut.

He rubbed hard between his legs. His groin throbbed in rhythm with his pounding heart.

Boom! Boom! Boom!

He stood at the entrance to the cooler and looked at the wrapped bundles. He'd always held back some of the moveable inventory from Hiller, but now it was very low. His eyes took in a heap of packages in the back, smaller packages, almost round. That pile had really grown over the past month.

No! He can't have those. They're mine, only for me.

He ripped off his grubby shirt, dug his nails into the already flayed skin that itched endlessly. He had to make it stop. No matter how many women he took, it was never enough. Never enough to make it stop!

He stumbled to the kitchen-lunchroom area. This was where his brat would come after school and do his homework.

Where are you? When I say I want more, that's what I mean, more!

MORE.

The monitor clock on the wall began to chime the hour. Time was running out. The hands of doom were sitting on his shoulder, like a monkey picking at his neck.

The cancer was stealing his life.

Jacob dropped heavily into a gray, vinyl-padded chair. He was exhausted from alternating between bouts of manic energy and deep depression.

He stared at the white marble kitchen tabletop. Spotless. He slid his fingers across the smooth surface.

Back and forth, back and forth.

Only three hours sleep and he was wide-awake and searching for answers. He lay his head down as though it were a delicate piece of china, studied the table surface, then his fingers.

Not even the hint of a smear marred the white expanse. Not the slightest indication that neither he nor anyone else had ever touched it.

Nothing there.

Nothing.

Did he even exist?

That thought moved him into action. He sat up, yanked at his hair again.

Watched the strands float to the floor.

His eyes throbbed, were as dry and gritty as a desert. Like the emptiness that came after a dust storm, one that cancelled any sign, any evidence of being.

He picked at his eyelids. Poked at his eyes. Not a drop of moisture was released.

The nothingness accelerated; he couldn't even feel his toes.

He grabbed for the small, round hand mirror he'd begun carrying everywhere; it teetered on the edge of the table. How many times did he check his image each day?

Every single day a part of his face disappeared, like a generous section of pie had been doled out to some unknown person.

Yesterday, his chin vanished.

He threw the mirror to the floor. A jagged crack sliced across the center.

"Seven years bad luck!" he screamed.

A harsh, mocking laugh rippled through the silence of the room, a crescendo that ended on a high, hysterical note.

* * *

Walter Cooke parked his car in a Tenderloin public parking garage, then walked through the tough the shoddy neighborhood with eyes in the back of his head. In almost every doorway there was some pathetic creature either sleeping or begging for money. The surrounding smells assaulted him, came close to making him lose his early lobster dinner.

Cooke knocked lightly on the back door of the mortuary. It was a very dark night and habit kept him looking over his shoulder even though he doubted anyone had followed him – most people tend to shy away from mortuaries, considered them bad luck.

He'd been around the block a few times in his sixty years and knew most people acted as if they would never die. And they stayed away from *anything* that smacked of death ... *especially* mortuaries. Death was for someone else, not them.

He was getting drenched. What had started out as a light rain was now a thundering downpour.

While he waited outside the mortuary, he tapped a foot on the asphalt to the rhythm of some crazy tune he'd long forgotten the name of but couldn't get out of his head. His sneaker made tiny squishing sounds on the wet pavement with each tap. He forced himself to stop focusing on the nervous, incessant music in his head.

This was only the second time he'd worked at Auston's Funeral Home. He briefly questioned his sanity for taking on a job in the Tenderloin, particularly at night and in this kind of weather. But the owner paid better than most, and next week he was scheduled for his annual trip to Tahiti.

The mortuary's security guy finally opened the door.

"Whadda you want?" He was big and stupid.

"He's expecting me."

101

"Yeah?" He peered out. "I guess I remember you." But he still didn't open the door all the way.

Cooke was losing patience. He'd left his umbrella in the car because it was windy and he was now soaking wet. His feet sloshed in his drenched socks and sneakers.

"So, are you going to let me in or what?"

Before the moron could answer, the door swung open and Charlie Auston stood there wearing a soiled morgue apron.

"Where the hell you been?" Auston shouted. "I expected you half an hour ago."

"Weather!" He snapped a nod at the guy holding door. "And I've been trying to get past your security goon for the past ten minutes."

Auston spun on his heel and motioned for Cooke to follow him down a painted concrete hallway. Cooke was relieved to finally be out of the foul weather.

No carpeting, paneled walls, or soft music playing in the working part of the enterprise. Instead, embalming fluid and the familiar odors of death assaulted his senses.

Cooke shucked off his drenched coat and hung it on a hook next to a line of rubber aprons. He took one, slipped the loop over his head, and fastened the ties behind his back. The floor was still wet from a recent hosing to get rid of someone's errant tissue.

The naked body of a 30-to-40-year-old woman lay face up on the drainage table. Someone had slit her throat long before she'd arrived at the mortuary. She laid there, bloodless, white as bleached bone.

Poor woman!

Cooke let the thought drift away as he slipped on a double pair of surgical gloves. A *déjà vous* moment placed him back in medical school ready to dissect his first cadaver. He may have failed his written exams, but he sure-as-hell was a whiz with a scalpel.

Sin & Bone

The older he got, the more satisfied he became. He was making more money than he would have as a practicing doctor, and without the messy emotional involvement.

As he worked, he thought about his upscale condo, the trips to Europe, the gorgeous women he'd landed in his bed. All that, and he would never have to worry about patients taking him to court and saying unkind things. He grinned at this take on an old mortician's joke.

Auston watched as Cooke made careful incisions and began removing organs, which were immediately fast-frozen.

"You won't be able to save *this*," Cooke said as he tossed a cirrhotic liver into a basin. "Big time boozer. Whoever slit her throat did her a favor. Probably would have conked out on her within a year."

Auston never looked up. Just continued packaging everything Cooke passed over to him.

"You've got to think positively, Walter," Auston said. "Seeing the destruction of the human body as a result of poor living habits is very instructive."

Cooke ignored the comment. He couldn't have cared less about other peoples' lifestyles, nor did he know or care to know anything about the final recipients of Auston's organs, limbs, bones, and other body parts. He simply assumed it was probably a broker or go-between who distributed the bits and pieces to private research labs and medical schools. This setup wasn't for fresh transplants.

Still, it was only the second time he'd been here. Who knew what the mortuary owner was up to? One thing was certain: nothing would be wasted, from collagen right down to fingernails and toenails.

An intact corpse meant a hefty wad of cash for everyone concerned, and even more so when the deceased was relatively young.

"Reconstruction or cremation?" Cooke asked, nodding at a bin of PVC pipe sitting in the corner. He was evaluating the various lengths Auston might want to use to replace long bones if there was to be an open casket.

"This one's scheduled for the burner."

"Got it!" He continued working, assumed Auston would fill the funerary urn with ashes from another source so the bereaved wouldn't be suspicious as to whether things were on the up and up. Again, that was none of his business.

By morning, Cooke was exhausted, but he consoled himself by remembering that the three corpses he'd dissected that night were for research, the good of humanity ... and cash.

* * *

Charlie Auston smiled widely after he let Walter Cooke out the mortuary's back door; the jerk had done a great job again. Cooke was a snobby idiot, thought he was the only one who could dice and slice a corpse with such finesse. But he was a top-notch skin and bone man or, considering the circumstances, *sin and bone* might be more appropriate.

Auston scratched his ear.

Yeah, well, maybe so, but he still has the personality of a dead fish.

Auston's legs were watery with fatigue. It had been a long night and he really needed to crash, but he was way too stimulated from assisting Cooke. Having downed cup after cup of hi-octane coffee, his adrenaline was pumping wildly. He went to his office, sat back in his chair, and plopped his feet on the edge of the desk.

He examined the inventory list centered in front of him. The monthly totals jumped out from the page. He took the pencil he'd stuck between his teeth – the favored one with all the tooth marks down to the graphite – and pointed at the columns as he absorbed the numbers.

Damn, looks like I'm short. Yeah, I am short.

He did some figuring in his head. He had legitimate contracts with three medical schools to process donated bodies, which had always been a nice side business. But since he'd thrown in with Milty Hiller things were getting very complicated, although he *was* making a lot more money. He'd had to raid some of the legitimate corpses in order to supply Hiller, whose demands had increased month after month. Auston was painfully aware that he had to fill those quotas first.

He could feel the stress building in his neck – soon he would have a friggin' headache. He tried to relax, stared at the picture of his wife, holding their granddaughter. Each time he looked at the snapshot, he was amazed by how much the two of them looked alike. His gaze zeroed in on his wife's soft, kind eyes. But he'd seen those eyes turn to stone, especially when she didn't get what she wanted, when she wanted it. Then, instead of "love" or "honey,"' it was "ex-con" or "loser."

And how many times after some nasty disagreement had she warned that if he ever stepped out on her, or went back to prison, it was all over?

Like *that* was something he really wanted to do?

Well, yeah, he wouldn't mind a little extra pussy now and then, if he dared, but he wasn't ever going back to the joint. The nickel he'd done in San Quentin for pushing drugs had messed up his head, to say nothing about his body. He wasn't going back there, no matter what.

He looked out the back window and watched daylight spread across the buildings, thanked his lucky stars that his Pops had been an undertaker. Man, he'd hated it when he was a kid, but now he realized how lucky he'd been to fall into this setup: A dead dad leaving his only child a great business.

And then he'd run into Milty, an old buddy from his cell block who was a big time black-market broker of body parts. Actually, Milty had found him. And it sure shot him in the right direction financially when the mug pointed out the piles of dough to be made. Auston knew when to jump right into a good deal. Hell, what did he have to lose? Stiffs were stiffs.

He turned back to the desk and looked at the photograph again.

Funny, nothing about the mortuary bothered her, and there was only the occasional complaint about the smell of the juice. In the beginning, he'd told her straight out: No matter how you try to cover it up, there's nothing to be done about the stink of embalming fluid. "It is what it is. It don't smell good, and that's that." After a while, she stopped complaining. She did have her good points.

Fresh out of the can, they'd met on-line. Hell, he'd fallen for the first available piece of ass after a five-year drought.

He visualized their summer home hanging over the ocean on the Mendocino coast, their fancy little estate in Belvedere, a nest egg of two mil invested in blue chip stocks, and a lot of cold, hard cash in the safe deposit box.

Unfortunately, she not only knew about his assets, she knew where everything was stashed. If he were ever caught, she'd sure as shit find a way to pocket it all after turning her back on him. She was that kind of woman.

Like, weren't they all?

He checked the telltale figures one more time. The money was still good, but for some reason it was getting harder and harder to justify what he was doing. It just didn't feel right anymore. Maybe he should quit the illegal stuff. But what was it Milty had reminded him on numerous occasions: "It's a rough business, Charlie, and once you're in it, you're in it. There's no getting out ... alive."

* * *

On the way to his car, Walter Cooke thought he recognized a guy coming down the sidewalk toward him. He started to say "Hi," then thought better of it. He felt safer not speaking to anyone in the Tenderloin.

After the guy was several paces away, the name came to him: Milton Hiller.

What's Milton Hiller doing around here this time of night? Could he be dealing with Auston?

Hiller had approached him once about doing some cutting, but when he'd checked up on it, he'd found out it involved stolen cadavers. He'd declined. Since then, he'd heard various stories about Milty. None of them good.

Cooke stopped and went through the motions of patting his pockets, both jacket and pants, as if he'd forgotten something. Without turning his head all the way, he barely caught a glimpse of Hiller entering the alley that led to the back door of Auston's Funeral Home. He retraced his steps and reached the alley just as Milty went through the same back door Cooke had just used.

Not good!

Cooke drove home, got several hours sleep and when he woke up, he called the police.

"Detective Yee?"

"Speaking."

"Walter Cooke. You talked to me a couple of months back, wanted to know if I had any information on the illegal trafficking of cadavers."

"Do you have something for me?"

"I'm not sure. It's just that something happened last night that caused me to be more than a little suspicious."

"And that was?"

He told her what he knew about Milty Hiller, and what had happened at Auston's Funeral Home.

"Milty Hiller, huh?" Yee said. "Tell me again about the funeral home. Auston's, right?"

"Yes."

"Anything else you can add?"

"That's as much as I know, Detective Yee."

"Hmmm. Tell me, Mr. Cooke, would you be willing to work with us in putting an end to this sort of operation?"

"This is as far as I go."

"Yeah, well, give it some thought. I'll get back to you in a day or so, okay?"

₪ CHAPTER 18

When Arina Diaz finished her shift, she raced out of Ridgewood. Just walking through the door energized her, gave her a sense of freedom that lifted her spirits.

She'd been having sleeping problems, hadn't had a decent night's sleep in more than two months. Most mornings she could barely drag herself out of bed.

Even the drab bus stop enclosure seemed inviting as she grabbed a seat on a long bench where two other hospital staffers were waiting. She watched traffic zip by for a while, then closed her eyes and let out a deep sigh as she focused on her feet. They were killing her.

She tried to see through the acrylic sheets that surrounded her, but some idiot had smeared white graffiti over most of the panels. It now looked more like an out-of-place country shed.

Her mood changed as she thought about returning to her lonely apartment. Being independent wasn't always what it was cracked up to be. When she lived with her parents there were always people around for company, ready to discuss anything that was bothering her. That was especially true of her mother. They could argue over the least little thing, yet she was still her best friend.

It was funny how people said the two of them looked more like sisters than mother and daughter; they even dyed their hair the same bright red and wore each other's clothes.

Arina missed not being with her mother, especially after working all day and dragging herself to an apartment that was filled with screaming silence.

All in the name of independence.

In the midst of thinking about Jorge and how he'd turned into nothing but a big pain in the ass, Katie Rifka from Labor/Delivery dropped down next to her.

"Hey, why didn't you wait for me?" Rifka said.

"Sorry! Couldn't spend one more minute in that place. I was so pooped all I could think of was cutting out before the Supe started pushing me to put in another extra two hours. I'd all ready done more than enough, thank you very much."

"That's what you get for volunteering for extra time in the birthing rooms," Rifka said. "Now you know why no one wants that gig."

"I thought it would be fun."

"Spoken like a cock-eyed Girl Scout, or the new girl on the block."

"Well, we both know I'm not a Girl Scout."

"Dumb, though. The last time the birthing room was laid on me," Rifka said, "there were twin eight-year-olds running around while the grandmother sat there with a blissful look on her face crocheting. She totally, I mean totally, ignored the friggin' brats."

"I can see how that would be frustrating."

"I don't dig the birthing room concept in the first place," Rifka said. "Why on earth would anyone in their right mind want to have their whole family around while they give birth?"

"Katie, you don't understand. Family is everything."

"All I know is if I'd spent nine months watching my belly grow like a weather balloon, I'd want a little peace and quiet before I had to take the screaming kid home."

"Maybe labor's not a walk in the park, but hell, we both know everything's a trade off," Arina said.

"For me," Rifka said, "the trade off is keeping the birthing room quiet so that mommy and the over worked staff can function and survive. If that means stuffing everyone under twelve in the linen closet and pumping them full of Stadol, I'm all for it."

Arina laughed. "You're way too cynical. And normally I'd argue the point with you, but after the day I've had, I don't have the energy."

"That's what I've been trying to tell you."

"I don't know … maybe if people weren't so self-absorbed, so-"

"Rude. Unappreciative. Uncaring," Rifka finished. "And remember, along with that trio comes, no good deed goes unpunished." She paused for a moment and then laughed. "Oh, for heaven's sake, Arina, don't listen to me. We both know I'm a real *kvetch*. I could go on for hours."

A bus pulled up and stopped, the doors hissed open.

"Lucky you. Saved by the bus." She stood, but Arina remained seated. "Hey, aren't you coming?"

"You go ahead. I think I'm going to veg for a while. Maybe I'll go shopping. Cheer myself up."

Rifka waved goodbye as she stepped into the bus. "See you later."

* * *

The bus stop enclosure emptied two or three times while Arina sat there. It was good to be in the fresh air even if it was chilly and looked like rain again. She began to relax a bit, but still couldn't decide what she was going to do with the rest of her day.

Screw today. What am I going to do with the rest of my life?

Her feet stopped aching and she was about to head for her empty apartment when a sleek, foreign-looking car pulled up to the curb. The passenger window slid down and the driver leaned over to look out at her.

"Need a lift, nurse?"

Arina studied the man. She'd seen him around the hospital – handsome, way too handsome.

"Thanks, but I don't ride with strangers."

He gave her a wide smile, looked at her with innocent, sea green eyes. "Hey, come on. I've seen you in L&D lots of times. Don't you remember me?"

111

"What if I do?" She unclipped her hair, ran a hand through it; it felt greasy. She stared at the man, the car, and wished again that she wasn't wearing her grubby scrubs. It might have given her the confidence she needed if she had on a pretty dress. Worst of all, she knew her deodorant was definitely failing.

"Then I'm not a stranger, am I?"

Arina was excited by the direct way he looked at her. It wasn't sexual, but it was probing. She wrapped her mind around the idea of getting into the sleek car and began to feel safe with the idea. Then she placed him: one of the drug detail men.

Maybe it's what I need. A real distraction instead of just hanging out, drinking wine, watching television, and waiting for Jorge.

She did some mental gymnastics, decided what appealed to her most was the possibility of not having to spend the evening alone.

He revved the engine. She gave him another glance, stood, smoothed her raincoat, and walked slowly to the car.

The door swung open. She hesitated. Then the honk of an impatient driver made the decision for her. She slid in and for a moment was enveloped by the musky aroma of lush car leather.

"Would you like to stop for a drink before I take you to where you're going?" the drug rep said. "I've had a long day and I'll bet yours wasn't a piece of cake either."

"You'll never know." She belted herself in and hunkered down into the seat. She leaned back against the headrest, her eyes closed in pleasure.

* * *

The waiter had just brought each of them an espresso, then offered dessert.

"Not for me," Arina said. "I'm absolutely stuffed."

St. George noticed she continued to look around self-consciously as she had for most of the meal. He'd watched her try to hide her nurse's scrubs under the raincoat that she kept

112

draped around her shoulders. She was obviously worried that she was underdressed for the restaurant.

He ordered chocolate-covered biscotti. She behaved as most women do, turning down a dessert they really wanted. He took a sip of the dark, heavily flavored coffee.

"That was a great meal, wasn't it?" he said, "Now aren't you glad I talked you into dinner?" He reached across the table and lightly placed a hand on hers. She didn't pull away.

The waiter returned, set down a silver tray of three biscotti. She lightly touched one of the sweets, then picked it up and took a tiny bite.

"You *would* order the one thing I can't resist."

St. George looked into her eyes. He could tell that the bottle of wine they'd shared was having its effect on her; her lips were relaxed into a lop-sided droop, and she was having trouble keeping her eyelids open.

He continued to fake-sip the same half glass he'd started with.

What a waste, He regretted having ordered a 2006 Palacios Remondo Placet Rioja and bypassing the less expensive 2005 vintage. She'd downed the fine wine it like cheap Chianti.

"What a wonderful evening," he said, pouring the rest of the rich, full wine into her glass, slipping in a roofie at the same time.

"Yes, wonderful." Her fingers softly caressed the stem of her wine glass.

₪ CHAPTER 19

The rain started as they left the restaurant. St. George helped Arina into the Jag and she immediately curled into the leather seat. In the short time it took him to get settled and start the car, she was sound asleep.

He drove around aimlessly for several minutes before heading for the butcher shop ... and Father.

As the engine purred to silence, he turned to look at the sleeping nurse. Her mouth was open, drool dribbling out, sliding down the side of her chin.

He felt sad for her.

Shouldn't trust just any man, Arina.

He took a deep breath; let it out slowly, slowly.

Maybe Father is right: I am a wimp.

From his teens, he'd been ready to run the moment Father expressed displeasure with him. A certain tone in Father's voice, a specific glint in the eye would send him flying out the door. He'd learned to run fast, very fast because Father was quick and devious. Once he tried to stand his ground, tried to fight back, and lost two teeth from a jaw-crunching fist in the face.

Jacob St. George's taunts—wimp, candy-ass, worthless asshole—assaulted him day-in, day-out. The epithet that hurt the most, though, was "son of a whore." Denigrating Mother sent him into a deep depression that lasted for days.

Eddie looked at Arina Diaz again, ran a finger down her neck, across and around her breasts.

She didn't move.

Drugs made people so pliable, so easy to deal with. He'd learned that while supplementing a partial college scholarship with a small, but highly profitable marijuana operation.

The *sub-rosa* notoriety of being the candy man, the man-with-the-cure, sat well on his shoulders, provided him with a sense of importance he hadn't felt since Mother had left for parts unknown.

He was *still* the man with the cures, the chemical fixes.

St. George unbelted the nurse before he got out of the car. He looked around the secluded parking area, made sure no one was watching, and opened the passenger door. Arina slumped halfway out of the car before he could catch her and scoop her up in his arms. She was like a limp rag, a heavy limp rag.

He tried to get her to stand, but had to half-drag, half-carry her into the shop. He hoisted her onto a long, stainless steel receiving table and began to wheeze.

Even with his inhaler, it took a minute or two for his chest to open up. He put his head down, held onto the table, and waited for his heart to stop roaring in his ears.

"What ... who ... .where," Arina mumbled.

Her voice was raspy, like dry rattling leaves. The aroma of stale wine oozed from her mouth, her skin and inundated the cold air. Bile crawled up his throat.

She sputtered something unintelligible. St. George placed an ear against her lips, listened carefully. The guttural sounds still made no sense.

Father appeared, limped up to Eddie and punched him on the shoulder, hard, viciously.

"What are you listening for little man? Think the bitch is going to tell you something wonderful, like you're a *real* man?"

Eddie straightened and gazed into the dark, unblinking eyes of Father.

"What do you see, little Eddie? And if you've got something to say, say it!"

The nurse interrupted with more mumbles.

Eddie's hands flew to cover his eyes; spikes of heat stabbed within his chest, hot rivers of sweat gushed from every pore.

Sin & Bone

Arina's long, red hair fell across her fluttering eyes as Jacob lashed out with a boning knife at the buttons on her raincoat, cut them away, and parted the belt with a single quick slash.

He continued to use the knife to slice through her scrubs, bra, and lacy black panties. He tugged and pulled at the destroyed garments until they were free of her, then tossed them on the floor.

He ran a finger down between her breasts, across her belly, and stopped at the edge of her pubic hair.

"God damn it, you moron! Can't you tell a dye job from the real thing?" He ran his fingers through the curly black hair. "A fucking fake red head."

Eddie's arms were covered in goose bumps, a huge wheeze burst from his throat. He clutched at his chest, couldn't breathe. The trap door in his lungs sprang shut. He groped for the inhaler.

As his eyes cleared, he watched Father snatch the nurse from the receiving table and carry her unsteadily across the room. Jacob's legs trembled from the weight as he dumped her onto the large wood cutting block.

Father grunted with effort, crawled up onto the table, and lifted her legs up and over his shoulders. He unzipped his fly and plunged into her, again and again.

"Mommy!" she shouted. "Mommy!"

Father stopped, stared at her unfocused eyes. Her arms reached out, pushed against his shoulders.

"Mommmmmmmmeee!" She used her small fists to pound against his face.

Father squeezed her wrists together with one meaty hand, grabbed a knife with the other, and slashed across her neck. Blood sprayed into the air and splattered down into the sawdust.

Bette Golden Lamb & J. J. Lamb

₪ HAPTER 20

Gina slipped and slid across the steamy bathroom floor, poster-nude for a one-legged search-for-balance dance. Dripping wet, it was all she could do to keep from falling flat on her face. Disgusted, she reached for a bath towel and stretched it across her rear-end before sliding it up to her back and shoulders.

"What a dork," she muttered. "Almost fall down and break my neck in my own stinking bathroom."

She ran a palm across the foggy mirror and stopped to stare at her reflection: Feathers of black hair lay flat against her forehead, bloodshot eyes stared with a "whaddayawant" kind of glare. To top it off, a huge zit was blossoming on her chin.

"Ugh!"

She shrugged on skuzzy flannel PJs and toed into the red rabbit slippers Harry had given her last Christmas; the little beady eyes rolled around in silly cartoon fashion before settling into a blank stare.

After turning out all the lights, she padded around the apartment, listening to the silence. She tilted her head and isolated different street noises, heard the staccato ticking of her Regulator clock, paused as it chimed the quarter hour. She walked across the deep-pile living room carpet that surrendered just whispers of sound.

The hot shower warmth she'd gratefully absorbed was quickly disappearing; allowing an invasion of cold sweat. She hugged her flannels close to her to stifle chills that swam up from the base of her spine to the top of her head.

Had it only been a little more than a week since her life had been turned topsy-turvy? She counted off eight days on her fingers.

Eight days since that first invasive, ghoulish phone call.

When she finally made it to her bed, she kicked off her slippers and gently touched the picture of Harry next to the telephone.

Seven days of a broken engagement.

"Dammit! I miss you, Harry Lucke."

She glanced at the clock as she crawled into the rumpled sheets, annoyed that she'd broken her promise to make the bed every day.

She counted every gong as the clock chimed eleven.

If she didn't get some shut-eye soon, tomorrow she wouldn't be able to concentrate on anything.

But she wasn't sleepy.

"What else is new?" She snuggled down into the bedding, bringing her knees to her chest, closed her eyes, and tried to think of nothing. Her eyes popped open again when she heard the musical bong-bong-bong-bong.

11:15.

So it's going to be that kind of night.

Even fully awake, she was still startled when the telephone rang. On the third ring, she picked up.

"Hi, Gina. It's me."

Harry. Her gut reaction was to hang up. Instead, she lay back and stared into the night.

"Please talk to me."

"It's late, Harry. I'm not up to talking to you, or anyone else right now."

"You know we'll have to figure out this mess sooner or later."

She bit her lip, refused to speak.

"Gina, if you change your mind, call me. Anytime. Please?" There was a long pause. "At least think about it."

What she really needed was to *stop* thinking about it, or anything else.

She hung up without saying 'goodbye,' stared into the darkness; it was like a solid wall—flat, unyielding. Nothing filtered through. Somewhere in the background she was aware of the clock rhythmically chiming off the time: **12; 12:15; 12:30.**

* * *

Crooked, broken streets. Raw garbage slopped around her ankles, lashed at her face, left a thick smear of stinking, rotting flesh over her arms, her legs. The nothingness made her ears ring, blackness curled its tentacles around her, consumed her, squeezed away every breath. She tried to fight it, but the blackness held on, a powerful emptiness that was swallowing, swallowing her fingers, her arms, her shoulders, her head.

* * *

A high-pitched scream melded into the ringing of a telephone. Gina bolted to a sitting position, a hand flat against her beating chest. She struggled to disengage from the dream, fell across the bed and grabbed for the phone; her body shook uncontrollably.

"Hel-hello."

Silence.

"Harry, is that you again?"

Pain stabbed through her head; her heart boomed in her ears.

"Harry? Harry … *talk* to me."

Wheezing, heavy wheezing. A raspy, wavering voice stuttered something she couldn't understand.

Her spine tingled with fear. "Who is this? What do you want?"

"Save me!" the voice whispered.

Gina trembled, stared into the dark, didn't answer.

"Please! Save me!"

She dropped the phone and ran to the bathroom, braced herself over the toilet, and heaved until there was nothing left but the clutch of spasms.

"Ohmygod! Ohmygod!"

She rose to the sink and splashed handful after handful of cold water onto her face, her neck, her shoulders until her PJs and the bathroom tiles were soaked. She fumbled for a towel, rubbed it hard across her face, threw it on the floor to mop up the splattered puddles. She took in long, deep breaths; the accelerated thrumming of her heart pounded in her ears.

She flipped on the bathroom light. "I'm all right … all right." She repeated the words mantra-like at her mirror image while rubbing hard at her arms, up and down their length.

Why is this man plaguing me?

Pepper Yee! She had to call the detective … immediately. If Yee didn't do something this time, she would become the cop's second skin. Something *had* to be done.

Resolve settled her stomach. She flipped off the bathroom light and stepped into the hallway, hesitated, and waited for her eyes to adjust to the shadowy corridor.

At first she thought it was dizziness—everything seemed to be moving. But like the black apparition in her dream, a billowing shadow separated from the wall.

She rubbed hard at her eyes, inched back as the dark cloud morphed into two arms reaching out to grab her.

She screamed, kicked.

"Let me go! Let me go!"

She was trapped, couldn't move forward or back. Her head roared; she twisted, squirmed

"Gina! Stop! It's me, Harry!"

When she finally recognized his voice, she went limp, began to sob.

He buried his face in her hair. "Don't … don't be afraid."

She took a deep breath. "Harry! Oh, Harry He called again."

"At work?"

"No, dammit. Here! Tonight!"

"Did you call the police?"

"I was on my way to do that when you scared the shit out of me."

He started walking her toward the living room. "Did he threaten you?"

"No. I think he's looking for help. I … I feel like such a fool freaking out like that. But it's the second time he's called here."

"Second time?"

"I didn't tell you about the first call because … because we were fighting."

Harry took her hand; she reluctantly allowed him to lead her to the sofa. They sat down together.

He wrapped an arm around her and squeezed her to him. "Maybe if we'd gotten married when we were supposed to–"

Gina flung his arm off and jumped up. "I don't believe you, Harry Lucke. A maniac is stalking me and all you can think of is marriage? You're an idiot!"

"You're right." He stood up to face her. "I am an idiot … an idiot for loving you, living with you, wanting to be with you forever. And you know what? That's all I've been thinking about for more than a year."

"Face it, Harry. That may never happen."

Disappointment clouded his eyes, new lines etched their way across his forehead. And she saw stubbornness in the set of his jaw that told her nothing had really changed.

Bette Golden Lamb & J. J. Lamb

₪ CHAPTER 21

"Shit, this is one real mother-fucker," Paul Lucke shouted down to his brother as he struggled to steady a dolly carrying a strapped-on refrigerator. The weight of the load was starting to defeat him as he tried to muscle it up a makeshift ramp and into a U-Haul van. But the whole load was inching backwards and he was going to be squashed when it let go.

"Damn it!" he yelled. "How about a little help?"

Harry jumped up onto the ramp and leaned into the fridge. "You said you could handle it."

"Forget what I said. Just push!"

"I warned you: keep this up and you're going to create one big, raging hernia."

Harry and Paul grunted in unison, shoved harder, and finally coerced the hefty appliance onto the level platform of the van.

Bent over, hands on thighs, they were speechless as they fought to gain control of their rasping breath and aching muscles.

"Talk about a great entrance," Paul finally said.

"Always happy to help out my puny older brother. Man, you *must* be getting old."

"Take you on any time." Paul Lucke's laugh was loud; a sound that filled the air with uninhibited joy. He grabbed Harry in a bear hug, pounded on his back.

"How's the old married man doing?" he said. "Must have left a dozen messages at your place. Ready to hunt you down."

"Don't ask. Haven't wanted to talk to anyone. Especially you."

"Fuck you, too, you little twerp."

"I knew you'd ask a lot of in-your-face questions I wasn't ready to answer." Harry reached into a pile of blankets and began covering the fridge.

"Do you ever plan on telling me what's going on?"

"We'll see."

"Whatever," Paul said. "And besides, you do look kind of beat, little man. And I don't mean from using those Twinkies you call muscles."

Harry raised both arms and leaned into the walls of the truck to stretch. He was done in.

"The Oakland docks don't give you enough work that you have to lug this stuff around?" Harry said. "Hell, if you're short on cash, just tell me. I'm always good for a fiver."

"Generous bastard." Paul pulled a blue bandana from his pocket and wiped the sweat from his face. "It's for mom and dad. They bought it from someone on Craig's List."

"So what's it doing here?"

"Gave my address. Guy dumped it off."

"You shoulda kept calling. I would have called back sooner or later," Harry said.

"Yeah, sure. And maybe you'd be in Reno, or New York. Hell, you're harder to catch than an ass-nipping baboon. Are you ever in town? Some job." He grabbed Harry's arm. "Come on, let's get a beer. Got a couple of cold ones inside."

Harry followed his brother into the two-bedroom condo. It was a mess, as usual. When they walked into kitchen, the smell of dirty dishes and garbage made Harry want to turn tail.

"Neat as always, Paulo."

"Shit, since Annie left, I just don't give a rat's ass." He reached into the fridge for the beers.

The open door gave Harry a view of spattered cartons of take-out – Chinese, Italian, deli, and some without identity. The odor wasn't too great either.

Harry twisted off the bottle cap, tossed it into an overflowing trash bag, and took a long swallow. His gut immediately balled into a knot. Alcohol on an empty stomach never sat well.

"What a pair," Paul said. "So you're obviously on the outs with Gina, huh? Tough one. Seems neither of us can hang onto a woman."

That wasn't something Harry was ready to own up to. He stared at his brother and finished off his beer with one long pull at the bottle.

"What did you do to screw things up this time, Harry?" He set his beer on the counter, slapping away some old onion peels to make room. "Shit! I like Gina and her goofy Bronx talk."

Harry started straightening up the area, ran some soapy water in the sink, and began washing the piled up dishes. Paul didn't offer to help, but after several pieces had drained on the rack, he reluctantly began to dry.

"I disappointed her, Paulo," Harry mumbled.

"Oh? Like you fucked-up-and-forgot-to-pick-her-up kind of disappoints?"

"No. More like the not-trusting-her-judgment kind. Problem is, she's into one of her suspicious phases … thinks there's a boogeyman going around doing bad things to nurses at Ridgewood."

Paul put an arm around Harry's shoulder. "Little brother, you're fucked."

* * *

"Thanks for dropping by and making me put this miserable place in order," Paul said. "Of course, it's only going to be a mess again in a couple of days, if that long."

"The hell it is," Harry said. "If I'm bedding down here for a while, I need neat." He pushed Paul's feet off the end of the coffee table.

"What do you mean bedding down here? No one invited you."

"I don't need an invitation. You're my brother, remember?"

127

"Yeah, yeah. Maybe you better think seriously about making up with that Italian beauty."

"She won't talk to me."

"And you're planning to move in here when?"

"Soon as I can get my clothes out of the trunk of my car."

"Wonderful. Just wonderful."

They lapsed into silence. The weak afternoon sun had disappeared and it looked like the promised rain might happen soon. Harry watched the second hand revolve on the clock Paul had bought at a garage sale for two bucks. It inched around the dial. His brother's head was nodding; he was starting to drift off, too.

"Did I ever tell you how I met Gina?"

Paul rubbed at his neck and straightened. "You mean when she encroached on *your* I'm-in-charge-here-territory in the ICU?" He laughed. "Yeah, you told me a million times."

"She was so cute, talking like a typical New Yorker—her hands going a mile a minute."

"And ready to knock your block off, right?" Paul said.

"Right. She's never been one to back away from a fight. Remember that union rally where the nurses took on Der Swartzenegger."

"That California Nurses Association is nothing but a bunch of rabble-rousing troublemakers. Damn unions."

"Knock off the phony right wing crap, bro," Harry said. "Where would you and your dockworker buddies be without the all-powerful International Longshore and Warehouse Union?"

"Yeah, but we really deserve the bucks we get."

"Oh, yeah? And nurses don't? Besides, if I remember correctly, the ILWU wanted the nurses to affiliate with them at one time."

Paul pulled at his curly hair, dark like Harry's, and gave his brother a big, lopsided grin.

"So, tell me again, little brother, what the hell was that Sacramento rally all about again?"

128

"Thought you remembered," Harry said.

Paul gave him an evil eye. "Talk to me about sex, I'll give you the most minute details. Talk about political rallies and I can snore with the best of them."

"The Terminator was calling them a special interest group."

"Yeah, I remember. Them and the cops and the firemen. Big mistake. They all hounded that fine movie-making man until his public image sank like the setting sun. Poor guy had to back pedal big time to re-gain all the ground he lost on that one."

"My little hell-raiser was smack in the center of that fight."

"So were you, buddy. Huggin' and kissin' all the pretty nurses."

"Just the one after I met Gina. And don't forget, your smarter, little brother is one of those 'pretty nurses'."

"Would I ever?" Paul tossed a section of the newspaper at him. "So what are you going to do about the Bronx bombshell?"

Harry took the newspaper, folded it neatly, and stacked it on some magazines on the coffee table.

"I wish I knew."

* * *

The brothers delivered the refrigerator to their parents' home later that evening, catching the first edge of a new storm system.

Paul said, "Told you we shouldn't have taken the time to clean up my place. Now we're going to get soaked."

"A little rain will do you some good. Wash away some of that cynicism. Make you a better man."

Paul howled, "I'm already the better man."

The elder Luckes came out of their run-down, faded blue and white Queen Anne to give their sons a menu of unnecessary directions on the best way to get what was now called the "white terror" up the steps and into the house.

Ike Lucke, dressed in faded jeans and a stomach-rounded t-shirt, came down the steps and was ready to push with his one good shoulder. His t-shirt immediately clung to his upper body, wet with rain. After only a couple of steps he was starting to grumble.

"Pops, will you please go back inside before you get blown away?" Harry said, as they put the makeshift ramp in place so they could unload the refrigerator. The elder Lucke scowled and ignored him. Their mother was getting ready to trudge back inside, but not before she had a thing or two to say to her sons:

"We expected you earlier." Her face was set in a prune-like frown. "And Ike Lucke, you better get yourself inside before you catch your death of cold."

"Can't let nursie-boy injure those delicate fingers," Ike said, patting Harry's head.

Harry and Paul said as one voice, "Cut it out, Pop."

The elder Lucke ignored both of them, yelled to his wife, "I'm just fine, Dorothy. These boys need some help."

Their mother, dressed in a pair of drab green, holey pants, stained with the same yellow that was freshly painted on the kitchen walls, led the procession inside and pointed to where she wanted her sons to put the new/used fridge.

"So you can help Paul and Harry with that heavy refrigerator, but the shoulder was too painful to help paint the kitchen?" She said it with a smile at the corners of her mouth.

The men were drenched but none of them complained as they sat at the kitchen table. Each had a cup of steaming English tea in front of them, and there was a pile of chocolate chip cookies on a bone china plate decorated with tiny, painted pink roses—it sat in the center of the oak table.

"Sit down and have a cup of tea with us, Ma," Paul said.

She poured tea into her cup and took a seat, smiled widely at Harry. "So I've got this awful pain in my neck for the last two months. What do you think it is?"

Harry reached over and touched her neck. "Is it here?"

"Nope. It's sitting in that chair right next to you. The man's become impossible since he went on disability."

"Can I help it if I got bashed with a container?" Ike glared at Dorothy. "Your picking on me isn't funny. Don't you think I wanna go back to work?"

"Leave him alone, Ma," Paul said.

They all quietly sipped their tea for a few moments.

"So, how's our little nursie doing?" Ike said, letting one wrist drop.

"You're pathetic, Pop," Harry said. "I'm a fully licensed registered nurse. And a damn good one. You should be proud of me instead of giving me all this girlie-girlie shit. Do I have to carry things on my back before you think I'm a man?"

Ike just smiled.

"Where's the little Catholic girl?" Mrs. Lucke said. "The one you were supposed to marry?"

"Yeah, I wanna hear what he has to say about that, too," Paul said.

Harry refused to answer. He scratched a fingernail on the wooden table, mainly to irritate his mother.

She reached out and pinned his finger.

The chair screeched as Harry stood. "She's not Catholic anymore – and who gives a damn if she is or isn't?" He leaned over the table and glared at his mother and father. "And you wonder why I don't come around more often?" He turned and headed for the door, Paul right behind him.

Their mother yelled at their backs.

"The way you boys get rid of your women, we're never going to have any grandchildren!"

Bette Golden Lamb & J. J. Lamb

₪ CHAPTER 22

Lexie Alexandros was sitting in the Advice Center when Gina arrived for work Monday morning. Tina looked smug and Chelsea was buried in paperwork at Shelly's desk.

Still no sign of the missing nurse. Now even her personal belongings were gone, taken away from the room.

Like she never existed.

"Right on time," the manager said.

"Aren't I always?"

Alexandros stood and motioned for Gina to follow her. When they were out of earshot, she said, "Alan Vasquez wants to see you at ten in Administration."

"What could *he* possibly want?"

"You tell me," Alexandros said.

"I haven't done anything."

"So you have no idea why he'd want to see you?"

"Not a clue," Gina said

The manager was jumpy, tugged at the usual loose strand of hair as she talked. "You haven't been going around scaring people with more talk about those calls, have you?"

"Lexie, we both know you have no faith in me or believe anything I say about this whole business. But at least treat me like a professional. I do know how to talk or not talk to people."

The manager's face flushed. "Haven't I always been fair with you, Gina?" She didn't wait for an answer. "But scaring staff—"

"And just whom have I frightened?"

"Tina, for one."

"You've got to be kidding. Tina complained about me *scaring* her?"

"She didn't use that particular word, but she asked for a transfer. *You* seem to be the reason."

Gina's hands waved around in the air as she talked. "I can't believe it. She wants out because of me? Did it occur to you that maybe Shelly's disappearance is what has her all upset?"

"The thought crossed my mind. But that's not what she said."

"That woman thrives on bushwhacking people. Didn't even have the stones to talk to me before running like some little kid to mommy." Gina hugged herself in frustration. "Would you tell that poor frightened thing that even the police don't believe me? Maybe that'll be enough to calm her fractured nerves."

Alexandros' piercing eyes made Gina uncomfortable as though she had broken some golden rule of behavior that she wasn't privy to.

"Anyway, the administrator will see you around ten. Do you want me to go with you?"

"Thanks, mom, but I'm a big girl. I can handle this all by myself. It's not like I haven't confronted the great Alan Vasquez before." Her stomach was doing flip-flops, but she'd be damned if she'd let anyone else know that.

Hell, they need me more than I need them. If I have to get another job, no problem.

The manager placed a hand softly on her shoulder. "If you want to talk, I'm here for you."

"Thanks, Ms. Alexandros, but I need to stand on my own two feet. And it's important for you to know that I'm not taking any crap from him, or anyone else in Ridgewood."

The manager flipped the tortured strand of hair out of her eyes and moved in the direction of her office. "Call me. I'll be here."

When Gina returned to her desk, she said nothing to Tina, who averted her eyes.

Maybe I'll be the one to go first, you sneaky little bitch. Try anticipating that!

* * *

When one of the inside lines rang at two minutes after ten, Gina was certain it was *the* call. She'd searched her mind since Lexie had told her about the pending meeting, but for the life of her she couldn't think of a single reason why the administrator would want to see her.

"Ms. Mazzio, this is Brianna in Administration. Mr. Vasquez is ready to see you."

Gina left the clinic building and used her favorite short cuts to crisscross through several of the Ridgewood departments. Her inner antennae tuned into the pace of the hospital unit nurses as they rushed around performing their duties. The vibrations were exciting, much different from the Clinic.

She couldn't help thinking about Oncology and how she missed working with her friend Helen. She also missed the nurse-patient relationships she'd enjoyed on that unit, and a sense that every procedure, every single moment was vital.

While the elevator made its slow rise to the Administration floor, Gina tried to compose her thoughts:

Why don't I just leave? I wouldn't need to deal with that bastard Vasquez. Just stop the elevator. Press the down button and walk out the door. Never look back.

"Not on your life," she muttered. Unfinished business was part of her past, not her future.

Brianna's desk was the first thing she saw when she stepped out onto the eighth floor. On one polished corner was a large bouquet of pink roses in an elegant cut-crystal vase. The flowers looked so fresh and beautiful it made Gina believe that summer really would return to the Bay Area. Brianna nodded as she read Gina's security tag.

"Let me take you into Mr. Vasquez's office," she said, moving toward an intricately carved oak door. She knocked, and without waiting for a response, ushered Gina inside.

When the door closed, Alan Vasquez stood and offered Gina a seat. He did not sit until she was in her chair.

"How are you today, Ms. Mazzio?"

She kept her gaze steady, taking in both him and the exacting cut of his very expensive suit. "I'm holding my own, thank you."

Vasquez steepled his fingers under his chin as he leaned back into his chair.

Gina was totally stymied. The man across from her bore no resemblance to the miserable person who had hounded her in the past. This man was ill at ease, almost humble.

"I have a problem, Ms. Mazzio. I'm hoping you can be of assistance."

What?

She'd been prepared for anything but *that*. She straightened in her chair. "If I can."

Vasquez turned away for a moment and stood to view the incredible cityscape from the expanse of his windows. Even though Gina was distracted, she couldn't help but notice how beautiful San Francisco was across the bay, even in the pouring rain.

As he turned to face her, his body language broadcast its own story: head slightly bent forward, shoulders drooping, fingers slowly flexing, eyes avoiding her. He remained silent until he slipped back into his chair.

"I'm a bachelor, Ms. Mazzio." He finally looked at her, seemed to be searching for the right words. "I'm not necessarily sorry about that ... I'm married to my job and that's good enough for me."

"Does your being a bachelor have something to do with *my* job, or me personally?"

"No, no. Not at all. But this meeting, the situation at hand, is very difficult for me." He looked quickly at the ceiling, then directly at her. "Our relationship ... yours and mine ... has been rather contentious in the past."

"To say the least."

"Yes, yes. And for that reason I want you to understand why I need to ask a special favor of you."

If he asks me for a date I'll scream.

"I have very little family left," Vasquez continued. "There's only my sister, her husband, and two nieces, Lupe and Arina. That's it. That's all the family I have."

"I see," Gina said, although she didn't.

A flash of anger crossed his face. "No, you don't see!" He held up a hand before she could respond. "Excuse me. I didn't mean to be harsh. I'm very, very stressed at the moment."

"Just tell me what you need from me," Gina said.

"I need your help."

"How I could possibly help *you*, Mr. Vasquez?"

He leaned forward, rested his chin on his hands. "My niece, Arina, is missing."

"Arina?"

"Yes, Arina Diaz."

"Arina Diaz is your niece?"

Vasquez raised bleak eyes to stare back at her. "Yes."

"My God! We were just talking in the cafeteria a few days ago. I had no idea she was related to you. I mean, she certainly never said anything about it."

"My sister talked me into secretly placing her in the hospital so I could keep an eye on her. I tried to tell her Arina was a grown woman, that we shouldn't try to direct her life. But my sister and brother-in-law insisted. I eventually agreed, provided none of us ever mentioned the fact to anyone within Ridgewood."

"Wise move," Gina said softly. "If people knew, it could have made things difficult for her."

"Exactly." After a long moment, he took a deep breath, let it out slowly. "She was supposed to attend a family dinner at my sister's house on Sunday. She neither showed up nor called to explain her absence. My sister hasn't been able to reach her by telephone, and there's no one at home at her apartment."

"Maybe she went out of town with Jorge, her boyfriend, for the weekend."

"I suggested that, but my sister didn't believe it. She said Arina would never do anything like that without first telling her. I wasn't convinced. But when my niece didn't show up for her regular shift this morning, I had to agree something was wrong."

He looked directly at Gina. "Now she's gone, disappeared."

"Do you think she might have run away?"

"There was no hint of anything bothering her." His thoughts seemed to drift for a moment. "She did mention that work was tiring, but there was a sparkle in her eyes. I could tell she was happy."

"Has anyone talked to Jorge?"

"My sister called him. He has no idea where she could be. He hadn't seen her for several days."

"Have you noticed any changes in her lately?"

"Not really. Well, since graduation from nursing school and going to work for Ridgewood, she may have become a little less communicative, doesn't seem to share everything that's going on in her life. But she's still devoted to her parents, and very close to her sister. "

Butterflies fluttered in Gina's stomach; the fear that had been with her since that first phone call returned with a jolt. Was Arina one of the caller's victims?

"Have you gone to the police?" she said, thinking of her own useless experiences.

"Of course. Her parents did that Sunday evening. We aren't stupid." He became the Administrator Gina knew from the past: superior, disdainful, and dismissive. But it was an ember, not a fire. His eyes moistened, looked sad. "The idea of her running away makes no sense whatsoever."

"I still don't understand why you sent for me. What is it you think I can do?"

"Truthfully, I'm not sure. I've talked to her manager in Labor and Delivery, and the Director of Nursing. All they could tell me is that she has good nursing skills and an exemplary work record. But no one seems to know anything about her personal life."

"The other nurses in her department?"

"Yes, well, I'm not at my best when dealing with the nursing staff."

Gina wanted to shout *Amen!* But she remained silent and waited for Vasquez to continue.

"My thought was that because of your union leadership, you have a good rapport with the other nurses. I would appreciate it if you would talk to the Labor and Delivery staff, see if Arina might have said something, anything, to provide some clue as to what's happened to her."

Gina's first instinct was to say, yes, that she would do what she could. But before she could open her mouth, her anger resurfaced.

"What about Shelly Wilton? She's missing, too."

Vasquez was obviously caught off-guard.

"Uh, yes, well, Ms. Alexandros did inform me about your concerns for Nurse Wilton ... and the disturbing telephone calls you had here and at home."

"And?"

"Please forgive me Ms. Mazzio. Initially, I let our past difficulties interfere with my better judgment. I shouldn't have."

"I know. Once a trouble-maker, always a trouble-maker."

It was a moment before he answered. "You did this hospital a great service last year, Ms. Mazzio, by uncovering the perpetrators of the bone marrow scheme. And you probably saved many evolving services that would have been dropped without enlarging our RN staff. The number of new nurses who have joined Ridgewood as a result of the new contract and benefits is more than impressive. And for that I'm grateful. Perhaps you deserved greater recognition, better treatment. Please forgive me."

Gina's anger was defusing. "I can appreciate what you're going through with respect to Arina," she said softly. "But I think you need to know that the police have shown very little interest in Shelly Wilton's disappearance. People seem to think she's a foot-loose, fancy-free kind of woman. What that has to do with anything is beyond me." Gina hesitated, then added, "I'm sure that isn't the situation with Arina, but—"

"But what?"

"Perhaps if *you* reminded the police that a couple of Ridgewood nurses are missing, maybe they would pay more attention."

"Do you really think it would make a difference?"

"Who did your sister talk to at the police station?"

"I don't know. Whoever it was said they couldn't do anything until Arina had been missing at least 48 hours. Or that there was evidence of a crime having been committed."

"I'd suggest that you call a Detective Pepper Yee. Make a big deal out of your being the administrator here, and that you're very concerned because two Ridgewood nurses are missing. Arina and Shelly Wilton."

"And why call this particular detective?"

"Because she's the one I spoke to about the man who called advice in the first place and scared the daylights out of me. She's also investigating Shelley's disappearance."

"I'll call immediately," Vasquez said.

Gina stood. "I'm really sorry about Arina. I hope she shows up soon, I hope Shelly shows up soon, also."

Vasquez came around his desk and walked with her to the door. "I would appreciate it if you could avoid revealing the relationship between Arina and me."

"I'll do my best."

"Thank you. I really do value your willingness to help."

He reached out to shake her hand. "I needed to talk to someone I thought would be one hundred percent straight with me, someone I knew would do the right thing, no matter what the consequences. Despite our past differences, I felt you were that person."

"Mr. Vasquez, I promise that if I hear anything at all, I will tell you immediately." Gina slipped her hand from his grip. "I hope Arina is all right. She's a very nice person."

The administrator opened the door. "Thank you for coming, Ms. Mazzio. I hope we hear from my niece, and Shelly Wilton, very soon."

Bette Golden Lamb & J. J. Lamb

₪ **CHAPTER 23**

Pepper Yee was mesmerized by the fuzzy, patterned socks on her feet, which were propped up on the end of her desk.

If the captain came in, he would stare her down until she planted her scuffed half boots back on the floor. But he wasn't there and with her charcoal gray slacks hiked up, her fuzzy socks were exposed to the world. She'd taken a lot of heat from her cohorts about the butterfly design crawling through the weave, but how anyone could see something sexual in insects crawling on your socks was beyond her. Leave it to a bunch of men—they could create some kind of sexual buzz about a half-croaked cricket on a stick, or a flattened frog on a tree stump.

It was almost noon and she was starving.

She zeroed in on a couple other detectives at the far end of the bullpen. They were arguing a case.

"Shoulda gone in, warrant or not."

"You're getting crazier by the year. Gonna find me a new partner. We ain't…"

Their voices trailed off. At first she'd listened carefully, pretending disinterest. But soon her mind drifted away and the men were only an irritating noise in the background.

Point of fact: they were talking about some ordinary, everyday break-in that shouldn't hold anyone's attention for very long.

She rubbed hard at her neck. The muscles were bunched and sore, making the prospect of tackling the pile of paperwork in front of her that much more grueling. She groaned and wiggled her toes.

Papers and notes of different colors and sizes were smeared across her desk like cheap props for a sixth-grade school play:

Here sits the busy, dedicated detective, who's very productive and always on top of everything.

On top of everything? In charge of her life? Uh-um. This mess told *her* a different story—it displayed just how out of control she really was.

Messy desk, messy life.

Her eyes drifted to the almost obligatory picture of the happily married couple right next to her against-regulation elevated feet.

Warren and Pepper. Another prop that had nothing to do with reality.

She eyed her husband, the computer wizard. Studied his handsome, sculptured cheekbones, black hair that outshone hers, and eyes that revealed no history, no future, no anything.

You fucking inscrutable Asian. How could anyone know what that stony mug of yours is saying? And look at me—grinning so hard my face is going to split in half.

Tears stung her eyes. Hard to believe the photo was taken only a year ago.

She slammed her feet to the floor so hard the two detectives stopped their cussing and instinctively reached for their guns.

She raised her hands in mock surrender. "Sorry!"

"Get a life, will ya, Yee."

"Broads!" Their voices were a duet of disdain as they turned away, diving back into their argument.

That asshole'll never know how close he is to the truth. I have no goddam life.

Who else would hang around this hole and eat breakfast, lunch, and dinner from vending machines rather than go out or go home?

Home? That's where Warren would be. Where he could ignore her, look right through her as though she didn't exist.

She studied the picture of the happy couple one more time before forcing her focus back to the pile of half-finished forms and reports in front of her. She ran her fingers through the mess of papers and tried to put them in some kind of order.

At the top of the pile were her notes on Gina Mazzio and the missing nurse problem at Ridgewood General.

Damn it!

She was so sick of these nothing cases, cases that were whispers of something but never developed into anything solid. If she wanted respect, she'd have to make a few headlines. Otherwise, she'd be nothing but a female grunt forever.

She conjured up an image of Gina Mazzio. There was nothing inscrutable about *that* one. Every word, every gesture was a sledgehammer.

Wonder how she'd do with Warren?

Yee had done little work in the past week. Even though she tried, she couldn't make her mind settle into deductive reasoning, settle down to even caring. All she could think about was Warren.

Why had he stopped loving her, stopped touching her, stopped talking to her? Was he having an affair?

She'd even followed him from work for two consecutive evenings. There was nothing out of the ordinary. Nothing.

Enough, you idiot. Focus! Focus!

Two nurses were missing, or at least unaccounted for.

Well, hell, people do not just disappear. Women in this age group? Usually there was some guy involved, tying them up in the bedroom, and she didn't mean a crime scene.

Shelly, the advice nurse was now missing for a week. Men. Shelly liked them. The gal slept around. But her manager said she was a steady employee. When she was sick, she called in. Where the hell was she then?

And Diaz?

Her uncle, the Ridgewood administrator claims she's gone missing. Didn't show up for a family dinner on Sunday, didn't show up for work this morning. And Mazzio was bugging her again—now about both of them.

The main problem: No bodies; not a single shred of evidence that a crime had been committed. In either instance.

And who the hell is this weirdo that's been calling Mazzio? Someone apparently was doing the deed. If you could believe her ... and she did.

Yee tapped the eraser end of a pencil on her desk, stirred a stray memo, which ended up moving a couple of inches closer to falling off the edge.

Yeah, she believed the nurse. Didn't want to, but she was solid enough.

Yee felt uneasy. She'd fallen down on the job. She'd let this and other investigations slide. Her personal problems were standing in the way of her good judgment.

Face it: you haven't done squat in weeks.

"Have to make things happen," she muttered to herself.

She quickly made neat stacks of the papers on her desk, but without any rhyme or reason. Again, sixth-grade props to make her look like the efficient cop that she knew she wasn't—at least not currently.

She picked up the phone, found the right Post-it, and called Walter Cooke, the human body parts man.

"You've had enough time to mull over my offer, Walter. It's time to get your ass down here and talk to me. Either that, or I'll send a car to pick you up."

In the process of straightening the paper mess, the notes on the missing nurse problem ended up buried somewhere in the midst of the stack.

₪ CHAPTER 24

Megan Ann's hands shook as she moved away from the entrance to the cafeteria. She watched the elevator clunk open and saw Gina move to the end of the line of impatient staffers wanting to get served.

She swallowed hard to drown the bitterness in her throat. Anger forced her into motion. She walked up to Gina, grabbed her wrist. Gina's mouth formed a perfect circle of surprise.

"I know," Megan Ann said.

"Hey, cut that out!"

"One of the surgery nurses saw the two of you at *The Hideaway*. She was more than happy to pass on that tasty tidbit."

Gina's eyes widened; she yanked her arm away. "What are you talking about?"

"You know!"

Megan Ann's legs trembled, her heart pounded; she had to shove her hands into her coat pockets to keep from slapping the advice nurse.

Gina's face morphed from puzzlement to irritation. Arching an eyebrow, she jabbed a finger at Megan Ann and said in a heavy New York accent, "Actually, I was wondering who on earth you were talking about since I didn't know you even *had* a boyfriend."

"Rotten smart-ass!" Megan Ann's voice was climbing in volume in spite of herself. "That's what everyone says about you."

"Take it outside," a voice piped up as people dodged around them to get into the busy cafeteria.

Another voice said, "Pretty unprofessional." The loudest and nastiest snapped, "For Chrissakes, get lost. Save it for the cat house!"

The staff bumped into, flowed around them, gave them dirty looks. Megan Ann was about to cover her face in embarrassment when Gina grabbed her arm and pulled her off to one side.

"Let's get out of here," Gina said. "We need to go someplace where we can talk and settle this."

Megan Ann's stomach growled, calling her attention to the painful, gnawing sensation deep down inside.

God, I need a drink.

Her thoughts went immediately to the stash of booze and drugs in her locker. She envisioned the vodka miniatures, the vials of Valium. She pressed hard against her stomach with both hands.

Gina tugged at her arm; she jumped at the touch. "I don't know what to think," she said, trying to speak above the hubbub of the lunchtime crowd. Embarrassed, she could see that people were still gaping at them, making rude remarks.

The advice nurse kept tugging at her arm; she relented and meekly followed Gina into an emptying elevator. Gina pressed "3" and they both sighed when the door finally slammed shut. The hubbub of the cafeteria crowd drifted away, vanished.

The elevator carried them to the surgical floor. Gina hurried them past the operating room area, guarded by large double doors and a bold warning:

DESIGNATED PERSONNEL ONLY

There was little activity or traffic in the corridor. Most scheduled surgeries had already taken place, or were well under way.

Gina led Megan Ann farther down the hall until at the very end they stood in front of the hospital chapel. A small doorway sign read:

All Are Welcome

Inside the dimly lit room was an abbreviated altar, set off by flickering candles. Soft, almost indiscernible music created a sense of tranquility. Megan Ann hadn't heard spiritual music in a long time. She'd turned away from religion when her husband and baby died. How could any God allow such a senseless loss of life?

They sat down next to each other on one of the three backless benches.

"I like to come here to think," Gina said. "There's rarely anyone around during lunch hour. I guess people pray or meditate on some kind of schedule."

The moment they were seated, Megan Ann covered her face with both hands, started to cry. "I don't know what came over me." She looked up at Gina. "I'm so sorry. And in front of all those people."

"Hey, that bunch has seen a lot worse. They'll buzz about it for a while until the next oddball thing comes along. You'll be old news by this afternoon."

"I was awful."

"Was this about Eddie St. George? He's the only guy other than my fiancé I've gone out with in a long time."

"Yes, Eddie."

Gina touched her shoulder. "Hey, we had a quick, friendly drink. He wasn't interested in anything else, and neither was I. And I certainly didn't know he was your boyfriend."

"He's not. At least if he is, *he* doesn't know anything about it."

Gina chuckled. "You got to admit it's really funny. I mean, two grown women fighting about *boyfriends.* Acting like a couple of silly teenagers."

Megan Ann tried to smile. "We're going out tonight, Eddie and me. But it's not like we're serious about one another. But I'm hoping."

"Well, let's forget about this. It was a drink. Nothing else. Honest!"

"Still, I behaved badly."

"Not important. Let it go."

"I know you'll say I'm a fool, but I think about Eddie a lot."

The music was beginning to soothe her. She took in a long breath and let it out slowly.

"Eddie looks so much like my husband Aaron that they could have been brothers. Every time I see him, my heart races. I can barely speak. It's like seeing Aaron across the room."

"Your *husband*? I didn't know you were married."

"Not too many people do."

"I can relate to that," Gina said.

"Aaron died two years ago, along with my two-year-old son."

"Oh, my God!" Gina put a hand across her mouth. "I'm so sorry."

"It was horrible. I keep seeing my little boy in Aaron's arms, the two of them igniting, dying in a flash of flames."

"Megan Ann-"

"I was at the movies with a friend. Neither Aaron nor I would allow baby sitters to stay with Timmy. We worried something might happen and we wouldn't be there." Megan Ann looked at Gina. "So ironic."

"Trying to second-guess yourself is way too difficult. It raises so many questions ... questions that most likely can never be answered."

"I would have gladly changed places with either one of them." Tears slid down her cheeks, dripped onto her scrubs. "And the worst of it, no one was ever able explain what happened."

"They don't know what started the fire?"

150

Megan Ann hunched over. "They had theories about the furnace, maybe a gas leak. But no one could say for sure."

Her insides were churning. She dug her nails into her arm until the tracks of old scratches were deep ruts of burgundy.

Gina took her hand. "It must have been terrible."

"Without them, I'd rather be dead."

Gina wrapped an arm around Megan Ann and said, "I'm glad you're not."

They sat in silence for a long moment before Megan Ann spoke: "If the tables were turned, I wouldn't be as nice to you."

"Oh, yes, you would," Gina said.

Maybe it was the kind words. Maybe it was just telling someone about her family and her loss, what she lived with every moment of every waking day. She did begin to feel better. Still, she burst into tears again.

"There's this … this huge hole inside of me and … and nothing ever seems to fill it."

Gina drew a tissue from her pocket, pressed it into Megan Ann's hand.

"It'll get better in time, Megan Ann. You have to stay strong and believe that."

Bette Golden Lamb & J. J. Lamb

₪ CHAPTER 25

Eddie St. George was exhausted. He trudged across the room, walked out of his clothes, left them strewn behind on the floor, and collapsed onto the bed. All he wanted was the oblivion of sleep. Instead, his mind spun in a whirlpool of activity.

Mother's face flashed into his mind, swept along through the years by ancient memories.

No matter how many times Father said that his Mother hated him, that she ran away with another man because she didn't want to take care of him, Eddie secretly thought of her as beautiful and kind. He remembered how she would sing to him even when she was in bed with her bruised, raccoon-like eyes. And she would hold him close despite her body being a mass of purple blotches.

"Mother fell down the steps," Father said each time.

Eddie had tried to hold on to Mother's music, the repertoire of popular songs that she sang to him over and over before she went away. But each passing year slowly deadened those memories. Pop music was no longer a part of his life. And when he danced, he was virtually unaware of the melodies, following only the beat, his involvement only to interest a woman, make her more compliant, easier to take to Father.

A sudden thought of Megan Ann Hendricks displaced the memory of Mother. He knew he shouldn't have agreed to see her even though he was drawn to her. He didn't want to risk being attracted to her, tried to shake off his vision of her.

She was just a tiny redhead. A nurse, like all the rest.

His breath filtered through prickles of needles that stabbed his chest; loud wheezes echoed off the walls of his apartment. He clutched the bed sheets, yanked until the wrinkled cotton was wet from his sweaty palms.

More. More. More!

The memory of Father's voice sliced through his brain like an electric knife.

He jumped out of bed, stepped in front of the mirror that filled the expanse of one whole wall. He watched his muscles pull, squeeze his ribs with every struggling breath until he was close to suffocating, was forced to reach for the inhaler on the dresser. He sucked in four long pulls of the medication, ignoring the directions on the container.

His heart raced, a rush coursed through him, followed by a creeping numbness that tugged at his lips. Soon the wheezing dissipated; he closed his eyes and rode with a momentary medication high.

The phone buzzed, shattering the moment like a popped balloon. He got up, stood in place, shaking as he listened to it ring.

Again, he wondered what would happen if he wouldn't do what Father ordered?

Wouldn't?

Hadn't Father taught him the consequences of not doing what he was told? Wasn't his back, his entire hide, criss-crossed with scars that deformed him with that knowledge?

He'd tried once to escape when he was in junior high, tried to run away. Found a hideaway in an old deserted film studio. Among the mold and dampness and rot, he'd found a traveling trunk, used it to store food and money that he stole from Father a dollar at a time. The day he was going to run away, Father found him. The cruel, harsh words still echoed in his brain: "Did you really think you could escape from me. Did you really think you could get away from your father, you little shit?"

Yes, he remembered everything.

The phone stopped ringing. The silence left the pounding of his heart echoing in his ears.

He paced the room, then frantically began lifting the weights he used to sculpt his body. The movements made him sweat, helped ease the painful memories.

The phone rang again, jarring him back.

He let out a small grunt of defeat, picked up the receiver, and held it far enough away to diminish the voice at the other end.

"Yes, Father. Yes, I understand," Eddie said. "I'm sorry. You need to rest. Remember what the doctor said."

Trickles of perspiration dribbled down the length of his rib cage. Every part of him was soon dripping wet. He watched the sweat splatter onto the bamboo floor.

"Yes. Yes. I will." He ground the heel of his hand into his chest, the tightening was beginning again. He nodded like a ten-year-old.

"Yes, I will," he repeated, his chest heaving in pain. "I promise."

He hung up. He dug into, tore at his scars; his legs collapsed beneath him, allowing his body to crumble to the floor. His breath whistled in short raspy jolts; without warning he vomited on the floor. Only by grasping a fist full of hair and yanking hard was able to stop retching.

He pounded the silent phone. "God damn it … hurry up and die … need to be rid of you. Die, you miserable bastard. Die!"

Bette Golden Lamb & J. J. Lamb

₪ CHAPTER 26

Pepper Yee looked across her desk at Walter Cooke, pointed her pen at him and said, "I need to hear more about Milton Hiller and his connection with Charlie Auston and his funeral home."

"I knew it was a mistake to call you. Must have been out of my mind." Cooke shifted in his chair, his balding head reflecting the overhead light. "I've told you all I know."

"Tell me again," she said.

Cooke raised his eyes to the ceiling, sighed, and said, "Like I told you the other night. I'm leaving Auston's Funeral Home after preparing a few donated cadavers for him." He tapped a long, delicate finger on her desk. "Legitimate, of course."

"Of course."

"I don't appreciate your sarcasm, Detective."

"Whatever. Just get on with it."

"So, I'm on my way to the parking lot and I pass this guy going in the opposite direction. Then I say to myself, 'Hey, I know that guy.' I stop, turn around, and see him going into the alley behind Auston's place. There's a street light and I get a pretty good look at him—Milty Hiller." Cooke shrugs as if to end the tale.

"And?"

"And what?"

"Weren't you just a little bit curious as to what Hiller was doing there?"

"Curious can get you dead, Detective. Milty Hiller is not a nice man." He put a palm to his forehead. "What an idiot! I should never have called you."

"But you did turn around and go look, didn't you, Walter?"

Another glance at the ceiling. "Yeah, yeah. Like I said before, just as I got back to the alley, Milty was going into the funeral home. That's it. End of story."

Yee scribbled a few words into her notebook, leaned back in her chair, and tried to intimidate Cooke with her eyes. He didn't so much as blink.

"And you called me, because?" she finally said.

"Look, Charlie Auston isn't one my favorite people, but I never suspected him of doing business with Milty Hiller. If he is, then that whole thing is screwed for me."

"My sources tell me that the clandestine sale of body parts is a very lucrative business. Is that right?"

"So I hear," Cooke said.

"Maybe … just maybe … it puts a few extra bucks into your pocket now and then, right?"

"No! No way! I don't get involved in that sh—, in that kind of thing, Detective. Never!"

"Good! If you're not into that kind of thing, you should be that much more willing to help me catch Milty Hiller. And maybe some of the people he's been dealing with."

"Detective Yee, I don't think I can do that."

"Yes you can, Walter, because I don't think you want me looking too closely into your supposedly legitimate business, right?"

"Not supposedly, Detective. My business is on the up and up. I've never knowingly crossed the line."

"Okay. Let's leave it at that."

Cooke tried to find help on the ceiling again, then slumped in his chair and looked across at Yee. "Whaddya want, from me, Detective?"

"Do you have an upcoming job at Auston's Funeral Home sometime soon?"

"I never know. He calls me when he's going to need me."

"Good!"

"Why 'good?' Like, you expect me to do what?"

"To tell me the day and time you're scheduled to be there, then give me a call as soon as you leave. We'll take it from there."

"I won't have to stick around?"

"No, Walter, you won't have to stick around. Now get the hell out of here and keep your nose clean. And you better keep your mouth shut."

* * *

Yee sat with her feet defiantly planted on the corner of her desk, glowering again at the morning memo passed down through the chain-of-command that had burned itself in her brain.

NO MORE FEET ON DESKS.
Merry Christmas!

Thanks for the sentiments.

She lost interest, kept her shoes on the desk anyway and drifted off into a daydream, thinking about nothing in particular. Mainly, she was still avoiding the piles of unfinished paperwork sprawled in front of her.

A two-bell buzz. The distraction repeated itself. She moved only her eyes, burned holes through the plastic facing that covered the four extension line indicators on her desk phone.

Transfixed, she tried to wish away the flash-flash on Extension 101.

Then 102 began to buzz-buzz, flash-flash, followed by 103 and 104.

Every goddam line! Why me? Where the hell is everybody?

She shifted her gaze from the phone to the wall clock and its herky-jerky minute hand: 4:50.

Then silence. When she looked back at the phone, all the calls had been answered.

Fucking miracle! Just like that!

Not an hour into her shift and everything was again quiet. Maybe too quiet. It gave her the creeps.

She slid her feet off the desk, sat up straight.

4:51 Click **4:52.**

Not long before Gina Mazzio would be getting off work.

Damn! Why can't I get that Ridgewood nurse off my mind?

She revisited the primary question: Did she believe Mazzio's story about the phone calls?

Yee didn't like ifs and maybes; she liked the safety of absolutes, hard evidence. Mazzio's story didn't fit into that scenario, yet there was no reason to doubt the tale she'd spun.

She thought back to the last time she'd stuck her neck out without hard facts. Her spine tingled with the memory: Verbally assaulted one of the other detectives when his wife confided—at a police barbeque no less—that she was being beaten by the lug. She'd stood up for the woman, who in the end, backed down, refused to testify – claimed Pepper Yee was drunk.

She defiantly clunked her heels back up on the desk one at a time. Yeah, *she* was the one who was hung out to dry, took a licking from her fellow palookas. Her compatriots shunned her like she was an Amish fornicator. Not only that, she'd lost a grade in rank. *That* really fried her.

No fooling around with second-hand evidence after that. She was only going with the sure bet if *she* was the one having to put a reputation on the line.

Yee looked at the clock again.

4:55.

What about the women Mazzio claimed might have been murdered by some maniac who called her on the telephone?

Back to the top of the list of her questions: where the hell were the bodies?

Most of her cases began with a corpse. And that's the way she liked it. Corpses were the real thing, the kind of stuff that made her sit up and take notice. A loose stiff was usually a murdered stiff. One plus one equaled two – a dead body equaled a perp.

She looked at her aching feet, frowned at the scuff-marked shoes and their three-inch heels.

Who the hell can work trying to walk on these stilts?

Well she did—she was too damn short. Usually wore heels around the station so her "buddies" wouldn't ride her for being a peanut. Out in the field, she didn't give a rat's ass; she would slip into sneakers, sometimes even boots to get the job done. Right now she was in her hurtin' heels.

Should have become a nurse, like Mazzio. Nice soft shoes all the time.

Mazzio!

Why does that chick and her weird story keep coming back to bug me? I should be concentrating on Milty Hiller and his ghoulish operation. Like where are all the extra bodies he sells coming from?

True, Shelly Wilton and Arina Diaz were missing. The nurse was right about that. And her boss backed her up.

She searched among the loose papers on her desk and found her notebook, opened it to a fresh page. She picked up a pencil and began to draw boxes—small ones, big ones, square ones, rectangular ones. Mindless doodling always organized her thinking.

After filling an entire page with geometric shapes, stick figures, and abstract flowers, she finally tore out the useless page, tossed it into the wastebasket and started from the beginning again.

1 – Serial killer?
2 – Telephone nut?
3 – Random disappearances?
4 – Coincidences?

Gina Mazzio, RN

A. Advice nurse at Ridgewood General Hospital

B. Co-worker with Shelly Wilton.
C. Knew Arina Diaz.
D. Contact with killer? (Telephone)
E. Stressed personal life.
F. Believable?

Alan Vasquez, Ridgewood Administrator
A. Uncle of Arina Diaz.
B. Acting for the family.
C. Pressing for action.

That filled one page and she was back to the little boxes before writing again.

Telephone Creep
A. Only contact, Gina Mazzio
B. Does he exist?
C. Cuts? Slices?
D. Breather. Wheezes. Deliberate? Physical?
E. What kind of nut is he? Nurses?
F. Female symbols?
G. Where does he stash the stiffs?
H. Where does he stash the stiffs?

Yee was getting a headache.

And still nothing to go on other than the word of one nurse at Ridgewood Hospital.

She shouldn't even be involved in this. Mazzio wanted to talk to Mulzini, only Mulzini was on vacation.

"Damn him and his lousy vacation! Damn him for leaving me here to get stuck with Gina Mazzio and her damn suspicions!"

₪ CHAPTER 27

Gina entered the Labor & Delivery Unit through the waiting room where three men were hanging out, two of them pacing back and forth, bisecting the area as though they were involved in a strange ancient ritual. The third sat casually reading a magazine, or pretending to.

She was a little surprised—most men stayed with their women in the labor rooms, and there was no end to her speculation as to why these three weren't inside.

Whatever.

She pushed through the swinging doors and headed down the hall, looking for Katie Rifka, her first stop to see what she could find out about Arina Diaz, the administrator's missing niece.

An RN in burgundy scrubs raced past her, yelling out IV orders to someone in the meds area. Rifka sat in the nurses' station, typing notes into the computer. She looked up at Gina with tired, red-rimmed eyes.

"Gina Mazzio! Haven't seen you for ages. Not since you left Oncology. Coming to work here, I hope, I hope, I hope?"

"Don't think so, Katie. Just stopped by for a quick chat."

A couple of doctors came down the hall, lost in serious conversation about a crash C-section. One complained how he'd had to start cutting a patient open before the woman was out of it from the anesthesia. Gina didn't hear the rest as they continued on until they exited the unit. Probably taking a dinner break.

"Okay, but make it quick. Don't really have a moment to pee much less chat. This place is a mad house."

"Yeah, I can see you're looking kind of stressed. Maybe I should catch you some other time."

"Honey, there is no better time. I may quit tomorrow, the way things are going." Rifka rubbed at her neck. "What do you need?"

"Actually, I'm a little miffed. Arina Diaz promised to get together with me last week, but I haven't heard from her. Is she out sick or something?"

"Don't even mention that traitor's name. If she's sick, she sure as hell didn't call in." Katie's eyes flashed, her cheeks turned a bright red. "We're all on 12-hour stints because she bugged out on us."

"Not too cool."

"Tell me about it! Staff was already down two bodies before she fell off the face of the earth."

"Is this something she's done before?"

"No, but right now, census is through the ceiling. And she knew that. We're fried!"

Gina sat down next to her. "Not a clue as to what happened?"

"Shit no."

"When did you last see her?"

"I can almost tell you to the minute." Katie signed off her notes. "Last Monday night we got off about five, after two hours of overtime, and we were supposed to ride the bus together. You know, the protection-in-numbers kind of thing. All kinds of creeps ride that damn bus."

"And?"

Rifka's face softened for the first time since Arina's name was mentioned. "The poor kid was beat. This is a rough gig for anyone, and she's about as green as they come. But she's been on it, holding her own. Fitting in, you know? Doing a damn good job."

"So?"

"I got on the bus, she didn't. Sat her butt down on the bus stop bench. Said she was going to go shopping, or something."

"And that was the last time you saw or spoke to her?"

Sin & Bone

"Yep! Our manager's called her apartment, her boyfriend's been around looking for her, and now you, for God knows what reason. What gives?"

Before Gina could think up a plausible explanation, Rifka was called away from the station. Relieved she didn't have to make up a story on the spot as to why she was looking for Arina, Gina sat on the tall stool and watched the swirl of activity in the L&D unit. Within a few minutes, Rifka was back.

"You gonna get off any time soon?" Gina asked.

Rifka gave her a cross-eyed look and stuck her tongue out the corner of her mouth, the accepted, if insensitive, "Q" sign for an expired patient. "Seven at the earliest, hon. Why?"

"Had a couple of more questions I wanted to ask you about Arina."

"Look, if you guys are thinking of recruiting her for Advice, forget it! We need her here. Besides, I don't think she's got enough experience to go on the phones."

Gina raised both hands and leaned back. Now she was stuck; she didn't want to cause any kind of problem if she could help it. "No, this isn't a staff raid. It's just that a, well, a friend of Harry's saw her and would like to meet her."

"Harry? Speaking of which, I heard you two were on the outs."

"Yeah, well, when did you start believing everything you hear?"

Rifka looked up and down the hallway. "Look, I was about to take a break … whether they want me to or not. If you want to go down to the cafeteria, we can talk there. I'll tell you what I can about Arina, you can tell me about this on-again, off-again thing with Harry." She grinned. "If he's available, I might be interested."

* * *

Gina swirled a tea bag around in a tall paper cup while Rifka sipped on a Coke and nibbled at a bagel, all the time repeatedly checking her watch.

165

"Is Arina close with any of the other nurses?" Gina asked.

"Not particularly. We usually ride the bus together because we live in the same   neighborhood. Other than that ..." Rifka broke off a piece of bagel, smeared it with cream cheese, and was about to stuff it in her mouth, then held the morsel in suspension, a couple of inches from her mouth. "Wait! I do think she's gone to the movies a couple of times with Shawna ... Shawna Jordan."

"Is Shawna on duty today?"

"Along with every other warm body we got."

"Point her out to me when we go back."

"Why all the questions, Gina? I thought you were trying to hook her up with a date, or something like that. But the Gina Mazzio I know doesn't get involved in the matchmaking thing. Besides, Arina already has a boy friend. In fact, he was here today looking for her."

"Jorge, right?"

Rifka's eyes drifted to the ceiling. "Now *there's* a piece of work."

"A character?"

"A male chauvinist pig! I know it embarrasses her, but she sort of shrugs and gets on with her work. The rest of us have tried stonewalling him, but he just keeps calling back until he gets her on the phone. Yuk!"

"You say he came by here today trying to find for her?"

"Around noon. Was real nasty about it, like we were hiding her or something. Tried to go looking into patient rooms. Had to call Security to get him out of here."

"Maybe she does need to go out with someone else," Gina said.

"I couldn't care less about her personal gig," Rifka said. "If she wants to be involved with that *shmuck,* much less live with him, that's her thing. I just want her ass back here on the floor." She looked at the wall clock. "I better get going before they send a posse out for me."

They collected and disposed of their trash before going out to the elevator.

"I'll point out Shawna," Rifka said. "But I'm not fooled, Mazzio. I *know* you're not giving me the real lowdown on why you're so interested in little Ms. Diaz."

* * *

Gina was able to grab Shawna on the run back in L&D. She practically chased after her down the unit's hallway.

"A couple of movies on Friday nights after work," Shawna told her. "No double dates or anything like that. Jorge takes up most of her time and he doesn't like doubles."

"She never complains about him, or anything like that?"

"Arina? I've never heard her bad-mouth anyone. Besides, I think their families are real tight, even though Arina did say her folks don't really like him."

When Gina finally got out to her car, she felt like she hadn't really achieved anything. Arina was a nice kid, good at her job, everyone liked her … and she was missing.

Gina wasn't looking forward to calling Vasquez in the morning.

She hoped that perhaps Yee might come up with something positive by then.

Yeah, sure!

Bette Golden Lamb & J. J. Lamb

₪ CHAPTER 28

Megan Ann stepped out of the hot shower stall into the steamy dressing area and dried herself with a large, fluffy bath sheet.

When she yanked off the plastic cap that protected her hair, billows of moisture turned her mass of red hair into a pile of Orphan Annie ringlets. She raked her fingers through it, trying to straighten out the tight curls, but they immediately sprang back into place, as she knew they would.

Tucking her towel around her, she walked barefoot back to her locker and stared inside at the contents. Her mind drifted into an airy nothingness.

"You're going to catch your death of cold standing around like that, Megan Ann. Get some clothes on!"

The sarcastic voice of the nurse wasn't lost on her. It was one of the same RNs who had witnessed her sharp exchange with Gina outside the cafeteria.

"Thanks for giving a damn," Megan Ann called out to the departing back.

She re-tightened the towel around her and reached out to caress the moss green woolen dress she planned to wear on her date with Eddie St. George. She had plenty of time to get ready to meet him at The Hideaway around 5:00. Her shift had ended at 3:30 and she was using every minute to ready herself. There was no way she would go out with that man in grubby, day-old scrubs. The shower had refreshed her, but instead of getting dressed immediately, she stared again inside her locker, specifically at a blue nylon bag. Her stash.

No! Not now.

She hurried to get into her underwear, pulled the dress out, and worked her way into it. The soft material fell around her, but her mind remained on the vodka minis and Valium tabs inside the blue bag.

Three doctors had contributed to the large Valium vial, now crammed with two hundred pills – a safety net and her perfect solution for when she absolutely couldn't stand her miserable life anymore.

When that time came, she planned to wash them down with alcohol. Every last one of them.

And there would be no heroics; she'd be well beyond any rescue effort that might keep her in the never-never land of a vegetative state.

But today she wasn't miserable, far from it. She was floating around somewhere up near the ceiling, looking down on herself. And what did she see? She saw a happy, expectant Megan Ann.

When her makeup was finished and she was ready to leave, she started to close the locker door, but at the last minute grabbed for the nylon bag. She yanked out one of the miniatures and downed the vodka without a second thought. When the liquor crashed into her empty stomach, a welcomed heat blossomed through her body. She closed the locker door and hurried from the dressing room.

* * *

Megan Ann hoisted one hip onto a bar stool, then the other. It annoyed her that most bar seats were about an inch or so higher than she could slip onto comfortably. The Hideaway stools were no exception.

She studied the lineup of liquor bottles on the back bar. So neat, so orderly.

Wasn't that the way life was supposed to be?

The liquors' many shades of color fascinated her, seemed to call to her; the small buzz from the miniature she'd swallowed earlier was long gone. Her mouth filled with a pool of saliva as she studied the offerings on the back bar.

She pushed up her sleeve and glanced at her watch. Eddie should have been here by now. He was more than a minute late.

Maybe he won't come.

Her attention shot back to liquor bottles. She wanted, no, she needed a drink. Now!

But she didn't dare. Not if she wanted to stay sober, to be with Eddie.

She looked around at the crowd. Bars had never been her thing; they were for people who wanted to hook up with someone, or to socialize their habit. When *she* drank, she wanted no interruptions from people who really didn't give a damn about her. Alcohol was about peace, oblivion; a night of not having to think about Aaron and her baby boy.

The Hideaway was rapidly filling and several men were trying to hit on her, vying for the seat she was saving for Eddie.

Two bartenders worked the crowd; the younger one gave her a big smile.

"What'llitbe, beautiful?" He waited patiently even though everyone around her was trying to capture his attention.

Before she could think about it, the order flew from her mouth: "Vodka gimlet, please."

"Coming right up!"

As he walked away and began putting her drink together, she studied his trim body, his taut buns. A flash of yearning rolled into an ache that started at the base of her spine and curled around into her groin.

"Is this seat taken?" asked a guy, about fifty. He slid onto the stool without waiting for a reply. "You don't mind if I sit next to you, do you?"

"No. Yes! That seat *is* taken."

The stranger ignored Megan Ann and held out a twenty-dollar bill for the bartender as the vodka gimlet was placed in front of her. Megan Ann immediately gulped down half the drink, ignoring the transaction.

The bartender reached for the twenty, but before he could snatch it up, the payer's hand was roughly pinned to the bar. The man grimaced in pain.

"What part of 'no' is it you don't understand?" Eddie St. George said.

Megan Ann watched, but her mind was on the drink in her hand.

The stranger pulled away and vacated the stool. "For chrissakes," he snapped, "you don't have to get violent over it."

Megan Ann stared into Eddie's eyes. They had turned a stony green, his handsome face a tight mask of fury.

The stool-stealer lingered behind them, slowly folded the twenty and intertwined it through his fingers, while continuing to stare at Megan Ann.

"Get your ass out of here," Eddie ordered.

The man finally moved, merged back into the after-work crowd without another word.

Eddie turned his attention to Megan Ann. "Way too beautiful. Can't leave you alone or you get into trouble." He was all smiles now, not a sign of anger lingered on his face.

She downed the rest of the gimlet; radiating self-assurance swam through her body, making her tingly and warm.

* * *

Pietro's, where Eddie had driven them for dinner, had an understated atmosphere of elegance. Megan Ann was aware of the upscale restaurant, but had never dined there. Eating out, like bar hopping, was not something she indulged in very often. When she left work she always went directly to the grocery, then to her apartment, ate dinner, and spent the rest of the evening trying to stay away from booze. And men.

It was a simple life, but the only way she could stay relatively clean and sober. Sometimes one of the AA people she'd met would drag her out to a meeting, but she avoided friendships because she knew that sooner or later she would disappoint anyone who cared about her.

She watched Eddie smile at the passing meal servers as though he knew them. Their table was near a bubbling fountain, where full-blossomed white, yellow, and pink orchids were tucked in stony niches; the air was sweet and fresh.

He selected a light appetizer of eggplant, tomatoes, and olive oil, then suggested for her a main course of salmon with crusted pistachios in white wine. His entrée choice was an order of breaded sardines, with sun-dried tomatoes, over a bed of arugula.

They started on the second bottle of Dry Creek fume blanc with dessert: a *torte di cioccolata* for her, but nothing for him.

"I haven't been this happy since my husband died."

"You were married?"

She took a long sip of wine. A moment of sadness filled her, but she looked into Eddie's eyes and felt a sudden peacefulness. It had been so long since she'd enjoyed that kind of moment.

"Yes. And I was so in love with Aaron." She reached for his hand. "You look so much like him. I can't begin to express how happy I am right now."

She was finally in that special zone where life and the surrender to mindlessness were woven into one blissful union.

Eddie had eaten less than half of his entrée, so she assumed he would probably share the dessert. But he kept his hands folded at the edge of the table while she ate every bite of the flaky pastry and its rich filling.

He watched her eat; she enjoyed the attention, feeling not a bit self-conscious. When he smiled, she looked at his lips and wanted to kiss them, kiss his green Aaron-like eyes that made her body throb with anticipation.

* * *

Eddie was fascinated by the twin rings of perspiration under Megan Ann's arms. The more wine she consumed, the larger the stains spread. He had to force his eyes away from the damp spots, just as he had to will himself to not look directly into her eyes. Her happiness made him feel unexpectedly strange.

He'd limited himself to only two half-glasses of the Russian River Valley white, while she'd consumed the rest. Part of him didn't want her to get tipsy, or drunk; he wanted to pretend this was just a date. A date with a beautiful woman he found extremely attractive. But he couldn't forget why he was here, couldn't forget Father.

The waiter brought the check and Eddie paid in cash. As they wended their way between the tables toward the front door, he held her elbow lightly, ready to grab her if she faltered. He was amazed that after all that wine she could even stand, much less walk with a steady, even gait.

When they were settled in the Jaguar, he worried that the motion of driving might make her car sick, causing her to lose not only her dinner but the roofie he'd dropped into her last glass of wine. But all she did was hum along to the latest Clifford Alden jazz CD playing on the cars audio system.

By the time he'd driven into the parking lot at the rear of St. George Fine Meats, she was asleep, snoring softly. Swallowed up in the peaceful silence, he wanted desperately to turn around and drive her home.

Why did she have to make herself so available? All he knew about this redheaded nurse was that she worked at Ridgewood, and unexplainably, he was very much attracted to her, to her beauty, to her tenderness.

His head hurt with all the things he didn't know or understand.

One thing was certain, one thing that couldn't be changed: there was no going back. What was done was done.

Sliding out of the car, he opened the passenger door and reached in to haul Megan Ann up and onto his shoulder. As her dead weight settled in place, she let out an animal grunt.

He could barely breathe as he moved with heavy steps through the shop and finally into the big cold room. When he placed her on the cutting table, her arms and legs splayed out in every direction; a glob of drool ran down her chin.

Back and forth, back and forth, he paced around the table. He had to get out of here. Had to leave right now. Her red hair was so soft, her skin like fine porcelain—clean and white.

"About time," Father shouted as he came into the room. "Put your ass on that stool, you miserable piece of shit."

Eddie's legs turned to water; he meekly sat on the stainless steel stool.

"You always think you'll walk out of here before it happens, don't you?" Father said. "Are you going to be that stupid forever? When's it going to sink into that infantile brain that whether you're here or not, you're just as guilty?"

Eddie was silent, a numbness creeping across his head like the delicate legs of a spider closing in on its prey.

"You always were a pussy, a scaredy-cat kid. Afraid of your own shadow."

Eddie wanted to hide, but there was no place to go. The usual inventory of hanging beef carcasses were gone, processed, and out of sight. Even the pitted plank floor, usually covered with a layer of blood-soaked sawdust, was swept clean.

He turned to Megan Ann—her face was expressionless; she was as limp as Raggedy Ann.

He didn't want to do this. He hadn't ever wanted to do any of it. Father made him bring them. Made him a murderer. Made him a monster.

"I'm sorry, Megan Ann," Eddie whispered in her ear.

"Stop blathering over her. Everyone dies. Everyone! Think about it, you idiot! No, don't turn your head away or try to wrack that pea brain of yours until it comes up with something pleasant to hide the truth.

"THINK!" Jacob yelled.

"From the tiniest mite, whom you don't give a rat's ass about, to the farthest star, which doesn't even exist for you except in books, everything dies. It's the moments before that should concern you, you miserable slug."

He leveled a large, bony finger at Eddie. "You! You, too, will die!"

Eddie tried to think, needed to act. But all he saw was Father—a black cloud of ugly reality circling the table.

"Get her clothes off!"

Eddie's fingers refused to move. Father grabbed the cutting shears and snipped away Megan Ann's clothes with one continuous movement. Goose bumps grew on her, an insult to the perfection of her pale, silky skin.

Father stared long and hard at her body. His hand shook as he traced a finger up her thigh and suddenly jabbed it between her legs. Megan Ann undulated to the in-out motion of his hand, began to moan.

"Aaron! I've missed you so much."

Eddie stared at her, his stomach cramped. Tears gushed down his cheeks.

"You chicken-shit cry baby. Cut the waterworks. Hiller will pay a bundle for a beauty like this when she's all cut up and packaged for those insatiable research labs he deals with."

Father used his tongue to lap at Megan Ann's skin, from thigh to breast. He bit down hard on a nipple but instead of crying out, Megan Ann sucked in her lower lip and smiled.

"Do it to me, baby. Do it to me."

Eddie stared at her in horror.

"You see, little Eddie? The tramp likes it. Wants it."

Father climbed onto Meagan Ann, pulled his pant zipper down, and plunged himself into her. She panted and thrust against him.

"Aaron! Aaron!" she cried out as she rotated her hips.

"Little Eddie finally gets it right." Father laughed, then let loose an animal roar as he climaxed.

* * *

Megan Ann was floating in a purple haze of happiness. Aaron had finally come back to her.

The room was a blur, the moment expanding. Soon she would explode. She moved faster, faster, tried to cry out but her voice was gone. She opened her eyes, saw only a blur of light that faded in and out.

She was undulating, rolling in waves of joy. Then she saw the shadowy figure over her. Aaron was there, where he was supposed to be. She radiated with happiness as she began to float.

"Aaron!"

Everything became a dazzling glitter. She reached out to take his hand.

Bette Golden Lamb & J. J. Lamb

₪ CHAPTER 29

"No!" Eddie screamed. He grabbed up a wooden meat tenderizer, swung it at Father's drooping head, hit a shoulder instead; the arm of the shirt blossomed with blood.

"Fu-u-uck!" Jacob roared. He pushed himself up with one arm and slapped his free hand against his shoulder. "I'll kill you."

Eddie swung the mallet again. Father countered the blow by grabbing Eddie's wrist, but the effort through him off balance; he rolled backward off Megan Ann and fell heavily to the floor.

Eddie dashed around the table, kicked Father hard in the gut, snatched Megan Ann up in his arms, and ran from the butcher shop.

Sweat drenched his shirt, circled down his legs until his feet were like fleshless stubs sliding in his shoes and socks.

Megan Ann was rolling out of his arms; the exertion of holding onto her nude body was tearing his arm muscles, tearing at his insides.

Stop! Have to stop.

He almost fell as he hoisted her dead weight over his shoulder. She was small, but her body seemed boneless; she shifted back and forth like a half empty sack of grain.

He stretched his neck, eyes strained as he listened for the expected rush of footsteps. But there was nothing. All he saw was the creepy corridor behind him; the same winding blackness he saw in all his nightmares.

Then he was running again, out the door.

His shoes pounded on the concrete, his breathing hard and painful as he gasped at air that wouldn't fill his lungs. His wheezing grew louder, the ragged sounds filling the space around him.

Black dots swam through his vision. He teetered on the edge of nothingness.

Move faster!

He struggled to stay upright as his legs grew weaker and weaker. At the Jaguar, he flung open the passenger door and dropped Megan Ann inside. She moved limply into the seat, her bare body slapping against the soft leather. He spread his palms across the top of the car to keep from passing out. Between gasps for air, he listened: Still nothing.

Nothing!

Everything was silent except for Megan Ann's soft moaning, in syncopation to the noises in his chest, his booming heart, and the eerie whistling wind that crashed into the overhead sign: *St. George Fine Meats.*

When his head stopped spinning, he hand-walked his way along the side of the car until he reached the trunk; he opened it, pulled out a blanket, and tossed it over the naked nurse. When he was safely seated behind the wheel, he fired up the engine and with a sharp screech of tires, left the parking lot. Stuffing his mouth with his inhaler, he took four rapid puffs.

He had escaped Father! He pounded the steering wheel with excitement.

Then it hit him: where would he hide this woman?

Megan Ann was now coming around, talking to herself in a singsong murmur.

Think! Have to think.

He slowed, pulled up against the curb. He felt the neighborhood's watchful eyes. Eyes that studied, looked to steal, hurt, cannibalize his car. He kept the engine running, locked the doors.

Dump her. Dump her here. Take off. She'll never remember what happened.

He pounded the wheel in frustration. No. She'd remember him, remember their date.

Can I forget?

180

"It's all your fault, Father," he yelled. "If it wasn't for you, I'd never be in this terrible mess. Why couldn't you leave me alone?"

As he drove away from the curb and back out onto the street, his thoughts took him back to the beginning of the horror. The quagmire started pulling him in the day he told Father about the scholarship his high school counselor had helped arrange so he could attend San Francisco State University.

* * *

"What's this crap? University? I don't have time to read some fancy shit from those dummies at your school."

"It's an invitation, Father."

"Invitation to what?"

"To the Honors Assembly."

"What fucking honors?"

"For outstanding students, Father."

"Outstanding? Hah! They should see you around here. Useless."

"Will you come to the assembly, Father?"

"Tell me, Eddie, what is it you're so goddam outstanding at?"

"I told you about being on the Dean's list all four years. The school sent you a letter about my four-point-zero grade average."

"Didn't put a nickel in *my* pocket."

"I applied to the College of Business at San Francisco State."

"What could *you* possibly know about business? This place would go belly up if I had to rely on you. "

"My counselor helped me get a scholarship."

"Scholarship, huh? Shit! Like I've always said: the more schooling, the dumber the man."

"I want to go to the college, Father. I really do."

"What school again?"

"San Francisco State, Father"

"Here in the city?"

"Yes, sir."

181

"What about work in the shop?"

"I ... I don't understand?"

"No free ride around here, damn it! Can you afford to hire someone to take your place, do your work?"

"No, Father."

"Will your stupid scholarship pay for your transportation, pay for your meals?"

"No, Father."

"No, father. No, father. Fucking A. You can't handle any of that. Where the hell would little Eddie get money if he didn't work for me, right?"

"Yes, Father."

"Oh, wait a minute! You could steal it, like that pissy-ass time when you thought you were going to run away, right?"

"Yes, Father ... I mean, no, Father."

"You don't know what you mean, do you, Eddie?"

"No."

"Where are the girls in your life, Eddie?"

"What?"

"Pussy, damn it! You date girls, don't you, Eddie? I mean, that's what you've been telling me these past couple of years. Maybe you're a flaming faggot?"

"I date girls, Father."

"San Francisco State's co-ed, right?"

"Yes. Why?"

"Why? I'll tell you why. We both can get what we want."

"I don't—"

"I'll explain it in terms even a genius like you can understand: you can go to school, but only if you work here the rest of the time. Got that part?"

"Yes, sir. Thank you."

"Suppose a lot of those giggling high school girlies have an eye for you, huh?"

"Maybe some of them."

"College girlies are so much better, so much riper. More available."

"I don't understand."

"You have a pretty dull brain for a wise-ass scholarship student. Well, let's smarten you up right here and now. You'll bring one of those college girls home now and then, for me, like a nice, dutiful son, right?"

"Bring one home?"

"Think I don't know about all those times you hid in the shop and watched me with those sluts. Sluts like your mother? You know what I want."

"No! I … I couldn't do that, Father."

"No? No? What makes you think you can say no to me? You do as I say, or you won't go to that stupid college."

"But—"

"You heard me. College for you, beautiful redheads for me."

"I can't do that, Father. I can't."

"You'll damn well do it, Eddie."

"No."

"Do it or I'll never tell you where you can find that whoring mother of yours."

* * *

Eddie pulled over to the curb again, this time a block short of the garage entrance to his apartment building. He tapped out a roofie from a plastic vial, then pulled a bottle of water from the cup holder in the armrest.

Megan Ann stared at him, but her eyes remained empty.

He tried to stay calm as he slid an arm around her waist.

"Hey, little girl," he whispered in her ear, "time to take your medicine."

"Anything you say, baby," she mumbled.

Megan Ann's eye lids fluttered; she reached over to Eddie and ran her fingers through his hair, pulled him to her and kissed him on the mouth.

183

Eddie was caught off guard as her tongue slid over his lips and her hand searched between his legs. He pulled away and gently squeezed her cheeks together until she opened her mouth. He carefully placed the pill on her tongue. She took a long drink of water before settling back in her seat.

He barely nudged the accelerator as he passed the front of his apartment building, stared through the glass façade of the complex, and took in the lobby with its shiny black marble floor and stark contemporary furniture.

The doorman usually parked Eddie's car for him in the building's underground garage.

Not tonight.

Eddie had to get Megan Ann into his apartment without anyone seeing her. Especially the doorman, a nosy, non-stop gossip. Because of him, Eddie knew all the dirt about the other occupants in the building. More than he ever wanted to know about anyone.

Where is he, where's the doorman?

Then he saw him, slumped in a leather desk chair behind a glass table, in napping mode: Head dipped, chin resting on his green uniform jacket.

The underground parking was only around the corner, on the side street. Eddie drove slowly, made the turn, and triggered the electronic button in the edge of the rearview mirror for the garage door. When the entrance yawned open, he eased the car down the ramp into the deserted, dimly lit area, pulled into his assigned slot, and doused the Jaguar's headlights.

Megan Ann moaned softly, clutched the blanket tightly around her, and snuggled deeper into the plush seat.

The engine shut down with a twist of the key and Eddie allowed himself the momentary luxury of silence. He eyed the perimeter of the area with its circle of evenly spaced lights. There weren't really any shadowed places, only deeper shades of gray around each parked vehicle. Most of the occupants of the apartment complex were tucked in for the night. He counted only two vacant spaces.

Before opening the door to get out, he switched off the interior lights. He edged around the car, opened the passenger door, but was startled by a pair of incoming headlights. He crouched low until he was half sitting on the door sill next to the nurse. He hoped the driver of the approaching car wouldn't be able to see him.

As his shoulder touched Megan Ann, she suddenly threw her arms around him, tilted her chin, and drew his mouth onto hers. She moaned and tore the blanket away, shoved his hand between her legs.

Warm. So warm and moist.

Eddie's groin ached with a flash of heat as her fleshy mouth surrounded his tongue. She yanked at his zipper. Her hot hand grabbed him.

"Do it to me … please do it," she whispered, her hips grinding.

The clunk of the closing elevator door jarred him. The arriving tenant was gone from the garage. They were alone again.

"We have to go," he said.

Eddie pulled up his zipper, scooped her into his arms, and arranged the blanket to cover her nakedness. In the elevator, he used his key to activate the penthouse button, then held his breath and worried that someone would be in the lobby waiting for the elevator as it came up from the garage.

Megan Ann laid her head on his shoulder, mumbled something he couldn't understand. The elevator moved smoothly past the lobby level.

He watched, almost frozen by fear when they passed each floor as they climbed their way up to the penthouse; he trembled each time the overhead panel signaled the next floor.

When the door finally slid open, he could see his answering machine blinking a furious red inside the penthouse. He carried

Megan Ann across the foyer, into the living room, and lowered her onto the sofa.

Still breathing hard and soaked with sweat from both exertion and tension, he listened to the message:

"Eddie!"

Father!

He stared at the answering machine, felt himself cower at the illusion *he* was right there in the room screaming at him.

Father's angry. No! This is worse. He's mad. Crazy mad.

Eddie tried to ignore the malicious sound of the voice that kept repeating: "Eddie! Eddie!" But he knew what always happened when he didn't listen to Father.

The voice tore at him, twisted inside, like someone had forced a fist down his throat and was blocking every pathway he needed in order to breathe. He sucked in a breath and a loud wheeze escaped from his lips and resounded across the room. Eddie yanked out his inhaler. Puffed hard at the plastic.

He stood in the living room, his legs shaking. He watched Megan Ann, who was splayed on the sofa, twisting first one way, then another. Her eyes flickered open, then closed. Opened, closed.

"What am I going to do with you?" he mumbled. "Tie you up? Stuff you in a closet? Chain you to the bed?"

He raced through the rooms, into the kitchen, frantically searching for something, anything that could be turned into a plan.

What am I going to do with her?

Then he saw the large laminated block of wood filled with an assortment of expensive knives, a rare gift from Father. As he walked to the counter, his eyes were on the glint of one particular stainless steel handle.

"BRING HER BACK, EDDIE!

"ED-D-DIE-E."

That voice, Father's unyielding voice, echoed throughout the apartment, making the hair on his neck stand, giving him the chills. He gagged as he grabbed for a 10-inch chef's knife, the longest and widest of the set. He raised an arm and chopped as hard as he could into a cutting board.

Not a butcher's boning knife. A killing knife that could rip her heart out.

* * *

Megan Ann's mind floated between the airiness of dreams and the hammer of reality. It was her special place, hidden among the soft shadows of a colorless fog-filled world of nothingness.

Here, there were no decisions to be made.

Here, she could be a numb, mindless creature. A jellied amoeba reaching out to everything and nothing.

Here was Neverland, where no one cared or pointed a finger at her for drinking, drugging, and screwing her way through whatever life tossed at her.

But she was cold. Very cold. And her head hurt. She tried to open her eyes, to remember where she'd been, but couldn't do it. Her lids were too gritty, too heavy.

* * *

The blanket had fallen off Megan Ann. She lay shivering on the sofa. Eddie tiptoed closer. Goose bumps had erupted, spread across her skin.

He stepped in closer and covered her with the blanket, then ran his fingers through her hair. She looked like a beautiful child.

But you aren't a child, are you?

He bent over, slipped his arms under her, and carried her toward the guest bedroom.

"Eddie, is that you?"

He remained silent.

"What happened?" Her face flushed a bright red. "Did I drink too much? Pass out?"

He continued on, ignoring her questions, and laid her down on the bed. The knife slipped from his hand, bounced off the mattress onto the floor with a dull thud.

He carefully raised her head and placed a pillow beneath it.

The telephone rang again. He tried to ignore it. The message machine picked up: BRING HER BACK RIGHT NOW, EDDIE, IF YOU KNOW WHAT'S GOOD FOR YOU. BRING HER BACK.

He ran into the living room, grabbed the answering machine, and threw it against the wall. The plastic shattered, flew in all directions.

Eddie returned to the bedroom, exhausted. He was so tired he barely had the energy to toss off his clothes and lay down next to Megan Ann. Her pale skin was mottled and her eyes dreamy as her fingers dug into the surrounding thick comforter, clutching, releasing, clutching, releasing.

"Aaron?"

She turned to look at him. "Stay with me, Aaron. Stay with me, baby."

Her hands were light like fluttering feathers moving across his face, traveling the length of him. Her body rolled, rubbed against him. She straddled his hips, her breasts slid up and down, undulating against the hairs on his chest. He moved inside her and was surrounded by a soft cloud of pleasure. He pumped harder, harder. But blackness was growing inside of him, turning his bowels to hot coals. It was roiling, building, exploding.

Even though it was smashed, he could still hear the message machine spewing out Father's summons:

"EDDIE! EDDIE! EDDIE!"

The evil voice reverberated in his head, bringing a tearing pain to his heart. He reached across the bed. Reached, reached down until his fingers curled around the long knife.

₪ CHAPTER 30

"I hope you have something positive to tell me, Ms. Mazzio," Alan Vasquez said even before the two of them could sit down. "The police sure haven't been of much help."

Gina had been waiting outside his office when he arrived at 8:00 a.m. She'd thought it was better to see him in person—you never knew who might be listening in on a telephone conversation. There were already way too many rumors floating around the hospital, some of which were probably her fault.

"Unfortunately, I haven't found out much of anything." Gina said. "The last person to see Arina was Katie Rifka. That was Friday after work, a little after 7:00 p.m. They were supposed to ride the bus home together, but Arina told Katie she'd changed her mind and was going to go shopping."

A look of keen disappointment spread across the administrator's face. "What about other nurses in the unit?"

"There aren't many others. Every department seems to be short-handed."

"As I know all too well," he said.

"Apparently Arina didn't hang out with the other nurses after work. A movie now and then, but that's all. The word is that she spent most of her time with her boyfriend."

"Yes, Jorge." He looked at her a moment before continuing. "And what do they say about, Jorge?"

"From all indications, he's as worried about her as you are. He's been calling, coming around the unit."

"I see," he said in a manner that made Gina think Jorge wasn't on Vasquez's list of favorite people.

"I wish I had something better to tell you."

189

"Yes, well, it's not your fault. It's just that my sister is beside herself with grief. And I've gotten no satisfaction talking to the police, although they now concede she's a missing person … for whatever good that does."

"Have you talked to Detective Yee?"

"Once. Now they only take messages. I've heard nothing back from anyone."

"I don't know what else I can do," Gina said.

"I only asked on the off chance you might have … found out something." He swiveled his chair around to look out the large picture window behind his desk, something he seemed to do under stress. After a couple of moments, he raised one hand, the index finger pointing upward. "I'd appreciate it if you'd let me know immediately if you hear anything else. Anything!"

She was certain she'd heard a tremor in his voice. She wanted to tell him how difficult it was to take care of her work obligations and still get around to talk to people in other departments; wanted to tell him how impossible it was to catch people after work hours, especially since her hours were different than those of the hospital nurses; wanted to tell him how difficult it was to ask about Arina without revealing why she was asking.

Instead, she said quietly, "Yes, I'll do that."

* * *

"And just where do you think you're going, madam?" Tina snipped as Gina clocked in and started for the door.

"Not that I have to explain anything to you, but I'll be back in a few minutes … after I talk to Lexie."

"You're taking time out for a chat while these phones are blinking and winking nonstop?"

"You know, Tina, you keep rattling my chain and you're going to regret it. Trust me."

"OOOOOH! I'm shaking in my boots." She turned to Chelsea: "The Bronx bombshell is going to get me."

Chelsea ignored both of them.

Sin & Bone

Gina gave Tina the finger and walked out. She'd made up her mind on the way into work that she needed some time off. The disconnect with Harry, the uncomfortable situation in the Advice Center, and, most of all, the fear that the mysterious caller might be abducting and killing Ridgewood nurses were all getting to be too much for her.

It was time to ask her manager for some personal time off.

* * *

Lexie Alexandros motioned Gina into her office, nodded toward a chair, and continued talking on the telephone without interrupting her conversation.

Gina forced herself to sit quietly, eavesdropping on a boring business call. But she was so antsy and sleep deprived, her eyes felt like two fried eggs ready to pop.

The image almost made her laugh out loud: yellow goo all over everything, maybe splattered across her manager's mauve silk blouse.

As she sat and waited she read the custom plaque placed prominently on the desk:

Lexie Alexandros, Manager OB/GYN

She again wondered why on earth a grown, professional woman chose to be called by a little-girl diminutive of Alexandra.

Okay, Alexandra Alexandros would sound pretty ridiculous.

Before she could ponder it further, Lexie concluded her conversation, looked pointedly at her watch, and said, "What can I do for you?"

Gina ignored the implied censure that she wasn't back in her cubbyhole, on the phones. She'd already decided there was no way to soft soap this.

"I need some time off."

The manager's chin tipped up, her eyes narrowed.

"When?"

"Now."

"You've got to be kidding." Daggers flew from her eyes. "Are we talking *immediately*?"

"I'm afraid so."

In some perverse way Gina was enjoying her manager's anger. Lexie was the kind of person who always had an answer for everything. Right or wrong. This time, she seemed almost speechless. She abruptly stood and walked to the office window, turning her back to Gina. The air was rife with her smoldering silence.

"Lexie—"

"You know, I don't think even you really understand how difficult it's become to deal with the nursing shortage. The new RN contract gave us some relief, but we're still stuck with minimum staffing to make everything function. And now, administration is talking about a six-month freeze on hiring."

Alexandros spun around to face Gina. "It's tough and it's getting tougher. All the hospital managers have been holding their breaths, sucking in their guts while they watch the toll it's taking, not only on patient care, but on staff morale. Bottom line, I'm at a loss as to how we're going to make everything function."

"Hey, maybe things aren't ideal, but I can tell you from my perspective that moral around here is better than it's ever been. I can also tell you that I don't need a lecture about the nursing situation. You don't get to dump that on my shoulders just because I need some time off."

"Oh, yes, I do!"

"I don't see it that way. I need to straighten out some personal things. I need the time."

"Well, I'll give you that. At least you asked first."

"What does that mean?"

Gina *was* feeling guilty. She knew what a hassle this was going to be for the department. Shelly was gone but that didn't stop the calls from coming in, and the advice center had been understaffed even before that.

"For example," Alexandros said, "several departments have nurses who aren't showing as scheduled. No call-in. No nothing. What kind of professionalism is that?"

Gina said nothing. She had no intention of sharing her thoughts about missing nurses with the manager again. Last time Lexie had made her feel like a nut case with half a brain. And she still didn't believe Gina about the caller.

"You know the Oncology manager, Leona?" Alexandros said, slipping back into her chair.

"Of course," Gina said. It was her old department and she kept close track on what happened there, who came and went.

"Today, she's down three people. You tell me how we're supposed to run a unit that way?"

"Why do you think there are so many nurses out?"

Lexie stared at Gina. "Don't tell me you still think someone is 'stealing' our nurses."

"I only ask the question."

"At the moment, I don't have an answer, but I'm looking into it." She paused, took a deep breath. "Anyway, let's get back to your time-off request."

"Good idea," Gina said.

Alexandros started twirling that stray lock of hair she always messed with. Gina couldn't help wondering why that particular strand of hair didn't just give up and fall out, considering all the abuse it took.

"Why do you need the time off?"

"I told you, it's personal."

"No family emergency, no illness. Just personal."

"That's right," Gina said.

Alexandros stood, making it plain their time together was over.

Gina also stood.

"I can't give you personal leave at this time. Not without more of a compelling reason than you given me thus far." She gave a hint of a humorless laugh. "Or rather, the reasons you haven't given me."

When Gina left, the door was slammed shut behind her.

She spent the rest of the morning paying minimum attention to the calls that came in, one after another like a fusillade of bullets. Mostly she was on autopilot; answering questions she'd fielded a million times. But when she broke for lunch, she regretted not being more diligent, and hoped she hadn't caused any complications for the patient callers.

* * *

Gina spotted Helen from Oncology as she moved through the cafeteria line. She'd half-filled her tray before realizing she wasn't hungry. She'd put most of the food back before sliding into an empty seat next to the Oncology nurse.

"Hey, buddy," Helen said. "If I didn't love you, I could have sold that seat for a hefty profit." When Gina didn't respond, Helen added, "You still ticked off at me? "

"Not really."

"That's great because I'm too freaking tired for a bloody fight."

Without another word, Helen dug into her salad, then took a huge bite out of a sourdough roll, if one could call consuming half the roll a *bite*.

While Gina watched her friend chew, she took a tiny bite of her macaroni and cheese, then used her plastic fork to move the food from one spot to another on the plate.

"Harry and I are still on the outs, if that's what you're wondering."

Helen's fork stopped half way to her mouth; it took a moment before she filled her mouth with salad. She spoke as she chewed. "You sure know how to let the good ones get away."

"Whose side are you on, anyway?"

Helen shook her head. "Harry Lucke is a good nurse and a good man. And they're both damn hard to find."

"Maybe."

"And what did that great guy do to keep your spirits down for more than a week now?"

"Good man or not, he doesn't believe in me."

Helen set her fork down on her plate. "You're not talking about that same screwball who called on the advice line, are you? Or those nurses you keep asking about, making it sound like something may have happened to them?"

"Yeah, I am."

"Excuse *me,* but between those two issues, I'd take ole Harry anytime. Girl, you are crazy!"

"Maybe I am."

Gina chewed slowly on a morsel of her cheese-slathered macaroni, decided talking about Harry wasn't going to make her feel any better. Besides, she was tired of fighting with everyone.

"So I hear you were down three nurses today," Gina said.

"Yeah. What a morning. Ran my ass off. We had four bone marrow infusions and three codes. Two made it."

"That's rough."

"But how'd you know about the shortfall?" Helen took another forkful of salad that made her cheeks look like a munching rabbit.

"Alexandros told me, while turning me down for a little time off. Seems I'm the biggest reason there's a nursing shortage, people like me taking time off."

Helen laughed. "Well, *aren't* you the problem?" She held up a hand. "Only messin' with you. You're not like that damn Megan Ann!"

"Megan Ann? What about her?"

"She's one of the three that not only didn't show, but didn't even call in. Not all that unusual for her, but still..."

₪ CHAPTER 31

Her naked body was squeezed against the length of him; her soft skin made his chest ache. Air whistled through his mouth, in and out, in and out. Each exhale made wisps of Megan Ann's tousled red hair float away from her face, then fall back on her temple like spreading feathers. She was sound asleep, barely moved as he slipped a hand around her full breast, gently caressed the nipple with his thumb. She stirred, ground her hip against the swelling between his legs.

Eddie forced himself to turn away, slid out from under the covers; what he really wanted to do was bury himself in her. He circled the bed, reached into the side table where he'd hidden the kitchen knife.

His heart raced, skipped a beat. He studied her face: mouth open, a tiny stream of drool seeped onto the pillow and was crushed under her head.

The knife felt heavy.

He reached out and touched her nail-bitten little finger.

So tiny.

A rush of warmth swept in before fear could follow. Could he trust her? He'd believed in Mother ... and she'd left him.

Would he lose Megan Ann, too?

He carried the large chef's knife out of the bedroom, tip toed into the living room and stopped. He balanced the blade on his palm; he'd had it since he was fifteen, just after he'd tried to run away – a gift, or threat, from Father. He was never sure which.

Eddie stared at the sharp edge, the long point.

He had never killed anything, animal or human.

Holding the knife like a weapon made him feel stronger. He lunged forward into a threatening stance. Father's face floated in his mind.

The target.

Jab. Jab.

Eddie then stared at his naked body in the mirror. He looked strong; bunches of muscles hugged his skeleton. But inside, he knew there was a soft, pliable nothingness. Fear snaked through his gut, settled in his belly.

After he returned the knife to the kitchen, he stepped back into the living room, stood naked in front of the picture window. He used thumb and forefinger to burnish an angel medallion that hung from a chain around his neck. Mother had given it to him the day she left. It was supposed to protect him, to keep him safe.

Safe from what? From Father? Why did I ever believe a silly piece of metal could do that?

He hadn't known Mother was going to leave that day. After she'd given him the medallion and told him what it was for, she stood for a long time just holding him by the shoulders. She'd looked at him with large solemn eyes, the same eyes he saw every time he looked at his reflection in a mirror. She'd opened her mouth once, twice as if to say something ... something important. Then she'd turned and gone out the door, didn't even say goodbye,

What was it she'd wanted to say? That she loved him?

No, he was almost certain that wasn't it.

His mind's eye slid over the memory, picked at it slowly, uncovered the minute details. Each time something would be different, revealing a new swatch of detail: The clothes she wore, green blouse, jeans that were baggy and hung away from her hips; stiff and tight body movements like she hurt all over; eyes that were sad, sadder than usual.

She'd looked both at him, and at something behind him, over his shoulder.

What?

Eddie remembered turning, trying to see what she saw. But he'd seen nothing, nothing but the door that led down to the butcher shop, with its ever-present smell of animal flesh.

He heard his cell phone start its distinctive version of *Take Five,* and he snatched it up from the counter so it wouldn't awaken Megan Ann.

"Bring her back!"

"No!"

"Wrong answer, Eddie. Do you think because you drive that fancy car you can turn your back on me? Think you can get out of it? Think you can run away like her, your mother?"

"No, Father."

"That conniving woman is in your face every time I look at you. The same mealy mouth, droopy eyes. And that hair? I want to tear it out of your head!"

"Yes, Father."

"I paid you unearned wages while you got all that fancy schooling. Don't forget that. Four long years."

"I thanked you for that, Father."

"Who cares? I'm talking about now, today. I need to deliver the packages. *We've* got to deliver them!"

"Yes, Father."

"I'm sick. Dying."

"Yes, Father."

"Maybe I can't beat this goddam brain cancer, but I'm still strong enough to take you on. Take you out! You know that, don't you?"

"I know, Father."

"If you know so much, why aren't you here? You have to bring her back. I need that one."

"I can take care of you, Father. I'll pay for everything. I will."

"When did you get to be so stupid? ... I NEED TO DELIVER THE FUCKING PACKAGES."

"Yes, Father."

199

"Milty Hiller doesn't take no for an answer. You know that, right?"

"Yes, Father."

"Remember, it's your ass, too."

Eddie said nothing.

"I can't hear you, little boy."

"Yes, Father. I know."

"Still can't hear you."

"I said, I know!"

"KNOW WHAT?"

"That I have to do it."

"That's better."

"But it's the last time, Father."

"WHAT?"

"No more. You haven't kept your promise."

"What promise?"

"For ten years you've been promising to tell me where Mother is. I want to know now.

"Now? Hah! Now little Eddie decides to grow a pair. Sorry, a little late for that. Should have tried that a long time ago. Now, just bring back the redhead. We'll talk about that two-faced mother of yours later."

"But—"

The line went dead.

* * *

The sting of hot water sprayed against Eddie's chest until his skin was a bright red. He ran the bar of soap across his body, took in the soothing steam.

From behind, Megan Ann clutched him, encircled his waist with her arms. She lifted the soap from his hands and slid around to nestle into his chest. He laughed at her. "Aren't you going to let me wash up?"

Somehow her presence gave him substance, like he was real, not somebody's nightmare. And she made him feel light and happy.

"I had a wonderful time last night, Eddie, even if I did get too smashed."

"I'll take you home after we clean up."

"No! Let me stay here, Eddie. Stay with you."

The large shower stall, with its half-dozen spray heads, was dense with steam, but it felt like the sun was shining on him for the first time. She jumped up, clamped her arms and legs around him, pressed her vagina against his erection.

"Do it to me, Eddie. Do it here. Now!"

She sl—id her breasts back and forth across his chest. His heart pounded in his ears.

"Do it, Eddie! Please!"

She moved her pelvis back and forth, up and down until he was inside her. He braced his back against the tiles as she rode the length of him.

"Eddie!" she screamed, her movements frantic, engulfing him in an undulating silken flow.

"Eddie!" she screamed again. He clutched her to him and laughed. Joy filled his entire being.

He was never, ever going to give Megan Ann back to Father.

₪ CHAPTER 32

The fourth floor nurses station was strangely empty, and then Gina saw Helen headed her way from one of the patient rooms. Helen gave a quick wave, scooped up the telephone, and punched in four digits. Gina edged silently around the desk, slid into a chair next to her friend … and waited.

Gina often wondered how Helen managed to do all the physical labor required of a floor nurse. She was barely five feet tall, yet the petite brunette had the strength of an ox. Gina once watched her hold up a fainting six-foot bruiser for several minutes until help arrived. Without her, the guy would have been flat on his face.

The silence was making her restless. Usually there was a hum of activity throughout the Oncology unit, doctors and nurses hurrying about, visitors coming and going. At this particular moment, though, there wasn't even the familiar sight of a patient pushing an IV pole up and down the hallway.

Helen was so absorbed in her conversation with the pharmacy that she didn't look up until she was finished with a string of med orders. Then, with a deep sigh, she turned to the computer keyboard, made a few entries, and hit save.

"I suppose someday I'll be more secure with computerized patient charts," Helen said. "But I'm still worried that everything I enter is going to disappear out into the ether someplace, never to be seen or heard from again."

"Know the feeling," Gina said.

"Okay, so what are you doing here, my friend? Didn't I just see you at lunch? Or have they finally thrown you out of Advice?"

"Not yet, but I'm working on it. I decided to take a real break from handing calls this afternoon instead of working straight through like I usually do. Besides, if I didn't get away from Tina, I swear I'd pull all my short, little curls out by their roots."

"I was lucky to even get away for lunch," Helen said. "Must be nice working in the clinic." She grinned at Gina. "Sounds like a good job to me."

Gina used a hand to sweep across the entire area around them. "Where is everyone? This is kind of creepy."

"Just the lull before the storm," Helen said. "The docs are in a budget meeting, which really means they're trying to find another way to toss my ass out of here, along with as many other RNs as possible. They seem to think they can get along without us. But I think they're going to have a big problem sliding it past the accreditation committee."

Helen put the computer to sleep and gave Gina a questioning look. "Okay. Now, what are you *really* doing here? You'd never waste time visiting me unless there's something specific going on in your devious mind. Spit it out."

"Does it even pay to have you as a friend?" Gina said.

"Uh-huh."

"Okay, okay. I need to know why Megan Ann didn't show up for work. Is she sick, gone AWOL, or what?"

"Pray tell, what does that trippy redhead have to do with you?"

Gina grimaced. "Busted."

"Hell, I know you like the back of my hand." Helen grinned from ear to ear. "*I* even remember the days when you sounded like a Bronx hooligan. Now, at least, you just sound like the displaced person you are. Most times I can even understand what you're actually saying."

"Yeah, yeah! Very funny."

"I am cute, aren't I?" Helen clicked her ballpoint shut and hooked it into her pocket. She pulled Gina out of the nurses' station into the drug storage alcove. "Come on, spill it."

"Tell me the truth," Gina said. "Do *you* think I'm crazy?"

"Oooh, that's a tough one," Helen said. "It all depends on what we're talking about, and what phase of the moon we're in."

"Right now, that doesn't even begin to tickle my funny bone," Gina said.

They stopped and waited while a couple of MDs wandered into the nurses' station to enter patient orders in the computer.

"Fair enough," Helen said when they were alone again. "I don't really think you're crazy, but you *are* weirder than those ER chicks on TV."

"Thanks a bunch."

"Any word from Shelly?" Helen said.

Gina winced at hearing Shelley's name. "The problem is, it's not only Shelly. Arina Diaz is also missing. I spoke to her mother; the poor woman is frantic."

"That's pretty creepy," Helen said.

"Yeah, like they've fallen off the planet."

"There still could be a perfectly reasonable explanation. Maybe just a coincidence," Helen said.

"Maybe, but I don't think so." She debated whether to continue, then blurted out, "Is this the first day Megan Ann's been out?"

Helen was toying with her pen again. She clicked it in and out, in and out. The noise jarred Gina; she placed a hand over the offending pen.

Helen gave her an annoyed look: "Well, yes. I mean I was off yesterday … don't really know what was what yesterday, but today, she didn't show up, didn't call in."

"She told me she was going out with Eddie St. George, that detail man from CHEMwest," Gina said.

"Why do you even care about her after the way she came after you in the cafeteria?"

205

"Just a silly misunderstanding," Gina said.

"If you say so. But it's really hard to like her. She never interacts with any of us, yet that wiggling ass of hers sure catches the docs' eyes." Helen turned her nose up. "When we're in the same space, I might as well not exist."

"You just don't notice the ones who have eyes for you." Gina gave her a big smile.

"Sure! But back to Eddie St .George. Did you say she was going out with that hunk?"

That's what Megan Ann told me."

"He'd be enough for me to call in sick. Anytime. Who wouldn't want to share their body fluids with him? I'd put out, too." She clicked her pen again. "You're not thinking *she's* gone missing, too?"

"Back up a minute," Gina said. "You just accused her of being a slut, right?"

"You have such a Bronx way of expressing yourself."

"I'm not the one who claimed she's an easy lay."

"Hey, it's all hearsay," Helen said.

"Well, tell me what you've heard."

Helen clicked the pen in and out again, made herself stop, then started picking at a cuticle on a colorless fingernail.

"Some of the nurses have seen her with a variety of lowlifes. They've also caught her drinking in the locker room."

"Uh-huh," Gina said. "And who was this observant informer?"

"Diane 'Big Mouth' Utterback. The float in med/surg."

"Oh, my God! You've gotta be kidding," Gina said. "That broad has something rotten to say about everyone. Catty little bitch. She'd backstab her own mother."

"You wanted to know who, didn't you?"

"Do you believe her?" Gina said.

"Actually, I do. There've been several instances when Megan Ann stayed away from work for two, three days at a time. When she showed up again, not a word as to why she was out—

not even a feeble stab at trying to make it right. Believe me, if we didn't need her butt slaving away like the rest of us, she'd be toast."

"No explanations at all?" Gina said.

"She keeps her mouth zipped," Helen said, "which makes what everyone says and suspects that much more believable."

"We both know lots of people who sleep around, but they still manage to come to work," Gina said.

"There's more to it than that. Face it: Megan Ann has a drinking problem, maybe a drug problem, too. Put that together with a bad case of hot panties and you've got a helluva situation."

"Demons," Gina said. It was obvious Helen knew nothing about Megan Ann's past, about her lost family. "Those demons plague all of us."

"Sorry!" Helen looked into Gina's eyes. "You asked and I'm only telling you what I know."

"No problem. You've been a great help. You don't need to apologize about anything." She glanced around the station. "Do you have Megan Ann's telephone number? She's not listed."

Helen walked to the employee data file and twirled the Rolodex to Megan Ann's card. She wrote the details down and gave the paper to Gina.

"Thank God not everything around here is computerized," Gina said. "You wouldn't happen to have the same kind of information for Eddie St. George, would you?"

"Are you kidding?" Helen spun the Rolodex to "S."

Gina was surprised, no, amazed at the availability of all data on the drug reps that called on Ridgewood. They could be reached at every imaginable place, at a moment's notice. Eddie St. George was no exception. He even listed his gym and dentist office numbers.

"Thanks for all the info," Gina said. She tucked the note into her coat pocket. "You're a real buddy, and there're damn few of those around anymore."

"Don't I know it," Helen said.

Gina checked her watch again. "Better get back before Tina sends Alexandros to ream my ass."

Helen giggled. "Spoken like a true thug."

Gina threw her a kiss with one hand and flipped her birdie with the other, then scooted down the corridor toward the elevator.

₪ CHAPTER 33

Where the hell is Megan Ann?

Maybe Helen was right: that redhead *was* in hyperdrive—drinking, drugging, getting laid.

She still ought to be able to answer her goddam phone.

It was the end of the shift, the end of what had been one truly stinking day. Gina was close to losing it. A gnawing feeling of fear and isolation was closing in on her. She had no one. No one to talk to about the missing nurses, no one to talk to about the frightening caller, and no one to talk to about the turmoil at work.

The Advice Center was a hotbed of discontent—Chelsea was silent and staying clear of all departmental tension, Tina was her usual sarcastic and bitchy self, and Lexie was scrutinizing her every move as though she had a couple of loose screws and might suddenly turn into a screaming banshee.

And just to add to the confusion, there were four messages on her voice mail from Harry. He was only going to want to talk about marriage, not talk about the things she needed to talk about.

On an impulse, she called St. George's office just before she left the Advice Center to see if he might know where Megan Ann was.

"Mr. Edward St. George isn't in the office at this time."

"Is there any way I can reach him?"

"Ma'am, I don't have that information. I suggest you call back tomorrow and ask for the sales department."

Disappointed, Gina ended the call.

Outside, she eased into her car, closing her eyes for an instant before punching in Megan Ann's phone number again. As with earlier attempts, the phone rang, rang, rang. Not even a pickup by a message machine. It had to be the right number, she knew that—it had come straight from the employee database.

She fidgeted in the car in the dark, watched the flurry of employee activity as everyone zoomed out to freedom. Yet, there she sat, going nowhere.

"Who doesn't have a message machine in the twenty-first century?" she muttered. Her nails scratched at the slip of paper where she'd written down bits of collected information.

Fear and anger had morphed into inertia. She rubbed at the back of her neck and was at a loss as to how to deal with all her suspicions, unhappiness, and…

She jumped when her cell belted out *"New York, New York."* Caller ID flashed Harry's name.

No! She didn't want to talk to Harry right now; she wasn't sure if she would ever again want to talk to him. After several choruses, the phone went silent. She let out a long, deep sigh.

Before she could relish the silence, the phone did its thing again.

Damn it, Harry, I'm not answering.

But the tiny screen said: *SFPD Yee.*

Maybe she finally has something to report. Anything would be a relief.

"Hello."

"Ms. Mazzio, Pepper Yee, SFPD."

"Detective Yee. Good! You're alive and apparently well. I'd almost forgotten about you. Or is it that you've forgotten about me? And you even have my cell number."

"You gave it to me."

There was a long pause, as though the detective was waiting for Gina to spill her guts—complain like she usually did during their encounters.

"What can I do for you, Detective?"

Heavy breathing. Was Pepper Yee nervous?

"Look, I really called to apologize. I know you think I've been ignoring you, but my investigation has been on-going ... and going on to nowhere."

"I don't believe this," Gina said. "Two women, Arina Diaz and Shelly Wilton, are missing. Someone, somewhere, must know *something*."

"Face the facts—there are no suspects or evidence of any kind," Yee said. "Employee photos of the women were passed around at The Hideaway, a bar Wilton and possibly Diaz were known to frequent."

"I've been there," Gina said. "Had anyone seen them?"

"A couple of people recognized Wilton, but not Diaz. That was it."

"That doesn't mean much," Gina said. "That's a busy place."

"True, but that's all I have to go on."

"It's also true those women are still missing."

"Missing doesn't mean murdered, Ms. Mazzio." The detective sounded miffed.

"What about the telephone calls? That crazy man calling the advice line, then my home? You don't find that disturbing?"

"I do find it disturbing. But I think we're dealing more with a stalker than anything else."

"And that's not dangerous?" Gina said.

"It bears watching, and I will be watching, Ms. Mazzio. Trust me! Other than that, I'm sorry there's nothing more to report."

"So you called to say you have nothing to say other than to apologize? Well, if that's it, I accept your apology. Now what?"

"I'll keep digging. That's all I can do."

"And while you're doing that," Gina said, "maybe another nurse will go missing. Maybe another nurse has already gone missing."

"What does that mean? Are you keeping something from me?"

Gina looked out toward the hospital, debated whether to end the call. She couldn't bring herself to accept that Megan Ann might be a victim of the caller. "It's an internal affair," she finally said. "We have this nurse who goes on benders and shacks up with guys for two, three days at a time."

"And why don't you think she's another Wilton or Diaz?"

"The circumstances are different."

Gina heard a rustling of paper, as if Yee were going through her notes.

"According to what I have here, that pretty much coincides with what people had to say about Wilton."

"Possibly, but certainly not Diaz."

Yee snorted. "What makes you think morals have anything to do with it? No, don't answer that. Just tell me how long this one's been missing."

"One or two days. I don't know if she was supposed to work yesterday. Today, no one's heard from her."

"So this bothers you, Ms. Mazzio, but not enough to let me know? Where's all that worry and concern for your fellow nurses that you've been laying on me?" There was a pause for a sharp intake of breath. "Further, who the hell are you to decide what deserves or doesn't deserve my attention in an on-going investigation?"

Gina blurted, "Telling you *anything* has been mostly counter-productive."

"Give me the details," Yee demanded, "or I'm going to have you picked up and brought down here and see what you have to say in one of our interrogation rooms."

Gina filled her in on Megan Ann's description, address, phone number, and background.

"Hmm. Interesting."

"What's interesting?"

It was a couple of beats before Yee responded. "From the information I've collected, all three of the Ridgewood nurses are redheads, or at least they were when they disappeared."

Gina thought about that for a moment. "You're right. The only difference is that Shelly and Megan Ann were … are natural redheads. I'm pretty sure Arina's color came out of bottle. Do you find that significant?"

"Maybe, maybe not. You got anything else I should know about?"

"The only other thing I can think of is that Megan Ann was supposed to have had a date Monday night with a drug rep from CHEMwest, Eddie St. George."

"Do you know Mr. St. George?"

"Yes."

"What's your take on the dude?"

"Seems like a nice guy, works for a reputable company. Went out with him once myself."

"And?"

"Just wasn't my type."

"Do you know if he dated Wilton or Diaz?"

"No. But every nurse I know thinks he's a hot number, and probably wouldn't say no if he asked."

"And still you're not suspicious of this guy? You're something else, Mazzio." There was a pause. "I'll send a couple people to check on this St. George guy as soon as I can. Work, home, whatever."

Gina took a deep breath, prodded again: "And you're going to keep looking into what's happened to Shelly Wilton and Arina Diaz, right?"

"I think our time for mutual cooperation is over, Mazzio. Unless I say otherwise, don't call me, I'll call you." With that, she hung up.

Gina lowered her cell and stared at it. The silence closed in around her. She decided to try St. George's home number. No one answered, but at least *he* had a message machine.

Everything was out of whack—Megan Ann, the missing nurses, St. George, Yee, Dominick, Harry—and no one seemed to really care all that much.

213

* * *

Gina found a parking place two blocks from her apartment. As she walked toward the building's entrance she saw something that made her slow down—Harry was leaning against the brick wall next to the entrance.

Her first reaction was anger, which was quickly displaced by a sense of relief ... and a momentary sense of safety. She hated herself for that feeling of dependence. Was she really that needy? She wanted to hold onto her anger. But was he any different than Yee, Alexandros, Tina, or anyone else she'd tried to get involved in the missing-nurse situation? Seeing Harry only confused her more—one minute she was angry with him and never wanted to see him again, the next minute, she was doing a complete turn around and wanting desperately to be safe in his arms.

"Hi, doll."

She walked up to him, looked into his eyes, and wondered if he knew just how much she had missed him. "Hi, Harry."

He held out his arms and moved toward her. She curled against his chest without a word.

"Things are bad, huh?"

"Like you wouldn't believe."

"Okay if I come up?"

She nodded, took his hand, and held it until they were upstairs. Silently, they worked side by side to fix a pot of tea, and when it was ready, they settled down on the couch with a box of Wheat Thins.

"I'm here to listen," Harry said. "And I'll do my best to suppress any negative thoughts."

"Okay, but when I'm through, please tell me what you really think, no matter what."

Gina started at the beginning, telling Harry once again about the original phone call on the advice line, and went on from there about everything that had happened up to the moment she'd come home now to find him outside.

He held her close, fed her a cracker now and then, and avoided any comment until she finally looked at him with questioning eyes.

"Vasquez, of all people, is the only person who agrees with your theory?" Harry said. "That's wild."

"And if his niece wasn't involved, I know I wouldn't even have *his* support."

"Do you think this cop, Yee, is really doing anything?"

"Yeah, she's looking into it, by the book and in her own sweet time. Just how diligently, I'm not sure."

"What if there are nurses missing other than Wilton and Diaz, I mean over a period of time, and from places in the Bay Area other than Ridgewood."

"I think that's a very strong possibility. It would get too risky for someone to keep taking victims from the same facility."

"A lot of my cop friends tell me they usually don't put in a lot of time on missing person cases unless there's actual evidence of foul play. Sometimes people just sort of *disappear* themselves—start over somewhere else because they want to run away from their lives."

Gina sipped her tea. "Right now, I feel like doing that myself."

Harry wrapped an arm around her shoulders. "That wouldn't solve anything. Besides, think how lonely I'd be without you?"

She turned, kissed his cheek, and gave him a small smile. "What you said about other missing nurses did start me thinking."

"Yeah? You mean I may be good for something after all?"

"You're good for lots of things, Harry."

"Just not marriage."

"Please, Harry, let's not go there right now." She gave him another quick kiss.

He nodded, but his eyes lost their sparkle.

"The police must have missing persons data computerized," Gina said. "Maybe they could develop a list of missing nurses by age groups, similar physical characteristics, that sort of thing?"

"That makes sense, and certainly something you should put to Detective Yee."

"If she'll talk to me again."

* * *

Yee had finally gotten her desk in some kind of order so she could feel as though she was somewhat on top of her game. She looked at Warren's picture on the corner of her desk and instead of feeling angry or hopeless, she felt nothing. She reached out and moved it to the bottom drawer, closing her husband inside with the tip of her boot.

"Pick up, Yee," the desk sergeant said in a loud voice that made everyone look in her direction.

"Yee here."

"Detective Yee, this is—"

"Yeah, I know who it is, Ms. Mazzio. I thought I made it clear that any communication between us would originate with me."

"Well, I wanted to ask you a question. "

"Listen, I've had more than enough of your questions and your innuendos implying I'm not doing my job."

"I just want to know if it's possible to bring up the stats on missing women who might have the same profile as Shelly Wilton and Arina Diaz?"

"And Megan Ann Hendricks?"

"Yes, and Megan Ann. The point is, maybe this whole business of missing nurses has been going on for a lot longer than we think, than *I* think."

"Still trying to do our job for us, I see."

"No, I—"

"I've tried to be nice about all of this, Ms. Mazzio. But now I'm giving it to you straight: Butt out!"

Yee slammed the phone down into its cradle. "Everyone wants to be a cop; they all think they can do our job better than we can. But none of them ever wants to take a bullet."

She'd complained loud enough that other cops in the room looked over at her. She waved them off with an impatient flick of her hand. She started to get up to go fight with the vending machines, instead, she leaned back in her chair and gave a second thought to something Mazzio had said. She reached out and pulled up the master Missing Persons file.

Bette Golden Lamb & J. J. Lamb

ℿ **CHAPTER 34**

Robert Merz glared at his assistant, who'd pulled him out of a CHEMwest national marketing meeting to take a telephone call. He rubbed hard at the back of his neck, every muscle and tendon a taut rope of steel.

"He hasn't what?" he shouted into the phone and looked at his watch: 9:55 a.m. "Where the hell is he?" Merz looked through the glass doors leading to the conference room. Everyone was staring back at him, waiting. "Find him!"

He couldn't believe that Eddie St. George had yet to arrive at Ridgewood Hospital with the sample doses of Pneucanex-CW. The bastard knew a TV camera crew from CNN would be waiting to televise the presentation of the free medication to the ailing father of an indigent family.

Everyone—the CEO of CHEMwest, Ridgewood Administrator Alan Vasquez, the new Oncology Chief Michael Cliffords, and who knew who else was there, waiting for St. George to arrive with the restructured chemo wonder drug.

CHEMwest's public relations veep in New York had spent several months convincing the network to document the story even though the product was really only a variation of their existing drug. Not a real break-through.

And now Eddie *Asshole* St. George was screwing up the best possible publicity opportunity they could ever hope for. He knew he should have gone himself, but he had this committee to chair, a damn important meeting, and to have postponed it would have been a major inconvenience He didn't like to be inconvenienced for one moment

Merz hung up on the caller from Ridgewood's PR department and had Michael Cliffords paged.

"I've just been informed that Eddie St. George is … uh … a little late for the presentation," he told the oncology chief, nodding to himself as he listened to the angry response

"Where is he?" Cliffords demanded.

"We're trying to locate him now, confirm his time of arrival."

"This is an oncology unit, Mr. Merz. We're trying to cooperate, but all these outsiders represent a significant danger to our immune-compromised patients. We need these people out of here as soon as possible."

"Let me get back to you."

But Cliffords wouldn't quit, started going over the same territory again.

"I know, I know," Merz said. "Mr. St. George explained the patient's circumstances when he proposed this gesture. We are certainly empathetic with the man's financial situation, and how the HMO wouldn't cover the additional cost of the new drug."

Merz wanted to hang up, but he needed to buy time. "The stats are solid, doctor. And they're exciting. The best cure rate out there."

"Yes, yes, but where is it?" Cliffords insisted.

"The medication will be there," Merz said. "I'm sorry for this inexcusable delay, and for upsetting your patient, you, the Ridgewood staff, and, of course, CNN. I promise we'll make it right. St. George will be there any minute."

"Forget St. George. Bring the drug over yourself. Now."

Merz tapped a pencil on his desk so hard the slim piece of yellow-painted wood splintered; he swept the pieces onto the rug and tried to rein in his fury. This was no time to let his short fuse catch fire. He had no choice but to confess another embarrassing fact to Cliffords. He took a deep breath and said, "St. George has the only supply of Pneucanex-CW in the area."

He cringed as the receiver at the other end abruptly clicked off.

"Get that son-of-a-bitch St. George on the horn," he yelled at his assistant. "Now!"

"He's not answering his cell."

"Well, for Christ's sake, don't just stand there like a limp dick. Look up his landline ... try his goddam apartment ... *send someone to his apartment*. Do I have to tell you everything?"

The assistant spun around and slid sideways through the doorway. Merz watched him depart, could tell he was pissed. For the umpteenth time, he wished he had a female assistant again.

Just as dumb but better to look at.

No, no more female assistants. One more harassment gig could cost him more than he cared to imagine.

His collar tightened the way it always did when his blood pressure was on the rise.

In the midst of all of this he pondered the nasty question again: Does it pay to fly the straight and narrow?

Fucking-A, it does!

His last female assistant, who was extraordinarily voluptuous, had threatened to go to the press. Cost CHEMWest a pretty penny to squash that whole sexual mess. Merz had thought she'd wanted it—he sure as hell knew he had! Stirred up a real hornet's nest when she claimed he assaulted her. What the hell did these women want anyway? Prince Charming? Couldn't afford to be in the middle of another mess like that again. Ever!

He took a loop around the desk.

Shit!

He wasn't going to wait for his assistant. He snatched up the phone and tapped in St. George's automatic dial.

* * *

Eddie stared at his cell phone; the chiming had been incessant. He gritted his teeth, finally answered.

"Why the hell aren't you at Ridgewood with that friggin' drug?" Merz shouted.

The question was shrill. Eddie held the receiver far from his ear. He'd expected it to be Father, not Merz.

"Angie's supposed to be handling it," he lied. "I'm sick, have a fever."

"I don't give a fuck if your balls are melting and running down your leg. You're due at Ridgewood. Past due! Get your ass over there!"

Eddie's hand shook as he let the phone slip from his fingers onto the glass tabletop. He broke out in a bubbling sweat, eased himself down onto the floor. This was the first time Merz had ever yelled at him.

A wheeze exploded from his mouth. He couldn't breathe. The harsh sounds grew louder.

Megan Ann, naked, rushed out of the bedroom, a glass full of vodka clutched in one hand. She sloshed the booze over the brim, ignored the spill

"Eddie, what's the matter?"

She grabbed for his hand, missed, and spilled more vodka on the polished bamboo.

He jerked his head towards the desk, where an inhaler was perched on the edge. She grabbed it, flipped off the cover, and put it to his lips. Holding it there, she lowered herself onto the floor next to him.

"Use it, baby." She compressed the inhaler. "Breathe!"

His eyes were swimming in tears, his chest collapsing. Megan Ann caressed his head, rubbed his back, crooned words he couldn't grasp.

...over the rainbow ...somewhere...

Sound contracted, expanded. Didn't Mother sing that song to him?

He gasped in air, and with it came the metallic taste of the medication that had saved him so many times. The room stopped its crazy spin.

Eddie got up, moved slowly to the dining room table, sat down, and remained perfectly still. He looked out at the penthouse patio. He was afraid to move, afraid to interrupt the even flow of air that was rhythmically filling his lungs.

"Feeling better now, Eddie?" Megan Ann asked.

"Yes. Thanks."

"I know there're better medications than this out there to control your asthma. You were in pretty bad shape."

"I'm supposed to be the drug rep, remember?" He smiled weakly at her as his shoulders sagged in relaxation. He was almost himself when his cell chimed—it shattered the silence

They both stared at it.

"Please don't answer it, Eddie."

He let it ring several times before putting it to his ear.

"You're fired!" Robert Merz yelled.

"Bob—"

"It's Mr. Merz to you, dickhead. When I told you to get down to that hospital, I meant right then. Not when you fucking well felt like it. And don't talk to me about Angie. I called her; she didn't have the foggiest idea of what I was talking about. You're a goddam liar. *You* have the dosages, not that simpering cunt."

"I can't help it. I told you before, I'm really ill."

"If you think you're sick now, wait till the bill collectors come after that fancy Jaguar of yours."

"How can you fire me?" Eddie said. "Haven't I always come through for you, for CHEMwest?" He couldn't stop himself. "Haven't I always done the job? My stats are better than any other rep."

"Well, Mr. Goodjob, that was yesterday."

"But I've never failed you," Eddie pleaded.

"Never's just a long time, St. George," Merz said. "And again, that was yesterday. Today, in case you've forgotten, I have a CNN reporter and camera crew at Ridgewood, ready to film our generosity in providing a drug that, goddam it, isn't there, or even close to being there."

"I ... I haven't forgotten."

"This whole friggin' affair was entrusted to you, Mr. Super Salesman."

"I can't move, Bob."

"Marketing's all set up to key this event into a national promo." Merz laughed harshly. "Fuck! And here I am, wasting my time yakking at an ex-employee who talks about never letting me down?"

"Bob—"

"Shove it, St. George! I'm sending a courier for the Pneucanex. You'd better be there!"

₪ CHAPTER 35

Before St. George could fully digest what had just happened, the phone rang again. He grabbed up the receiver, hoping against hope that Merz had merely lost his temper, thought it through, and changed his mind.

"WHERE IS SHE?"

"I ..."

"YOU WERE SUPPOSED TO BRING HER BACK YESTERDAY."

"Father!" He dug a fingernail into a scar under his arm, making it burn like a cigarette ground against his naked skin. "I've been sick."

"BRING HER!"

"I'm too sick."

"SICK?"

Father's voice exploded in his head, reverberated through his brain. "I'm the one who's sick. You're the puny little nothing who can't stand the sight of blood."

"Yes, Father."

"My head's on fire. Do you hear me? I need the woman; Milty wants his packages."

"Yes."

"What?"

"I'll do it."

* * *

Jacob St. George slammed down the telephone, cutting off his pathetic son's voice.

"Whiner!" he screamed at the sides of beef awaiting his attention. "Always making excuses."

225

Goddam it, why couldn't I have gotten a real son, one with backbone?

He smacked one of the slabs of beef with the flat of his hand.

Yeah, but what else could I expect from that bitch? She never did anything right.

He hated his son, had hated the kid right from the day he was born—a redheaded, sickly, sniveling, mama's boy.

He'd found it disgusting that Lola made excuses for the boy's sissy ways, for his nightmares. She would even take the punches that were meant for the kid. Then he discovered that he enjoyed beating *her* much more than he did smacking around his pantywaist son. Her lily-white skin would turn bright scarlet, then flip into multi-colored bruises. And each time he worked her over, it became more difficult to stop himself from doing it again.

The effects became so exciting, one day he covered her with cow blood and finger-painted fiery patterns across her nude, shivering body, all the time whispering gutter talk about his contempt for her.

She became his personal punching bag. Spunky Lola? She stopped fighting back, changed from defensive to submissive.

And her thick, flaming hair? Every time it grew out four or five inches, he would hack it all off, making the ritual a part of whatever new fantasy jumped into his brain.

Humiliating her became the only way to make him feel *anything*.

After the last time he beat her, he awoke in the middle of the night to find her standing over him, her eyes wild and fierce. She was ready to stab him with a large chef's knife.

"You think you're going to kill *me*?" he sneered.

"You're through being cruel to Eddie! You're never going to yell at my son again! I'm going to stop you from making him cower. From beating him. You're an evil man, Jacob St. George."

She thrust downward with the knife; he rolled out of the way, leaped from the bed, and squeezed her tight against his body with one arm.

Her eyes widened into pools of hatred; he grabbed her wrist and twisted until she dropped the knife. He scooped up the weapon and slit her nightgown from neck to hem, leaving a thin line of seeping blood down her chest and stomach.

"I'm not the adulterer," he shouted.

St. George threw her onto the bed, positioned himself over her, and lowered his body until her stiffened nipples rubbed against his chest. He entered her and thrust in and out of her limp body until he climaxed with a guttural, wall-shaking roar.

After a moment, he rolled off the bed; he picked up the knife again, and jammed the blade up between her ribs and into her heart.

There was only a slight gasp as her breath caught and ceased. He watched her life ebb, come to an end.

Jacob St. George leaned over his wife's face, licked her cheek, and swallowed her last tear. *She* was dead. *He* was alive. Alive with … with joy!

He had the power.

He stood, hovered over her—a beast with a new kill.

His skin was taut, every pore tingling. He admired her attack, her defiance; he wondered if there was even a hint of that hidden strength in his son. But to what end? He would always prevail.

Standing at the bedside, looking down on his wife's wilted body, the joy ebbed. He already missed that feeling of exaltation and power.

In the wee hours of the morning, he snuck his wife's body out of the apartment and took it to the butcher shop. He wrapped the body in butcher paper and stored it in the back corner of the walk-in freezer, piling boxes of steaks and chops in front of it.

By the following noon, Jacob St. George and Milton Hiller had found each other. They'd come to an agreement on what was supposedly a one-time deal.

* * *

Jacob tugged at the collar of his turtleneck, loosened it from around his Adam's apple. He was burning up, even in the refrigerated air of the cutting room. He looked at his knives, all honed razor-sharp, lined up, and ready to use. Next to them were the cleavers and handsaws.

His cell vibrated inside his pants pocket. He slipped a hand under his blood-smeared apron, pulled out the phone, and read the caller ID.

Fucking Milty Hiller again.

He kicked viciously at the padlocked cooler where he stored the packages. For the first time in years it was almost empty on a day Hiller was scheduled to make a pickup.

Damn Eddie!

His right foot felt numb, or was it his imagination? No, his toes felt icy, hard; the fingers of his right hand were tingling; and his tongue seemed large and floppy. The radiation wasn't working.

"Yeah, yeah!" he said into the phone.

"It's time," Hiller said, his voice firm, threatening.

"I don't have the whole order, yet. How many times a day do I have to tell you?"

"Listen, I promised those packages for tomorrow," Milty Hiller said. "One of my best accounts. You let these universities down and the money disappears forever. It's not like I'm the only show in town."

"Don't keep singing that sad song to me, Milty. I told you, I don't have it all put together. Maybe later on today, or tonight."

St. George's tongue was suddenly so swollen he couldn't speak.

"That's not good enough. Do you understand?"

228

St. George tried to respond, managed only a soft, unintelligible sound.

"Jacob? Are you there?"

St. George folded the cell, returned it to his pocket. His heart thumped in his ears, pounded like a locomotive gone wild. He pulled a vial of tablets from a pocket, tapped out four into his palm, wondered if he could even swallow them.

May have waited too long.

He placed the pills one by one on the back of his engorged tongue, uncapped a bottle of water, and tried to swallow. After three attempts, the pills finally washed down.

He sat on the stool, laid his head on the wooden table, and stared at the array of cutting tools. It was hypnotic the way they shone back at him. St. George's eyes drooped shut.

As he drifted off, he thought about his father, who long ago had given him the matched set of knives, said they were the best in the business. He then unexpectedly demonstrated their quality and efficiency by slicing open Jacob's forearm. Cruel, but instructive.

Oh, yes, my knives are sharp; they hold their edge. I can fillet any piece of meat without tearing or damaging the flesh, or anything else.

He awoke with a start, checked his watch. He had conked out for almost an hour. His tongue was almost normal again. He pulled the phone out of his pocket and punched Eddie's number. It rang and rang.

"Pick up, damn you!"

When he heard the phone at the other end click on, he said, "Don't give me a bunch of bullshit excuses, Eddie. I need a woman tonight. Hear me? Tonight!"

"Yes, Father."

Jacob St. George hung up, shivered. No matter how much he tried, he couldn't stay warm. He watched his right arm jerk uncontrollably as though it didn't belong to him; he was starting to have trouble talking again.

He'd complained loudly about the symptoms the last time he'd gone to his doctor, but it was the same old spiel—pills to make him comfortable, retreat to some kind of home where they'd feed him, tuck him in, and watch him in to die.

What did they call it? Not a hospital. Not a hostel. Hospice! That was it. Well, no matter what they called it, he wasn't ready to go there.

The phone rang. He read the display and saw Milty's name again. "Shit!" But he lifted the receiver to his ear.

"Jacob, what's with you? Don't ever hang up on me like that again."

St. George said something garbled that didn't even make sense to him.

"What's with the mumbling? I need answers."

St. George cleared his throat, swallowed more water, and croaked out, "Haven't been feeling too great lately."

"None of us are as young as we used to be. Hell, you're just getting old, Jacob."

"Can the stupid jabber. I'm doing what I can."

"You promised, Jacob. No time for excuses. Is this gonna affect our deal, or what? Gotta know. Ain't got no time to fool around. Need those packages. You got 'til midnight!"

Jacob kept shivering, but could feel the sweat dripping from under his arms. For the first time in years he was scared, scared of dying, scared of Milty.

"I ... I'm working ... on it."

"You're not shitting me, are you Jacob?"

"No. You'll have the packages. Tonight."

"Don't play games with me."

"What're you going to do Milty, kill me?"

There was a long moment of silence.

"You know, Jacob, I've always thought you were a sick fuck, and I never asked you any questions that might mess up our little deal. But if you don't come through, I'll stuff your prick in your mouth and turn *you* into a package I can sell. A deal's a deal."

Before Jacob could stutter a reply, the line went dead.

₪ CHAPTER 36

It was almost noon before Pepper Yee found the time to request a plainclothes team to go find Eddie St. George and have a talk with him. In the meantime, she telephone-chased CHEMwest's HR director to find out the extent of the drug rep's sales territory. She wanted as much background on St. George as she could get, as quickly as possible.

Yee caught the pharmaceutical company's HR department head just as she was sitting down for some kind of professional luncheon meeting at the Fairmont Hotel.

"Sorry to inconvenience you, ma'am, but I need the information right now," Yee said. "Later this afternoon might be too late." Not exactly the truth, but…

"Everything's in the computer," the woman said impatiently.

"And you can't access that data with your iPod or Blackberry, or whatever is in your purse, or perhaps the hotel's computer?"

"Well, yes, but …"

"How long could it take?"

"I hope this is as important as you say it is. Hold on. I can't do it here at the table."

In less than ten minutes Yee had the information she wanted. If Megan Ann Hendricks was alive and well and shacked up with the drug rep, that would take care of that. But if the nurse wasn't there, then she wanted to be prepared. St. George was the first real lead in what she'd come to call the "Mazzio Muddle."

Yee called the SFPD's IT computer geeks to find out if she could get data on all local female medical personnel who had been reported as missing persons over the past five years, women who had never been accounted for.

"No problem, lieutenant," said the on-duty nerd. "But we'll need the request in writing."

"Yeah, yeah! Soon as we hang up. And while you're at it, could you limit the printout to redheads, age 20 to 40, trim, no more than 150 pounds? It would speed things along."

"If the info's available, we can get it for you."

"How long?"

"You set the priority."

"ASAP."

"You got it."

"Good," Yee said. "Now, what about other metro and county jurisdictions throughout the Bay Area, say as far south as San Jose?"

"We have pretty good synergy with most of the police and sheriffs in the area. That'll take a little longer, though."

"Just get me what I need. I'll bring the written request right down."

Once she had the data from IT, she'd coordinate it with the info she'd been given by the CHEMwest HR director. She doubted it would take very long to catch any kind of a pattern that might make Eddie St. George a prime murder suspect.

When Yee returned after taking her written request to IT, the switchboard had a message from Walter Cooke: he'd been tapped to do another dismemberment job at Auston's Funeral Home. Tonight.

Mazzio, Hendricks, and St. George would have to wait. She called her lieutenant.

"This could be the night we catch Milty Hiller ass-deep in illegal human body parts," she said. "Could you give us the leverage we need to shut down the entire operation."

"Go for it," said the lieutenant. "How many people do you need?"

"Soon as I locate Hiller, I'll put a tail on him. He usually hangs out during the day at his discount camera shop on Market

Street. I'd like to take Daniels with me, and I could use a couple of uniforms for backup."

"Sounds like a plan. Good work, Yee!"

* * *

After work, Gina Mazzio drove to Solomon's, a local deli; it was almost as good as the ones in New York. She bought a turkey sandwich with onions and mayo on pumpernickel, and a cream soda to wash it down. Then she continued on her way to St. George's apartment building.

She was somewhat surprised to find that the drug rep lived in very posh Pacific Heights. She'd always assumed that people in that profession made a very good living, but this was beyond her expectations. She found a parking spot across the street from the building, nibbled on her turkey sandwich, and waited for some kind of plan to pop into her head. It was already dark so she didn't feel quite so conspicuous sitting in her ancient Fiat in what was probably a very security-conscious neighborhood.

While she was chewing on the last bite of her sandwich, a tan four-door sedan pulled up in front of the apartment building and double-parked. Two guys got out who looked and acted like cops. When they reached the lobby door, they pounded on the glass and flashed badges at the doorman.

Yee had certainly taken her time.

* * *

"Mr. St. George, Edward St. George?"

"Yes."

"I'm Detective Sorenson and this is Detective Delgado. We're trying to locate a Megan Ann Hendricks. She's been reported as a missing person."

"I don't understand," St. George said. "She's only been staying here a couple of days. Isn't there some kind of waiting period before the police act on a missing person report?"

"Not when we have probable cause, sir. Now tell me, do you know where I might find Ms. Hendricks?

"Well, she's—" St. George looked back over his shoulder in the direction of the hallway leading to the master bedroom. "She's in the bedroom."

"Do you mind if we come in, Mr. St. George?" Sorenson said. He eased one foot inside the doorway without waiting for an answer.

St. George opened the door wider and allowed both officers to step into the penthouse foyer. "Who filed the missing person report?"

"I have no idea, sir. We just need to see Ms. Hendricks and determine if she's unharmed and not being held against her will."

"Okay. I'll go see if she's, uh, presentable."

"If you don't mind, sir, one of us needs to go with you."

"Just give me a moment, please. She was taking a shower when I came to answer the door."

"I'll go," said Delgado. She gave her partner a wry smile.

Just then Megan Ann stepped out from the hallway, wearing a man's t-shirt that covered everything, but hid nothing. She had an empty old-fashion glass in one hand. "Oh, goody! We have company."

Sorenson stared, mouth open, Delgado glared at her partner, and St. George felt himself flush.

"Megan Ann," St. George said softly, "don't you think it would be a good idea for you to go back and put on some clothes?"

"Are you Megan Ann Hendricks?" Sorenson asked before she could say anything.

"Yep!"

"Are you here of your own free will, Ms. Hendricks?"

"You damn betcha!"

"What do you think?" Sorenson said to Delgado.

Delgado looked at her clipboard. "She certainly matches the description … and then some."

"Okay," Sorenson said. "Sorry to have bothered you, Mr. St. George. Everything seems to be in order here. Is that correct Ms. Hendricks?"

Megan Ann raised her empty glass in a toast. "Would be if I had a little vodka and ice in this glass." She turned and giggled her way back down the hallway toward the bedroom.

Delgado spun her partner around and St. George escorted the two of them back to the elevator. He waited until the indicator showed the car had reached the lobby level. Before he could begin to think about what their visit meant, the phone rang.

Again!

And again.

St. George paced back and forth, covered his ears. Father had been calling consistently every fifteen minutes since yesterday. It seemed like the ringing would never stop.

He tore at his hair, gouged the scars under his arms until blood trickled down his sides.

"Stop it!"

The incessant ringing was like nails being hammered into his skull.

"Eddie!" Megan Ann called from the bedroom.

He ignored her, grabbed the telephone. "What do you want, Father?"

Silence.

"I know it's you. Leave me alone!" Eddie clutched at his chest; the tightness was squeezing him unbearably, his wheezes expanded to fill every space in the room.

"Wimp!"

"Stop it!"

"Bring me that woman or you'll take her place. Do you hear me?"

Eddie hung up and reached for his inhaler, pulled in four quick puffs. His heart raced while he waited for air to fill his chest.

"Eddie!" Megan Ann yelled.

He moved into the kitchen.

"I'll be right there."

He took a new bottle of Absolut from the cupboard, filled a fresh glass with ice cubes, and left for the bedroom. Megan Ann was sprawled across the bed, eyes unfocused. He left the glass and vodka on the bedside table.

Back in the living room, looking out across the city, St. George gave serious thought to who could have prompted the police to come to his place looking for Megan Ann. Somewhere along the line he'd made a mistake, left a trail.

That worried him. Really worried him.

If it could happen with her, could someone make a connection between him and the others he'd taken to Father?

Tears ran down his cheeks. It was over. He should have stood up to Father years ago. It was time to break away, force Father to tell him where Mother was. Once he knew that, he could leave, close out his accounts, disappear.

"Eddie!"

Her voice lanced him like a sharp knife. One more decision to make. He walked slowly back to his bedroom.

Megan Ann was sitting up, leaning against a pile of pillows stacked against the headboard. She was well into the bottle of Absolut he'd brought her only a short time ago and the t-shirt was gone.

She squirmed against the pillows, invited him to take her. He sat on the edge of the bed, gently lifted her head, and slipped a roofie into her mouth. She reached for the glass of iced vodka and took a long drink.

"Come to bed, Eddie. I need you. Real bad." She ran her fingers slowly up and down the mound between her legs.

St. George took a deep breath, let it out slowly. "Soon."

* * *

Gina sipped her cream soda, checked her watch, and waited. She assumed the next thing she would see was the pair of cops coming out with St. George between them.

Ten minutes later, the cops exited the apartment, laughing, and alone. Where was St. George? Where was Megan Ann? And what was so damn funny?

She felt pretty stupid. All this because St. George had gone on a date with Megan Ann. It looked like Detective Yee, Harry, and all the others were right—it all added up to a case of hot pants, nothing more.

She studied the area: Tall buildings, all facing either a nearby park or the bay. What did the drug rep see from his windows?

St. George: an elegant name. Well, he *was* kind of classy, just like all the other reps in their expensive clothes. Smooth and good-looking, they all looked more like celebrities than business people. There wasn't an ugly duckling in the batch, at least not that Gina ever saw. Every one, man or woman, caught your attention.

But there was something unusual about St. George. Yes, he was handsome, but his smile was forced and his eyes were almost always sad.

Men! Always an enigma. And that made her think about Harry. What was she going to do? She couldn't keep putting him off forever. She had to make a decision, one way or the other.

Harry had tried hard last night to be objective about this whole business of the missing nurses. But it was really more than just that—he was tired of the tension over the getting/not getting married issue. And while he was sympathetic to her complaints about working in Advice rather than being involved in direct patient care, the kind of nursing that really meant something to her, her bouts of depression over her work situation had to be a real drag.

Harry's suggestion that she resign from Ridgewood and get into travel nursing with him was sounding better and better all the time. But was that the answer to their relationship problems? Or was that just doing another geographic and hoping for the best?

Tears rolled down her cheeks. As soon as she found out what the real deal was with Megan Ann, she would have to get serious and do something about putting her life into some kind of order.

₪ CHAPTER 37

Gina took a napkin from the take-out food bag and blotted each eye until she started to quiet down. She was tired of sitting, thinking, and staring at the apartment building. Now that the cops had come and gone, she wanted to find out for herself what was up with Eddie St. George and Megan Ann Hendricks.

She forced herself out of the Fiat, ran across the street. The same gray-uniformed doorman was still there, sitting behind his desk, working a crossword puzzle. He looked up when she tapped on the glass door. He buzzed her in. The door swished closed behind her.

"May I help you?"

"Yes. I was going up to see Eddie St. George." She stood there, certain the guard was scrutinizing her swollen eyes and rumpled clothes.

He glanced from her to his puzzle, quickly filled in three or four squares, looked up again, and said, "Popular man this evening. I need to give Mr. St. George a call to let him know you're here. Name, please?"

"Mazzio; Gina Mazzio." She smiled and pushed at her hair, waited while he punched in the number.

When he hung up, he got up from behind the desk. "He said it's okay." He started toward the elevator and indicated she should follow.

"I don't need an escort," she said.

"It's the penthouse," he said, as if that explained everything.

"So?"

He held up a key ring. "Have to unlock the floor button for you."

241

On the way up, Gina fished in her purse for her lipstick, then used the polished brass plate of the floor selection panel as a mirror. She'd just zippered her purse together when the door opened and Eddie St. George stood there in front of her, smiling.

She was caught up short. But he filled in the silence.

"Ms. Mazzio! It's so nice to see you again. And to what do I owe this unexpected pleasure?"

"Is Megan Ann here? I need to talk to her."

"Oh?" He stepped away from the elevator door. "Yes, she's here. Come on in."

She followed him into the living room, immediately noticing the sparkle of city lights through the penthouse windows. Megan Ann came down the hallway wearing only what was apparently Eddie's V-neck tee shirt. It was obvious she had nothing on under the thin white cotton shirt. Also obvious that she was unharmed and perfectly happy. Looking at Megan Ann's outfit, it made sense now why the two plain-clothes cops were laughing when they came back down.

Yee's right. There's nothing going on here to make anyone suspicious. Just good old sex!

"Gina Mazzio, RN, what are you doing here?" Megan Ann said, waving an empty old-fashion glass. "If you're looking for a date, you're too late. He's mine!"

"I got that," Gina said. "I just wanted to see if you were all right … we've been worried about you at work."

"Yeah, I know. Shoulda called in." She gave a big double-shoulder shrug. "But that's nice of you. Come on in and have a little drinky."

Gina smiled, shook her head, and looked at Eddie. He was fidgety and his face was bright red. But as far as Gina could see, there was nothing for him to be upset about. Maybe a little embarrassed, which she could understand. He was dressed in gray slacks and a midnight blue silk shirt; he could have stepped right out of a page in *GQ*. All he needed were wrap-around sunglasses, a Laguna Beach tan, and his usual gelled and spiky red hair, which was now flat against his head.

Gina sat down on a plush love seat; Megan Ann plopped down beside her. "I was worried about you. Helen told me you've been out sick. Guess I wanted to see for myself, make sure you're all right."

"That's so nice of you," Megan Ann said, each word articulating into a slur. "Did you meet Eddie? He's so sweet. Treats me like a queen."

Gina looked up at Eddie; his green eyes were moist and he looked as if he were about to cry.

"And what made you think you'd find Megan Ann *here*?" he asked softly.

"I knew she had a date with you the other night," Gina said with a self-conscious laugh. "And we haven't been able to reach her since then."

Gina tried for an innocent look, hoping Eddie would buy it. "Just a shot in the dark, really," she said.

"Don't mind if I do," Megan Ann piped in. "A shot or two sounds exactly what we could all use about now." She waved a hand at Gina, then Eddie. "She and I had a fight over you, didja know that?" She curled up into the corner of the sofa.

Eddie looked confused. "No, I didn't know that."

"She's exaggerating," Gina said.

"She does that sometimes," he said, trying to make light of it. "But I'm forgetting my manners. May I get you something to drink?"

"No, I don't think so." Gina emphasized her response with a shake of her head. "I really should go. I'm imposing."

"Not at all." He smiled again. "You certainly have time for a glass of Pellegrino, with a touch of lemon?"

"Or how about some vodka, for me," Megan Ann said. "With a touch of Eddie." She giggled and started to doze off

Eddie never looked away from Gina. "Okay, vodka for Megan Ann, and for you, Ms. Mazzio?"

"Pellegrino is fine."

Gina watched as Eddie ran his fingers through Megan Ann's hair as he walked past her towards a large wet bar. She could see he was taken with her. Maybe this was what Megan Ann needed, someone to really care about her, treat her with respect and love.

Gina decided to be polite and take a couple of sips of the sparkling water, then be on her way.

* * *

Eddie could hear the buzz of their voices in the living room: Megan Ann, awake again, but getting quieter and quieter; Gina telling Megan Ann how worried everyone at work was about her absence. He guessed Gina was the one who had instigated the missing person report.

Eddie prepared their drinks, taking more time than necessary while he looked out the window at the patio trees and their blinking Christmas lights.

They say your life flashes before you just as you're about to die. What will I see at that moment? Father, who hates me? Mother, who is long gone, who deserted me for someone or something more important than me?

He listened to the wind outside whistling through a partially opened window.

Did Mother ever care what was going to happen to me?

Before he picked up the drinks, he dropped a Roofie in Gina's glass to match the one he'd given Megan Anne after the cops had left, then carried the two glasses into the living room.

Gina drank half her Pellagrino in a single continuous gulp. "Didn't realize how thirsty I was."

"I'm always thirsty," Megan Ann mumbled, looking up at Eddie, but unable to lift a hand to take the glass from him.

Eddie knew she was drunk, doped up, and being silly, but the way she looked at him lanced his heart. No one except Mother had ever looked at him that way.

"I do have to be going," Gina said.

He nodded, took a seat, and watched. Gina and Megan Ann's eyes glazed over at the same time. Experience told him that really shouldn't happen, given the difference in their ages and physiology, factored with the rate of alcohol consumption for one vs. none for the other. But there it was, both of them nodding off at the same moment.

Bette Golden Lamb & J. J. Lamb

₪ CHAPTER 38

Jacob St. George glared at his son, watched him struggle under the dead weight of some bitch slung over his shoulder. Eddie's steps were heavy, his knees sagged, and he was drenched in sweat.

Just like the dumb ox he's always been. And goddam if he isn't making those disgusting squeaking sounds he's made ever since he was a little brat.

He watched the veins and cords in Eddie's neck bulge as he lowered the woman onto the hardwood cutting block. His son clutched at his chest, tried to catch his breath, then slumped onto a stool, wasted.

Pinpricks of hatred crawled up and down Jacob's skin; he wanted to lash out at his son, tear his eyes out, knock him to the floor, stomp him. But there was no time for any of that. Milty would be here in less than an hour, expecting all the body parts to be packaged, individually labeled, and ready for delivery. He needed Eddie.

Jacob turned his attention to the woman on the block. She sure as hell wasn't the one his son brought to the shop Monday; the one Eddie stole away.

This slut didn't even look like a nurse, and she sure as hell wasn't a redhead.

Miserable wimp. Nothing gets done the way I want it. Have to tell him over and over and over what to do, how to do it.

Jacob stared at the woman: big, tall, and dressed in goddam purple.

Detest that color. Goddam! What happened to nurses' uniforms? Skirts, damn it! They're supposed to look like women, angels of mercy.

This one's dressed like Lola. Lola the fornicator. Lola the adulteress. Always wearing purple, taunting me with it, said it made her red hair look sexy. Sexy my ass. Only wore it because I hated it. She wanted to be pretty, wanted to fuck someone, anyone. Just not me.

He could still see her, still hear her in his head, like she was alive and torturing him. Until that voice shut down, other nurses would keep paying for her sins. That or until the crusher chewed up his brain, grinding it to mush and oblivion.

Jacob tried to eviscerate Eddie with a penetrating glare.

The purple bitch left behind a useless, ten-year-old sissy. Looking at Eddie only made Jacob hate her all the more for what she'd done.

Rotten cunt

"What the hell took you so long?"

"No more, Father," Eddie said, avoiding Jacob's eyes. He stood and rearranged the dark-haired woman on the table.

"Why'd you bring me this one? She's not right and you know it. Not even a nurse."

"She's a nurse, Father."

"Doesn't look like a damn nurse."

Jacob limped around the table, put a hand on the unconscious woman's breast, then took heavy poultry shears from his hip pocket and cut away her clothes.

"Too big! Too tall!" He yanked the clothes from under her, like pulling a tablecloth from under a set with dinner dishes. "You know that. Dammit!" He reached out and tugged hard at the black hair on the woman's head, then reached for her pubic hair. "Does this look like a redhead to you, dumb ass?"

He walked up to Eddie, who backed away even though his son towered over him. Jacob jabbed a finger into his chest.

"Where's that little red-headed number you stole from me, took to that fancy uptown apartment of yours?"

Eddie continued to back-peddle, but his eyes were rebellious. "You can't have her. She's mine."

248

Jacob laughed at the tall blob of nothing that was supposed to be his son. "Yours? What would you do with a woman, any woman? You'll do what I tell you … you…" He tried to concentrate on the next word but his brain refused to focus. "Pussy," he finally said. "Pussy! Pussy!"

"Say whatever you want, but you can't have Megan Ann. She's mine. I love her."

Jacob's tongue was thick; he couldn't swallow his own spit. He reached into his apron pocket, opened the vial of pills, and without even counting, tossed several into his mouth, forcing them down by dry-swallowing over and over. Some of the pills flew out of his mouth; most went down his throat.

"*Can't* have? You lost that fuckin' pea brain of yours? This is a business, little Eddie St. George. You're not walking away after all these years. I need those packages."

"Take this one, then. She's got what Hiller needs, same as Megan Ann."

"Not the same. And fuck Hiller. They have to be right for *me*, you idiot. Right for me! Right for me! I want them small. I want their red hair. Real red hair. Is that so fucking hard to understand?"

The silence lengthened before Eddie replied: "No matter what you do to me, you're not getting Megan Ann."

Jacob's stomach churned, threatened to erupt. His son was stupid. Puny and stupid.

"You're the one who brings them here; you're just as guilty as I am, Eddie. Somewhere in the back of that puny brain you gotta know that. The crusher's going to get me; I'll be dead, but you'll get the big needle if you don't do what I tell you. They don't disappear without me."

Jacob's legs wouldn't hold him; he dropped down hard on the stool Eddie had moved away from. His throat was still swollen. Why did all of this suddenly seem so funny? He laughed and laughed. "You talk to me about killing?"

Eddie looked at him, his face forming a big, fat, friggin' question mark.

"Don't go acting high and mighty. You're a drone, a slave owned by those pill pushers."

"We help people."

"Even you don't believe that shit. I'm dying because a blob of something no one can kill is eating away at my brain."

That sounded really funny. He roared with laughter, croaked out, "Maybe I have mad cow." He pointed at Eddie. "Do you get it? A butcher with mad cow!"

"Father! Stop it!"

The laughter was gone as quickly as it came. "What have your brilliant drug big shots done for me? What have *you* done for me?"

"I … I've tried to find a treatment for you."

"Yeah, yeah, yeah! You work for a pack of hyenas. You lie to the docs, lie to the public. And for what? *Money!* Well you're not the only one who can make money."

"We do some good," Eddie said.

"Well so do I, little boy. The body parts I sell do more good than those phony studies you scream about."

"You *murder* people, Father."

"*We* murder people, Eddie. *We! Me, you,* and that slimy drug company you work for. Don't *ever* forget that."

* * *

A velvety layer of green lifted Gina as she moved through tuft after tuft of scattered cirrus clouds. It was a balmy summer day; she was lying on her back, her body spread out in the long, soft grass.

Nice.

A piercing light jolted her out of the peacefulness. She stared out into a telescopic dot of light while spasmodic whispers of pain circled her muscles.

Where am I?

250

She'd gone to Eddie St. George's penthouse, been there with him and Megan Ann. And what? The last thing she remembered was the glass of Pellegrino Eddie had served her.

Her mind started to float again, drifted off before she could reason out the details of what had happened, what was happening.

Purple clouds floated all around her and she dug her bare toes into the grass to feel its softness.

Ouch!

Someone yanked her hair, top and bottom. Cold air blanketed her; she shivered so hard her teeth chattered.

Where are my clothes? Need to cover myself. Can't budge my arms or legs.

An explosion of voices assaulted her, the volume building from near subliminal to something like a sonic blast.

Two people. Arguing. One voice stirred a memory—the crazy one who'd called the Advice Center ... called her apartment. What was he doing here?

This is important ... have to get out of here ... have to tell Yee.

Frigid air fanned her, curling her muscles into tight, painful knots.

Panic roiled over her.

She was back in her apartment, flat on her back. Dominick had come from New York to kill her.

No!

She wanted to scream. Couldn't.

What's in my mouth? Stuck. Big. Like a ball. Oh, God! It's my tongue.

* * *

Eddie stared at Father. Blinked. Stared harder. Father had changed. When had he become such a little man? He was just a shrunken version of his former self; his face was a chalky, shoe-polish white.

Bette Golden Lamb & J. J. Lamb

Was this the man who had beat him, made him a slave by promising over and over to tell him where Mother was? Was this the same man who'd raped and killed all those women Eddie lured to the shop? How many women had there been?

He couldn't remember. Didn't want to remember.

Desperation crawled up his throat. The wheezing became more intense, louder.

He was eighteen when Father forced him to bring the first woman to the shop. Her and all the others were cut up, frozen, and sold. The packages.

Eddie inched around the table, looked at Gina, then peered into Father's eyes.

"Time to stop, Father. Time to stop the killing. Now!"

The shriveled man expanded to fill his loose, sagging skin; what started out as a roar of anger turned into bellowing laughter.

"Who do you think you're talking to, Eddie?"

* * *

Gina listened to the exchange between the two men, one on either side of her. She allowed her eyes to slit open when she finally established which one was *that voice*. She squinted, saw him. Eddie St. George! *He* was the caller! The room echoed with the wheezing sounds bursting from him—sounds she'd only heard before over the telephone.

On the other side, an older man Eddie called father, stood next to the table. He laughed viciously at the drug rep. At the same time, he looked down at her, poked her with a fingertip from time to time.

Where am I?

She shifted her eyes, moved her head slightly, afraid to draw attention to herself.

Ugly beef carcasses patterned with blue veins and yellow fat hung from hooks only a few feet from her; the fresh smell of blood and the acrid aroma of fear made the frigid air heavy. Next to her was a huge wooden rack of knives and saws.

Butcher shop? Why am I lying here naked in a butcher shop?

252

"I won't do it!" Eddie shouted.

The older man ignored the protest, looked down at Gina again. "I need packages for Hiller. Tonight! And not just this one. Go! Bring me that redhead while I get this one ready. There'll be plenty of money in it for you. You can buy a new Jaguar."

"I've never taken the money, Father. You know that. And I never will; not tonight, never!"

"Dumb ox! Always said you didn't know your ass from your elbow."

Gina couldn't unravel what they were talking about, couldn't make the day's events fit together. The father sounded insane as he yelled at Eddie. The words were garbled, difficult to comprehend.

A sharp pain jolted her hip. Eddie's father had grabbed her leg, twisted it. She pushed hard at his chest with the other leg, surprised that she could move it. The kick barely fazed him except to produce a mild look of annoyance.

"Father! Leave her alone!"

Gina felt the hand release her leg. The older man started around the table after Eddie, who moved in the opposite direction. She inched carefully to one side of the table, eased off the edge, and let herself fall to the floor. Her fingers splayed out in mounds of wet, blood-tainted sawdust.

"Get her back up on the block!" the old man roared. She could see foam bubbling from his mouth, sliding down his chin.

She had to get away from them, had to hide.

Eddie yelled something back, and while the two men screamed at each other, she snaked across the floor towards a large meat locker. The door was open just a crack.

* * *

Jacob glared at his son. "*You* are telling *me* no?"

"Father. Let her go."

"*Weak*! Just like that whore mother of yours."

"Leave Mother out of this."

253

Jesus, how he'd wanted to kill this whining piece of shit almost from the day he'd flopped out of his mother's cunt. But torturing him had been almost as good as beating down Lola every time she fought her way up.

"Leave her out of it? She left me, goddam it! She found another man. The bitch left you behind. How many times do I have to tell you that? That ungrateful slut left you here for me to take care of. You belong to *me*. You've always belonged to me. When are you going to get it? Now go bring me what I asked for, what I need. The redhead!"

* * *

A large meat locker, its door barely open, was within inches of Gina's fingertips; she was certain she could squeeze inside.

Her mind kept drifting, thinking of Harry, her brother Vinnie, and Dominick. Their images hung in the air like layers of floating thoughts fogging her mind.

If she could just make it into the locker and close the door, maybe she could keep them all away. Escape when she could think again.

She clawed her way through the narrow opening, was almost inside when she heard Eddie's father bellow:

"Come out, come out, wherever you are. We need to cut you up for Milty."

He grabbed her before she could close the door, yanked on one ankle, then the other. She reached out for something to hold onto. Anything!

Her fingers dug into a heavy plastic bag. It didn't stop her from being dragged out; the bag made no difference at all. It was dragged with her as he pulled her back into the room, into the glaring light.

"Give that to me, you bitch!"

Gina clutched the package, held onto…onto…

"Oh, my God!" she screamed.

Sin & Bone

The ice-crystal-coated plastic bag was filled with a human head. Large, bulging eyes stared out, framed by a head full of red hair.

The old man let go of Gina's leg, crawled forward and grabbed the plastic package away from her. He stood and held the bagged head up in the air

"Here, Eddie! I've kept my promise. Here she is. At last! Your mother's been here with us all the time. And you know what? She's going to stay here. The slut stays where I can see her adulterous face every time I open that door."

He started to reach down for Gina, stopped, clutched his chest. A grimace contorted his face; his whole body shook as if hit by a powerful electrical charge.

Gina scooted away, watched as he tumbled to the floor, lay there twitching. She stared at Eddie, *the caller*. She was angry with him, but scared out of her wits by the father, and horrified by what she'd heard and seen. She needed to run, to get as far away as possible.

Eddie reached past her, picked up the bag, looked closely at the contents, and released a bone-chilling scream. Tears ran down his cheeks, his shoulders shook in agony.

"You killed her!" he yelled. He held the plastic bag out in front of his father, shook it at him. "You killed Mother!" His voice was like a huge rasp tearing through the air.

The father slowly raised his head, a look of satisfaction spreading across his face. He rolled over, reached up, grabbed for the cutting block, and pulled himself upright.

"I'd do it again if I could," he screamed. "She was going to run away with some skinny teacher she met at that friggin' night school. Wasn't happy to be a butcher's wife. Said she never would have married me if she hadn't been pregnant with you. Both of you are nothing but two putrid peas from the same rotten pod."

The room echoed with a primitive howl that ripped from Eddie's throat. He grabbed a large butcher knife, leaped at his father.

Jacob held Eddie's arm away from him. But Eddie twisted and turned until the knife hand was free.

"This is for Mother." Eddie plunged the blade deep into his father's chest. Again and again and again.

Gina watched the older man look down at his wounds; he sank to the floor, a creepy laugh bubbled from his throat.

"Finally did something worthy of a real man. Now you'll pay the price. Pay in hell for what Lola St. George did to me."

And then Jacob St. George's eyes went blank and a final breath escaped his body. A mean smile remained etched on his face.

Eddie was wheezing even harder now, air struggling to get into his lungs as he turned towards Gina.

"You!" she said. "You're the son-of-a-bitch who called me at the clinic ... at home."

"It had to stop," Eddie said, sobbing. "I wanted to stop Father from harming anyone else, to stop making me bring him women."

Eddie's eyes pleaded with her as he knelt down beside her and collapsed across her lap.

₪ CHAPTER 39

"Okay, St. George, I'm here," yelled a gravelly voice. The rear door to the shop slammed closed with a loud bang. "Where the hell are my packages?"

Gina watched a tall, beefy man push a hand dolly through a row of hanging sides of pork on the far side of the room. He came to an abrupt halt in the middle of the shop.

"Jesus!" the man said hoarsely. His eyes bulged as he looked down at Jacob St. George, the handle of the large knife protruding from the butcher's chest. He toed the body, scratched at a two or three days' growth of beard.

Gina was still down behind the large, thick cutting block in front of the locker. She pushed at Eddie, tried to budge him off her lap. She didn't know whether to remain silent and hope the man didn't see her, or to call out for help. Before she could make up her mind, Eddie raised his head, looked around at the man, and motioned for Gina to keep quiet. He slowly got to his feet.

"There's nothing here for you Hiller, go away," Eddie said.

"You and Daddy have a little disagreement?" Hiller said. "Looks like *you* won. Man, that's a laugh and a half."

"Just go away."

"Don't think so, Eddie." Hiller swiveled his head to look around the room, caught sight of Gina. "And who's this little dolly? Don't tell me the late, crazy Jacob St. George didn't get the job done before he went to meet his maker?"

Gina scooted back against the door of the walk-in cooler, tried to cover her nakedness with her arms. Both Hiller and Eddie were staring at her.

"I told you, there's nothing here for you," Eddie snapped. "That's it!"

"Huh! Little Eddie thinks he's finally got a pair. Well, wrong time, wrong place." Hiller started toward Gina. "Your old man was supposed to have a delivery for me. Several packages. Wrapped and ready."

"No!" Eddie shouted and stepped between Hiller and Gina.

"Get the fuck out of my way, kid." Hiller pulled a small pistol from his coat pocket, aimed it at Eddie's midsection, and took another step forward. "Unless you want to join daddy in never-never land," Hiller said, "I suggest you move. Now!"

Eddie glanced back at Gina, then spun quickly around and swung a fist at Hiller's head. Hiller easily dodged the blow and smashed Eddie's face with the gun.

"No!" screamed Gina, scrambling up from the sawdust-covered floor. "Leave him alone."

Hiller looked at her; his eyes glistened. He pushed Eddie aside and started toward her.

"Not Jacob's usual taste, but a very usable package. And all stripped and ready for the axe. Right, Eddie?"

Hiller reached behind him and grabbed Eddie by an arm. "Got a problem here, kid. The package is still on the hoof, so to speak." He looked over at Jacob. "We can save your ass. Do big daddy, too." He yanked hard at Eddie's arm. "Get busy!"

"Wh ... what?" Eddie said.

"I'm telling you, get busy. I got commitments. Your old man made me a promise. And since you got rid of Daddy, it's up to you to make good on the contract. You dig?"

Eddie's mouth dropped open; he shook his head rapidly from side to side, his eyes large and terrified.

"Come on, kid. The slicin' and dicin' isn't my shtick. You've got to do it. Jog those memory cells ... pretend you're papa."

Eddie didn't move; Hiller glared at him. "Hey, if you're too chicken to make the kill, I'll shoot her for you. Tell me where so I don't damage the goods."

"Screw you, buster," Gina blurted. She dashed into the cooler, slammed down the long-handled latch, and peeked through the small, heavy glass window in the door.

She watched as Hiller reached the door in three long strides. As he grabbed the door pull, she rose up on her toes and smashed her bare rump against the inside latch bar to prevent him from opening it.

The icy-cold metal impressed itself into her flesh, and stuck. She could feel pressure on the latch from the outside, then came a pounding on the door, all accompanied by muffled, angry shouting. There were a couple of gunshots, one big thud into the door, and a push at the handle, but the door held.

She wanted to look out the window again, but she would have to move away from the door latch, and that wasn't about to happen.

She waited-seconds, minutes, an eternity.

* * *

The gunshots and flying sparks from the bullets slamming into the door latch sent Eddie charging forward, one shoulder lowered to catch Hiller in the small of the back. When he fell, Eddie kicked him in the solar plexus. The impact knocked the wind out of Hiller and sent the pistol sliding across the floor.

"I told you to go away," Eddie said to the fallen, gasping gunman. He reached out and tried to open the cooler door. When it didn't move, he knew Gina was holding the latch on the other side. He tried to peer in the window, but the glass was fogged.

"Gina! It's okay. You can come out."

No response.

Hiller, groaning, tried to sit up. Eddie kicked him back down, grabbed the loose end of a ball of twine suspended from the ceiling and wrapped the rough sisal cord around Hiller's wrists and ankles.

"I'll ... I'll kill you," Hiller mumbled.
"Not today, Milty." He stuffed a wadded paper towel into the man's mouth and moved back to the door of the walk-in freezer.

* * *

Gina shook, cold, tremors that rippled up from blue toes to her pounding head. What if she passed out, couldn't continue to hold down the latch if there was another attempt to open the door?

Her mind was sluggish; she didn't want to think about it. She didn't want to think about anything. But she had to do something. Much longer in the freezing storage room and she would pass out. Already she could barely move her hands and legs.

She unstuck herself from the metal handle, tearing skin in the process. She massaged hard at her buttock while she looked outside, peered through the tiny window as far as she could to the left, then to the right. No one. Her breath fogged the glass even more.

She heard someone tell her it was safe to come out.

But was it?

She took a deep breath, tried to stop shaking, and unlatched the heavy door. Slowly, trying not to make a sound, she pushed outward. The heavy door creaked open and there stood Eddie St. George.

"Don't touch me!"

She jumped back inside the meat locker and hit the latch.

"Gina, can you hear me?" Eddie shouted. "It's okay. You can come out. No one's going to hurt you."

Her teeth chattered so hard she almost couldn't respond. "I … I d-don't t-trust you."

"Father's dead," Eddie said.

"S...so?" "Th … that other m … man," she called out. "And you? Wh … hat about you?"

She felt St. George pull at the door handle.

"Milty's tied up," he shouted. "And I'm ... I'm ..." A moment passed. "You have to trust me, Gina. I'm not going to hurt you."

"No! I'm not c … coming out. You k … killed Arina and S … shelly.

260

"No-o-o!" he groaned. "Father! Father killed them. Made me bring them."

"I d ... don't care who did what," Gina said, slapping at her upper arms.

"You can't stay in there," he pleaded. "You'll pass out. Die."

"In here, out ... there, what difference does it ... make?"

"The killing's over," St. George said so softly she barely heard him. "Never again."

She knew he was right. She was going to pass out soon. It was either die here or take her chances outside the locker.

"What do you want to do?" St. George called. "You can't stay in there."

"Go away!"

"I'm going," he said. "I'm going to Megan Ann. Count to ten and come out. I'll be gone."

* * *

Gina lost track of the count at three, paused, started over again, then again, but couldn't seem to get past three. Finally, she started shoving on the heavy door, unsure whether enough time had gone by or she had enough strength to open it.

"Hold it right there!" It was a no-nonsense command.

Gina stopped leaning into the door, but couldn't stop shivering.

"Come on out, hands high and in front of you."

Gina pushed the door a little more, stumbled through the narrow opening, and raised her shaking arms, palms out. At the far end of the room, two uniformed cops were crouched, pistols aimed in her direction; a sullen, handcuffed Hiller stood off to the side.

She looked around for Eddie St. George, but instead saw Pepper Yee, who rolled her eyes and told the officers to lower their weapons.

Yee snatched a bloodstained butcher's coat from a wooden peg, stepped out to block the cops' view of Gina, and walked across the room.

"Do I … finally have your f … full attention?" Gina said as she passed out.

₪ CHAPTER 40

Gina kept trying to open her eyes. Someone was talking to her, telling her she was going to be fine, but she couldn't remember why that was important or why she wasn't fine in the first place. Slowly, she climbed through a dense layer of confusion to a reassuring level of time and place. Then she was able to open her eyes.

She stared into the concerned face of an EMT, who smiled widely at her. "Becoming a polar bear means you should stop and get the fur coat first," he said.

"Don't listen to him," a female EMT said, recording her body temperature before checking each of her fingers. "Close your eyes and get some rest. You're going to be okay."

"Just how cold did I get in that freezer?"

"Not too bad. And your vitals are all stable."

She was now alert enough to be scared. What had the hypothermia done to her? "What about my fingers and toes? Am I going to lose them?"

The female EMT reached under the pile of blankets, took her hand and squeezed it. "Everything looks good. I think with some basic medical treatment you'll cruise right through this."

Well, at least she wasn't shivering anymore. That had to be good. Gina shifted her head at the sound of a deep sigh, saw Yee standing at the back of the ambulance. The detective smiled when Gina looked at her.

"You manage to get yourself into the strangest situations, Ms. Mazzio."

"What are you doing here?" Gina said. "Lose your cruiser?"

"Nope. Just not letting you out of my sight this time."

Gina tried to read the continuous ECG strip they were running on her, count the drops running into the IV port hanging above her head. No deal. She couldn't concentrate.

"Detective Yee?" She was becoming light headed, had trouble organizing her thoughts. "I'd appreciate it if you called my ... my...fiancé." She was suddenly very, very tired. She could barely get Harry's cell number out of her mouth.

* * *

"Neither one?"

Gina awakened, looked around to see who was talking. It was Yee, a cell phone tight against her ear. She shifted her eyes, saw that she was on a gurney in the ER

"Yeah! Yeah! Keep looking." Yee folded the cell and put in her pocketbook.

"Can't you find Harry?" Gina mumbled.

"Looking for St. George and the Hendricks woman," Yee said. "That call came from one of my people at his penthouse."

"They aren't there?" Gina remembered why she'd been trapped in the freezer and fought a sudden shiver. Even though blankets were piled on top of her and the fluid running through the IV was warmed, she didn't believe she would ever really be warm enough again. She squirmed around, wished she had some underwear and socks to put on.

"Been and gone, from the look of things," Yee said. She leaned back and gave Gina a stony-eyed stare.

"What?"

"What? Well, for starters, whatever possessed you to go to Eddie St. George's apartment in the first place?"

"I told you, I was trying to find Megan Ann. Wanted to make sure she was okay."

"You're goddam lucky, do you know that?"

"That's the third or fourth time you've said that since you picked me up," Gina said.

"And you didn't know anything about this God-awful business the St. Georges were involved in?"

264

"Of course not! All I knew was that a couple of our nurses were missing, and that maybe Megan Ann was missing too."

"Damn lucky!"

"Agreed!" She rubbed her palms on her thighs, tried to create more heat under the covers even though she suspected her actual temperature was normal again. "But how did you happen to show up at the butcher shop? I'm pretty certain you weren't looking for me."

"To quote someone I know, damn straight about that!" Yee made a couple of notes on a pad. "We had a tail on this guy Milty Hiller, a sub-human type we were onto for dealing in illicit body parts."

"That's what the butcher was doing?"

"Yup!" She made a couple more notes. "We'd set up a sting at a funeral home and were going to take down Hiller and his accomplices there. But he surprised us. Took off in the opposite direction. Lost him for a while. Had to call out an APB. A patrol unit finally spotted his truck parked outside the butcher shop. By the time Daniels and I got there with our backup guys, Eddie St. George was gone. But we did find Hiller, all trussed up like a Thanksgiving turkey."

"The guy kept threatening Eddie with a gun, wanted him to cut me up for body parts. They kept calling them 'packages.' Yuck!"

"Yeah, we found some of those in St. George's freezer, but the ones we found in slime-ball Hiller's truck should be enough to put him away. He apparently made another stop before going to the butcher shop."

"Lucky me you showed up when you did," Gina said.

"That's what I've been trying to tell you."

Gina tried for a second time to sip some warm water the nurse had brought her, but she couldn't get the fluid to go down. "So," she said. "You caught Hiller, Eddie's father is dead, Megan Ann and Eddie are missing, and you still don't know what happened to Shelly Wilton and Arina Diaz."

"That isn't quite true," Yee said.

"Which part?"

"The missing nurses part."

Gina grit her teeth, took a deep breath, and said, "At the butcher shop?"

Yee looked away from her. "The crime scene people discovered that the late Mrs. St. George's plastic-wrapped head wasn't her husband's only trophy."

"How many?"

"More than you want to know about, all packed nicely in pork loin boxes," Yee said. "The late Mrs. St. George was the only one on display, so to speak."

"God!"

"Should close out a lot of missing person files throughout the Bay Area," Yee said. "What I need from you is every single thing you know or think you know about Eddie St. George, no matter how insignificant you may think it is."

"What would you say if I told you I feel kind of sorry for the guy? He—"

"Knock it off, Mazzio. Eddie St. George is either a mass murderer or an accomplice to mass murder. And if I get the smallest inkling you're not telling me the truth, Ridgewood Hospital is going to be missing the services of another nurse."

* * *

Gina was still wiping tears from her eyes when she was released from the ER, almost two hours later.

Poor Arina, poor Shelley. And all those other women.

Yee had offered her a lift home, but she'd declined, lied and said she had a ride. She wanted to get away from any semblance of crime and the police as quickly as possible.

The staff had found her some used, disinfectant-smelling clothes to wear, none of which fit very well. She didn't want to think who might have worn the scratchy garments before she got them. But the hospital scuffs were great, except that they kept falling off her feet.

When she reached the sidewalk, using one hand to keep her drawstring pants from falling, she looked for one of the taxis usually lined up at the ER exit.

And there stood Harry, leaning against the passenger door of her Fiat, holding jeans, a sweater, and sneakers.

"They found you," she said.

"Yee chased me down, but a couple of EMT friends picked up on her operation on their scanner and let me know even before she did." He opened the car door. For a moment they just stood and looked at each other.

Gina grinned, ran into Harry's out-stretched arms, grabbed him around the middle, and squeezed and squeezed and squeezed.

The End

Bette Golden Lamb & J. J. Lamb

About the Authors

Bette Golden Lamb, an e-Bronxite, writes crime novels and plays with clay in her home studio. Her artistic creations appear in juried exhibitions, galleries, art associations, and retail stores. She also hangs out with her 50+ rose bushes and sneaks out to movies when she should be writing or sculpting.

J. J. Lamb switched from engineering to journalism just in the nick of time, then on to an Associated Press career. Army intervention provided a top secret clearance, a locked room with table-chair-typewriter, and the time to write short stories. This led to a PI series featuring Zachariah Tobias Rolfe III before collaborating with Bette.

The **Lambs** make their home in Northern California where they are busy at work – individually and together – on many more creative projects. You can check on them at Left Coast Crime and at www.twoblacksheep.us.

Bette Golden Lamb & J. J. Lamb

www.ingramcontent.com/pod-product-compliance
Lightning Source LLC
Chambersburg PA
CBHW062134170626
46813CB00002B/697